Love and Other Euphemisms

LOVE
AND OTHER
EUPHEMISMS

by Norma Klein

G. P. Putnam's Sons, New York

For Erwin

Contents

Pratfalls

Chapter One

HER mother took her to the San Francisco airport since her father was working.

"Who will you stay with? These friends you mentioned?"

"I'm not sure they're there. . . . Look, I can stay at a hotel till I get settled."

"Do stay at a good one, Rachel. . . . It's so foolish taking chances."

"I will, Mom."

"You know, your father is very worried about you."

"Oh?" She hated this tendency of her mother to put things into other people's mouths which often were her own thoughts.

"He never wants to say anything. . . . He doesn't want to upset you."

"That's nice of him."

"He just can't understand why you seem to lack an orientation in life. . . . Why, we look at Julie and Dan—"

"Oh, Mom, come on. . . . Dan has some routine job in the DA's office, and Julie is a tough dykey little type who's managed to worm her way ahead." She really didn't believe this, but under duress it came tumbling out.

"Well, I admire Julie tremendously. . . . As for Dan, he—"

"Mom, turn right here. . . . Oh, Jesus, you missed it!"

"What did I miss?"

"The sign! It said airport. Well, you take it from here."

"I thought we got off at Exit Seventeen."

"We do. . . . That *was* Exit Seventeen."

11

They didn't miss the plane. In fact, they arrived half an hour early. While waiting stiffly on the edge of their seats for the boarding announcement, her mother suddenly said, "I spoke to Edward. . . . I called him last night."

Rachel stared at her in disbelief.

But her mother went on imperturbably, "I wanted him to know you were coming East. I knew you wouldn't bother to call him. . . . It's his right to know of your movements."

"His right! Look, who decides what his fucking rights are? Are you a lawyer or something?"

"I think Edward is repelled when you use language like that, Rachel," her mother said.

"Mom, will you stop quoting other people? . . . Say *you're repelled*."

"*I'm* not repelled. . . . I mean, I know it's part of the new generation. *I'm* not repelled. . . . But Edward, it's different. You have to understand. His family, they want to attain a certain style of life, a certain elegance. Now, of course, your father and I don't totally approve of that, but I think we have to understand it, we have to understand its roots."

Rachel raised her eyes to heaven. "Listen, Mom, for one thing, if it means anything—I'll put Edward's family aside—he says fuck, too . . . not in front of you, maybe. He's too polite."

"He says it to please you."

"He says it because he feels like it. He was saying it long before he ever laid eyes on me, and I'll wager he'll be saying it and a lot of other things long after."

Her mother was silent. "I think Edward wanted in you a certain dignity, someone who would conform to certain—"

"Mom, listen . . . how in God's name do you know what Edward wanted?"

"Edward is not a man who would be driven to infidelity unless he was—well, driven."

Rachel smiled. "You know, I wish . . . I mean, Edward should be here. Because either he'd fall flat on his nose hearing all this or he'd be happy beyond belief. I mean, he may be an egoist, but even he never invented these noble motives. If he has to shit, he shits. If he feels like screwing, he screws. I just don't know where you get this picture of the noble savage or whatever. It's laughable."

Magic! It was boarding time. They both looked at each other. "I will write," Rachel said. "Don't worry. . . . Listen, when you next hear from me, I'm going to have such a big deal job Julie will run screaming with shame under the nearest couch. They'll be quoting me in the New York *Times*."

"Darling, the only thing we want for you is for you to attain inner happiness and self-respect."

"Sure, Mom. . . . That sounds easy enough." Rachel bent over for a kiss and grabbed her luggage. "Thanks a million."

Walking to the plane, she thought: You're the one with these great, intellectual, noninterfering parents? . . . Well, I mean Dad, mainly. . . . Anyway, compared to other people's. . . . Why didn't *she* marry Edward? She knew so much about him! Incredible, did he put this over on everyone or was it the old Aging Liberal views (through squinted eyes, rose-colored glasses, etc.) the black son-in-law. Of *course* he's a combination of FDR, Olivier, Paul Robeson, and—oh, who else? I mean, what other kinds are there? . . . Her parents had been delighted she married Edward. There weren't enough Communists left— in any case, too many people were left-wing now to have it a very significant trait. That your daughter should marry a black and you approve wholeheartedly was one of the few areas in which you could comfortably feel a sense of moral superiority in a world where such satisfactions were becoming increasingly scarce. Despite the irony that at the wedding it was Edward's parents who cut them or, at least, acted with sufficient disdain and coolness to make their point. It was a class difference—pure and simple. They didn't care if he married a white girl or even a Jew, but she should have been a debutante, an heiress, someone who would lend style, tone, not eat steak bones with her bare hands. Her parents were high school teachers in Oakland. What did they—or she, their product, for that matter—know of town houses and color TV and corporation law and mink stoles? It wasn't just a matter of money—they disdained those things as representations of a way of life Edward's parents had all but glorified into heaven on earth. But now, despite this—how brief their memories were!—the fact that she and Edward had split automatically cast her as the Villainess, he as the Wronged. . . . That's what parents are for, my dear. Have you forgotten?

The plane had engine trouble and circled Kennedy for fifteen minutes. Rachel was sitting next to a businessman type with a briefcase who wondered if she was an actress "because of her voice." Her voice! What voice? I mean, like, she'd never heard her own voice. It was great to think it was more than just an instrument for conveying speech. "I think I'm getting a cold," she said. "I probably sound more hoarse than usual." In fact, she had just got her period and had a bloated, irritable feeling.

They ended up looking at photos of his wife and six children.

"Don't you believe in the population explosion?" Rachel said, she hoped, humorously.

"Oh, I don't like children," he said, straight.

"You don't?"

"No. . . . My wife doesn't either, really. . . . It just kind of happened."

And they call *me* disorganized.

"I got sterilized three years ago, and I've never felt better in my life," he said. "I wish I'd had it done twenty years ago. . . . You know, when you're young, there's this pride thing. You think people will look at you in a funny way. . . . Who cares? It's safer than the pill and there you are, you can travel. . . ."

"So your life is a waste," she said sadly. After two daiquiris she was glad to indulge, under the usual nervousness of—will the plane crash?—the fleeting intimacy of transiency.

"Whose life isn't a waste?"

"God, it's surprising." She peered out the window, trying to figure out if they were going lower. "You look like this typical sort of Babbitt type. You know. Very self-satisfied."

"Well, I am, in a way."

"You don't seem to have a sense of humor."

"Well, not when I feel I'm about to die."

She did a double take. Did he have some dread disease? He looked so pink and plump and fit, as though he'd been working out at the New York Athletic Club every Tuesday for the last ten years.

"No, I mean, the plane could crash."

"Oh, the plane!"

"Death could come at any moment," he said. "I think one should be aware of that."

A philosopher to boot! He began describing a course his daughter was taking in Boston, taught by a Tibetan monk. He had become interested in it. Rachel's mind wandered. Mention of the transcendental made her vaguely nervous.

"I'd like to go to India someday," she said to try and bring the conversation back to a more practical level.

He said, "My wife had to have a breast removed two years ago. . . . Now she's all right. But that's what I mean."

"Yes, I can see."

Where, where were all those round, pink people that you were told existed? Where? Did they flee when they saw her coming? Did they turn like little beasties in the night into tormented Kafkaesque types? She wanted to meet normal people!

The airport was crowded; it was four in the afternoon. People were greeting people. Her own lack of direction suddenly hit her. She was arriving from somewhere, going to somewhere, and as usual, she had scarcely worked out those connectives which were, if you came down to it, the key to everything. Well, she would call Jacques Ibert.

When she had said to Edward and her parents that she was thinking of "staying with friends in New York," whom had she been thinking of? Now that she was here, it struck her that the few people she might have had in mind could well have moved. There was no one with whom she'd kept in contact, no former roommate, now married, or friends. Not that either alternative was the kind toward which you ran, arms open. But Jacques Ibert fulfilled two qualifications: He was likely to still be in New York; he would not be nonplussed at her not having called or written earlier.

She had met Jacques Ibert five years earlier on the boat coming home from Europe with Stef. It had been one of those not very good student boats that took fourteen days, where the food was a little too greasy and everyone seemed to be meeting in little groups to discuss what they'd got out of the trip. And Stef was going mad. And the weather was rotten. They had been placed at a table with Jacques and his "friend" Quentin, just the four of them uncomfortably tête-à-tête. She had felt neither interested nor friendly to the two evidently gay men who made small talk about cathedrals in France and were too well dressed and refined-seeming for this student boat. Then one afternoon, two days before they had landed, Stef had been unable to come to lunch and Quentin laid low by some combination of flu and seasickness. She had sat through a dull, polite meal with Jacques Ibert, but suddenly, as they were having coffee, he had begun an "analysis" of Stef, whom he said he had been observing during the voyage. Usually she would have been enraged at such presumption. But he spoke so precisely, with such a combination of understanding and detachment, that she found herself spending the entire afternoon with him, sitting in deck chairs, listening to him talk. What made it palatable was that he didn't seem a psychologist type, didn't use jargon or fancy phrases. Nor did he seem to be taking a kind of malicious, chuckling pleasure in the idea of other people's suffering. But he had seen everything. Noticed each little gesture which she thought only she noticed. It was a relief, partly, to have someone from the outside make such a "diagnosis." ("He is already mad," he had said very calmly as they sat watching the gray, flat sea.) It relieved her of all the guilt of the past months, thinking maybe everything was just her own overactive imagination, morbidity. She had thought at first that being homosexual, he might be inwardly sneering at the thought of "young love gone awry." But in his tone, in everything he had ever said then or later, there was none of that. He was rather, allowing for certain national differences, that Chekhovian-doctor type, pince-nez, thoughtful frown, steady, merciless gaze on human foibles. It spoiled it a little for her that he was homosexual. Spoiled it, but also made their whole friendship possible because anything with even muted sexual overtones would have destroyed the sense of objectivity, the lack of guilt, with which she could listen to him and, after their talk, exchange glances at the table when Stef said certain things.

She had invited him to her wedding to Edward, and he had come, not with Quentin, but alone. Since then she had seen him just four or five times, occasionally exchanged a card—he was always traveling and sent beautiful shots of madonnas from Italy almost every summer. What he thought of Edward, of her marrying a black, she hadn't the slightest idea. But she suspected he would neither approve nor disapprove, and that indifference was what she wanted just at the moment.

"Are you in New York now, right at this moment?" he said when he answered.

"Well, right at this moment I'm in a phone booth at Kennedy," she said.

"You sound so far away."

"We may have a bad connection." She was already feeling hesitant. Sure, just call anyone, they'll drop everything and rearrange their whole life around you!

"Is it correct that you are looking for a place to stay?"

"It is."

"Well." A pause of several seconds. "I have a class tonight which meets at my home from seven to nine. . . . But you are welcome to stay here."

"Well, listen, you're sure? Because I have money. I mean, I can stay at a hotel. . . . So say if it's not convenient."

"It is perfectly convenient."

What had made her think of it was that she knew he always lived alone. If, as a homosexual, he was a misogynist, he was also, to almost as great a degree, a misanthrope. Not the type to be living in one of those fuddy-duddy "you wash the socks, I'll sauté the snails" kind of middle-aged queer relationships. He would be alone. She would stay briefly, get her bearings and find an apartment. . . . She liked the way he said "perfectly convenient." That Gallic precision. "Well, then, I'll come. . . . Will you be there?"

"I'll be here briefly. . . . Then I must go out."

"Fine. . . . I can make it in forty-five minutes, I think."

In the cab she felt pleased. But wished she had brought something for him, some really fine wine or cheese. She could tomorrow. After all, she hadn't known he would be there. He was a fantastic cook. Even when he ate alone, she imagined, he didn't, ever, open a can of chili or munch on devil's food cupcakes. He always seemed totally unrushed, as though he could spend an hour gently patting dry a head of Boston lettuce leaves. And why not? What better occupation for anyone's time? . . . Of course, he was a scholar too, but his articles, so she'd gathered, were horrendously dull, precise works, the kind you wrote to keep a good job and which someone, presumably, read. But he never seemed to care about them or take much pride in them, except for those on French Provençal songs, a topic he genuinely liked.

The apartment—the same one in which she and Stef had had a drink with him before getting the plane to California—was one of those old Riverside Drive apartments with a lobby so huge you could have given a grand ball in it. But seedy. You suspected roaches.

When she rang the bell, he came to the door immediately, but his hat and coat were on. "I must rush. . . . I'll be back in an hour."

Rachel pulled off her coat and collapsed in his living room. The furniture looked old, some of it deliberately antiquy, the rest just "shabby but serviceable." It was overheated, and she threw open a few dusty windows to let air in. She had planned, while he was gone, to shower and make herself presentable, but sitting there, she grew so sleepy she actually fell sound asleep in the chair, having half-confused dreams about Berkeley, Stef, the past and the far past drifting together. She started when his key turned in the lock.

He was carrying a large paper bag. His cheeks were pink. Without his coat and hat he looked just as she remembered. He was one of those people you never expected to age.

"I'm afraid I can't offer you a very resplendent dinner," he said. "The students are coming in an hour."

"Oh, that's okay. . . . You shouldn't feel you have to—"

But of course, in twenty minutes she was sitting at his small round table with a perfectly sautéed minute steak, sprinkled with parsley, immersed in some shallot-wine sauce, crisp potatoes, marinated green beans, what he called "some leftover wine" but which was, she ascertained from a glance at the bottle, a quite good Châteauneuf du Pape. What kept her from feeling guilty was the feeling that he probably would be eating like this anyway.

"You know, it occurred to me when I was calling you," she said, "that it is a little weird, just bursting in like this. . . . I mean, I should have written."

"You never plan ahead, as I recall," he said.

It struck her that they were stuck, both of them, for good or bad, with the images formed that afternoon on the boat. She would always think of him in his Chekhovian-doctor role, musing with detachment on the ways of the world while staring out at a gray October sea; he would always think of her as the post-adolescent girl, very intense with lots of emotional problems, not quite knowing which end was up.

"I've been visiting my parents in Berkeley. . . . My husband and I are separated," she said quickly. She hated starting out that way, but holding back the information or knowing, as might be true with Ibert, that he would wonder but be too polite to ask, was awkward. On the other hand, it reminded her of a time when she had been looking for a psychiatrist and had gone around telling her life story so frequently that it became not only humiliating but dull. "You remember Edward," she added.

"Of course I remember Edward. . . . I was at your wedding."

"No, I just thought maybe. . . . How is Quentin?" she went on, wanting to forestall any more involved discussion till later.

"He's in Prague at the moment," he said.

He said it flatly, not seeming to imply there was any rift between them. If only she could have those kinds of emotional relationships: cool, civilized, each person doing his own thing, going his own way.

"You know, I don't really have a separate bedroom. You can sleep on this sofa bed. . . . But if you want, during the time the students are here, to go inside, please do. . . . You can stay and listen, if you like. It just may be a bit tedious."

Coffee he made in a very large quantity, evidently for the course, and laid out a platter of cookies. She went into his bedroom to wash. At seven she heard the bell ring, and after that it rang several times in short succession. She looked at his clothes in the closet. A little dull and shabby like the apartment. That was a pity. Of course, in a way it suited him, but in another way she could imagine him rather well in some Renaissance costume, purple velvet doublet and pointed shoes with a very elegant silver sword. It struck her, too, how atypical of academia her life with Edward had been. It was the family money, of course. Not that Ibert was poor—he certainly ate exceedingly well, traveled a lot, and had everything in life he considered important. If you handed him a million dollars, no doubt he would still continue living in this old apartment with his books and the rug that slid out of place in the front hall. It was more that the rest didn't interest him.

She came out to listen to the last half hour of the lecture. Seeing her emerge from the bedroom, several of the students looked up in surprise. She saw two girls exchange glances. Ibert went on imperturbably—he was quoting some French poetry. How delightful that they should imagine she was his mistress! It was worth staying just for that. All the chairs were taken. She sat on the floor, leaning against the wall, next to another student.

They struck her, all seven of them, as a dreary lot. Was it the gray of the apartment, casting off shadows, was it New York after California, was it her mood? They all looked faded, industrious, not especially brilliant. Some would get their degrees; some wouldn't. Maybe graduate students more than undergraduates always had that look. You wanted them to expose themselves just to prove they had genitals, that they might even be capable of some excitement, sexual or otherwise.

She helped Ibert clear up after they had left. "Do you have a protégé?" she asked, half-mockingly.

"Oh, no one special. . . . Well, maybe Henry—did you notice him?—that little fellow who sat near the door. His thesis is almost finished, and I think it might be interesting. The rest—" He waved his hand.

She got into pajamas, and he helped her fix up the studio bed. "I may be up early," he said, "but please do sleep as late as you want."

"I'm going to start looking for a place," she said. "Do you get the *Times?*"

They had no long discussion about life, which in a way relieved her. She fell asleep instantly, despite the lumpiness of the sofa.

She stayed there a week. It worked out very well. Ibert always went his own way, never made her feel a burden. In the morning after breakfast she would look through the *Times.* The apartments were invariably too expensive, nearly two hundred dollars, even on the West Side. A few times she went to look at ones that sounded promising. In one case it was already taken. In another the building was so seedy it hardly seemed worth it. She became uneasy about supers, especially after Ibert told her the following story about the one in his apartment. The super was worried because several robberies had taken place in the building. One night he saw a stranger heading for the elevator who, when questioned about his destination, gave a false name. When he came down, half an hour later with a TV and camera in hand, the super tried to stop him, the man resisted, and the super killed him with a paring knife. A few days later the same sort of incident, and again the super killed the robber. The police, hearing of both events, were pleased at having a criminal out of the way and didn't press charges. Then, a week later, the super killed himself.

"With a paring knife?" said Rachel. They were walking along Broadway to Ibert's butcher.

"No one knows the weapon. . . . He was quite a nice man, a very retiring fellow." He smiled at this discrepancy, the kind of thing which amused him.

"What a strange denouement. . . . I was expecting something different."

"I was fond of him," said Ibert as they walked into the butcher's store.

It was a small store, but there were articles from the New York *Times*, citing the excellence of this man's sweetbreads and filets. Ibert was evidently well known in the store. He took a number from a stack and waited patiently as a little old lady requested a quarter pound of ham and two sausages. All the time several men in bloody white coats bustled back and forth, weighing, carving, yanking immense sides of beef out of a freezer in the back. When it came to Ibert's turn, he had quite a discussion with the owner of the store about the particular cut he wanted. Different roasts were brought out, inspected, squinted at. Rachel much admired the care and expertise that went into both the examination and the discussion. There was talk of what the cows were fed, how this affected tenderness.

Mr. Bruneheim began paring off some chops while a lackey wrapped Ibert's roast. Rachel watched him in fascination. She loved butchers. Was it some repressed sadism? She'd always remembered a story someone had written in her high school class about a little girl in love with her mother's butcher. They seemed so graceful, the way they took those huge sharp knives and with such delicacy whisked off bits of fat, created chops, roasts out of what previously had been a shapeless hunk of flesh. In that shape they saw patterns, as though their minds could dissect the beef mentally before a cut was made. It reminded her of Edward. Why, dear? Could you please go into that. Well, it was—no, it wasn't any sadistic thing; it was the knowledge of something abstruse. It had always seemed to her typical that she'd married an astronomer when math was her worst subject. But she admired people, like butchers, like astronomers, who had at their fingertips some fund of esoteric knowledge. Ibert with his French Provençal poems she could not admire, at least not for that. Anyone could learn about French Provençal poetry if he put his mind to it, she thought. But it took something more magical to make a crown of lamb or gaze at the stars and know why and when and how the universe was put together. And so, the romanticist will out. No, no, it's not that.

From the butcher they went to the open-air market where Ibert squeezed melons, examined fresh asparagus. Then to a Hungarian pastry shop for strudel. He was really like one of those French housewives with their little baskets. You couldn't imagine him doing anything as prosaic as wheeling a cart around a supermarket. Perhaps he liked having someone to cook for. This appeased her conscience, for although she was contributing to the food, he was doing all the cooking, having rejected out of hand her efforts to help. He only allowed her to make the coffee, and even then he watched her carefully, as though she might make some horrendous wrong move.

She decided not to get an apartment. There were none. They were too expensive. She would rent just a room. In a bookstore near Columbia she saw an ad for a room on 116th Street between Broadway and Riverside. The room was small, but adequate, not filthy. It was in an apartment evidently owned by a little old lady who let other rooms to students. There was furniture. It would mean that she could just move in and be instantly settled. Somehow it seemed a great relief, as though she'd bypassed a hurdle without having to exert herself. An apartment, even if she could have got one, would have meant buying furniture, studio beds, curtains, little pillows at Bloomingdale's. Here, it was true, you couldn't entertain very well, but there was a communal kitchen everyone could use, and she did have a table in her room. It would work. The other would have seemed so career-girlish, those chic little East Side apartments with girls all dressed, scurrying off to nine-to-five jobs. Of course, she'd have to scurry off to something to earn some money, but that could be worked out later.

She had Sunday breakfast with Ibert before moving into the new place. He was in his dark-blue bathrobe. There was a relaxed, casual feeling. Could marriage be like this? Would you want it to be? Even in this one week, while enjoying the comforts of gourmet cooking and civilized conversation, she'd had moments of claustrophobia, of wanting to get drunk or run screaming, naked, through the apartment and rape him, not because she was really sexually attracted to him but because everything seemed so neat and orderly and ultimately stultifying. But now, sipping the excellent strong coffee and munching on a stack of Swedish pancakes with lingonberry jam, she felt completely at one with the world. And didn't even mind when he said, "You shouldn't be married, Rachel."

If her mother had said this, she would have bristled instantly, sensing some implied insult, no matter how it was put. But he said it very calmly, just stating an observation.

"Why shouldn't I be?"

"Because marriage implies depending on other people for your happiness. And that's no way to live. . . . It never works anyway. . . . Even if it does, it's pernicious."

She sighed. "Well, I don't know. . . . The thing is, what alternative is there?"

"You live alone, you create your own life."

"Ya, that sounds good only. . . . Can women do it? Maybe men can, but women—"

"Don't be absurd! It may be more difficult for a woman—"

"But, like, what about sex?"

"She has lovers if she wants them."

"But what if she can't find them? After thirty, you know, it's not so easy."

"Nonsense. . . . That's such an American attitude. . . . In France women have lovers till they're seventy. They keep themselves in shape; no one cares what their age is."

Oh, dear! She had to admit the image he painted was intriguing, herself as a kind of Madame de Staël, "mistress to an age," sipping cognac in a wine-red velvet gown, "growing old gracefully."

"What about children?" she asked defensively. She was feeling that claustrophobia again, almost a dislike of him.

"What about them?"

"What do you mean, what about them?"

"People say that automatically. I wonder how many really think it through or really want them. . . . Anyway, even if you did, they let single women adopt children nowadays. I have a friend who has done it."

She felt frustrated. On the one hand, she was flattered by what he said in that it seemed to be a matter of: become a female version of me. On the other hand, even with her mother she felt a greater sense of shared goals. With her mother she was forced to act the *enfant terrible* and show contempt for the bourgeois. But with him, here she was defending respectability, conformity; it made her annoyed with herself.

"Do you think if Edward hadn't been black, it would have made any difference?" she said. She had not, throughout this entire week, referred to him except for her opening remark about being separated.

"*Was* he black?"

He was smiling, but she said, "What do you mean?"

"No, I just meant—what difference could such a thing possibly make? You sound as though you're boasting."

Again she felt that contradiction. With other people she had to beg, plead, and cajole to make them see that Edward's being black made no difference. Here was someone who just blithely assumed it was irrelevant and she—was it just out of perversity? —felt angry, as though he were belittling her.

"I don't *think* I'm boasting." She set down her fork.

"You try to make a drama out of your life."

"No, well, if I do that, it's bad. I shouldn't."

She felt as though she'd just swallowed something saying "Drink me" and was now the size of a small mouse sitting on an overstuffed armchair.

"Edward was a perfectly fine, conventional fellow," he said. "But what does he matter?"

Somehow in his life he seemed to have managed this trick: cutting himself loose from human ties, floating like a big rubber balloon which would not burst, would not sail away, would just float imperturbably onward. But was she, even if she decided such a goal was a worthy one, capable of the same?

"I'd better start moving," she said and shuffled into the bedroom to gather up her things.

Ibert went up to the new room with her, although the little old lady who had rented it to her, Mrs. Wally, gave him a suspicious look. "It's not the most elegant thing," Rachel said, "but I thought—"

"It's adequate."

After he'd left, she sat in a chair, looking out the window which overlooked the Columbia campus. Everything looked gray, for September, dreary. . . . Well, she was grateful to Ibert. What had she wanted? He'd put her up for a week. Did everyone have to do an emotional striptease? Sure, he must have moments of lying awake in the dead of night and wondering about ultimate things. But why should he reveal these to her? Why should she insist or even want him to?

She bought a few groceries at a local store and tried to squeeze them into the already-overstuffed refrigerator. The kitchen itself was small and smelled obscurely of Chinese vegetables. It was clear that eating out was going to be a frequent occurrence—or just eating things raw.

Her first night she lay in bed, aware now that the bed was too narrow and too soft, listening to the other noises in the apartment—someone practicing a flute, someone typing—and had just that feeling she'd thought of earlier—I'm floating. She awoke to the alarm from someone else's clock.

The first thing—this after breakfasting at Chock Full o'Nuts and skimming the New York *Times*—was to decide what job she ought to get. It was easy enough to decide what she didn't want. She didn't want a job in a publishing house or as a nursery school teacher or social worker—not that she had the training for any of those, but she didn't even want to *get* the training. She didn't want to be a sprightly girl graduate in a tweed suit, taking dictation, going for coffee breaks, helping humanity, being useful. What did she want? Well, she would have liked being a brain surgeon or a lady astronaut or a Senator, so she thought anyway, having never done anything remotely resembling these things. She would have liked to wield tremendous power, to have people shudder and gasp at her every word, to be brilliant and earn vast sums of money. The trouble was, leaving aside the luck which made people attain these positions, even after years of effort, they all took work. And training. And long years of doing things she had no desire to do. If only she had started training for something at fifteen, now, at twenty-five, she would be skilled, adept. But to start now was too much of a bother.

There was the reasonable alternative, the one everyone would have approved of, getting a job as a laboratory technician, but that would end up being nine-tenths dishwashing, and even more it was too connected to zoology, which she had once thought of seriously pursuing. She would be reminded every minute of lost opportunities, wasted chances, the ghosts of former women professors lamenting the fate of those like her. Nopey pope. What she would like was something different, something she'd never thought of before.

The *Times*, that day and in the days subsequently that she scanned the employment section, revealed nothing. Haphazardly she answered a notice she saw on the Columbia bulletin board about someone who wanted typing done. She could have her parents mail her typewriter out; it was the kind of mindless work that she would not object to part of the time. She could set her own hours. But it was scarcely a way to live.

Then one day, about two weeks after she'd started looking, the women's page carried an article on women clowns. There was, the article claimed, a college of Clowns. If you went for six weeks, five days a week, you could, at the end of that time, graduate as a clown. A great idea! First of all, she would be acquiring a skill—the article referred to learning yoga, juggling, unicycle riding. Even if you never used all those skills, they would be great to have. And perhaps, even if you didn't join a circus, you could do entertainment of some sort, for children's parties or the like.

Rachel the entertainer? No, it was true, at school she'd always hated performing, but mainly, she decided now, because it had usually been a case of trying to look beautiful—ballet dancing, say, or acting in Shakespeare. In fact, the one such thing she could remember enjoying was dressing up as a mustachioed old man for a second-grade costume party. The teacher had chided her in private that her fly was open, and she had won no prizes; but she had felt comfortably screened off, beyond criticism on any of the usual grounds.

That night she was excited by fantasies of herself in various fantastical getups, face painted blue with eyebrows like stars. And magic tricks? Maybe she could learn to do magic tricks!

"We don't, as a rule, take very many women," Mr. Perse, the man behind the desk, informed a crestfallen Rachel, "but it does happen that we've been experimenting more with that idea recently. For instance, in our present graduating class, we have three women to thirty men."

The College of Clowns had turned out to be in Florida. The closest thing resembling it Rachel had been able to track down was this organization in lower Manhattan: Magicians and Entertainers. The training fee did not seem extravagant: Rachel decided she could use part of the thousand dollars she had saved.

"We have a rotating system," he was continuing. "Each six weeks a new series of classes begins, but you can start certain ones one week, others another week. . . . Or you can wait and enroll in all of them from the beginning."

School! She was back in school! Yet it struck her that odd as "the subject matter" appeared to her, it was not odd to anyone here. You could have been at the Columbia School of Journalism or the New York School of Social Work. There was the same official-looking building, the same people rushing from room to room, looking intent and harried. Apart from the high percentage of men to women, there was nothing unusual. Even that was not unusual.

In her first class she met Beatrice. Besides herself, Rachel had noticed only one girl, a slight blonde who looked just in her teens. Beatrice stood out immediately because she was nearly six feet tall. Of course, it was funny, but typical, Rachel thought, that now she tended to compare everyone to clowns she had seen, and Beatrice, at first glance, struck her as a kind of female Jacques Tati. She had that kind of gangling body and thin poker face. Possibly she was pretty or could have been, but her height made you not judge her on those conventional standards. The men looked more conventional—oh, some were very short or very fat, but on the whole they might have been a group of men gathered for induction in the Army, except that the age range seemed wider. Most were young, at least under thirty, but there were a few who had a kind of beaten, tired look, as though they had tried several professions, none of which had quite worked out.

Beatrice said—it was the end of the first week, and they were removing makeup after a greasepaint session—"I don't think this woman really understands the first thing she's doing."

Rachel was scrubbing at her cheeks with a Kleenex soaked in cold cream. The cream dissolved easily on her skin and smeared off, but she still felt that for the rest of the day her face had a sticky, clogged feeling. "About the materials, you mean?" she said.

"About everything! The whole essence isn't to paint on a face like out of a book. I mean, you can start with that, but you have to go beyond it."

"Maybe she's planning to go beyond it."

"I doubt it." Beatrice peeled off a red star she had affixed high up on her forehead. "I've studied mime, you know, and so maybe this seems terribly overdone, exaggerated."

"Ya, well, I thought that was the point."

"No, it's not! Well, of course, it depends on what your goals are. For most of them it's probably quite sufficient."

It turned out that Beatrice had nothing but contempt for about eighty percent of the apprentice clowns and a goodly number of the teachers as well. The man who taught yoga, a small Japanese with black eyebrows that looked as though they'd been slashed on with india ink, she admired. "He knows what he's doing. He has a respect for it. But the rest of them!"

Beatrice walked with Rachel through part of the Village, partly on a quest for certain health foods which she felt were essential to her well-being. "You're not going to make it if you don't take good physical care of yourself," she said to Rachel. "You're *much* too flabby."

"That's what my mother says."

"Without a decent body, you're dead. Especially in entertainment. You're not going to get up there and tell jokes. It isn't a verbal thing. You have to use your body like a tool."

"Ya, I see what you mean," Rachel said. Already she was coming home at night as sore as if she'd been cracked over a wheel. Muscles she never knew existed were suddenly being forced into use, and they rebelled, yelping.

Beatrice lived alone in a five-floor walk-up in the East Village. It wasn't that she liked the Village scene, she explained, just that "it was all she could afford." It seemed that she worked evenings in a local coffeehouse.

Rachel felt ashamed that her own motives in taking this course were so ambiguous and so hazy. Beatrice was dedicated. She wanted to be a kind of female Marcel Marceau, for which, she immediately added, one really ought to go to France. Something as crude as going on the road with the circus, which many of the other students considered as an opening, she rejected out of hand. "The pay's lousy," she said, "and who wants to live that kind of bummy life, always packing and unpacking?"

"What do you think of doing with the training, then?" Rachel wanted to know.

She shrugged. "I suppose I'm impractical. . . . I didn't take this just to get a job. . . . I have money saved. I can live. . . . I've thought of entertaining at children's birthday parties. They're usually so cruddy. Have you ever been to any? My sister has six kids, and every year she goes through this thing of trying to find someone to organize it for her. The best she can do is get some fly-by-night magician, nothing the kids like."

"How does it pay?"

"Not enough to live on. But if you got started. . . . Are you interested?"

"In what?" Rachel was trying to digest a portion of tuna sprinkled with wheat germ that Beatrice had insisted she try for quick energy.

"Well, it occurred to me—if you felt like it, we could be a team. If you want to. . . . It's easier that way. Not so tiring. And there's more variety."

"How could we—I mean, what would we—"

"Oh, I have a dozen programs," Beatrice said, tossing one of her cats a piece of fish. "I've thought about this for years. The main thing is not to condescend. People are always condescending to children. Act exactly as though they were adults. They always prefer that. . . . You could fit in very well," she said. "I think you'd be a good buffoon."

"A buffoon?" Rachel felt a little hurt.

"Yes, you know, like in that costume you wore in class the other day. . . . You tumble rather well. I see you plumped up a little, you know, kind of floppy, with a big hat. . . . I'd do the magic tricks."

It was true, Rachel had noticed, Beatrice was superb at magic tricks. Was it her hands? She had those long tapering fingers you associated with pianists or violinists. But it was her manner, too. Her long poker face with its thin, almost invisible eyebrows, her disdainfulness. Rachel always felt a little guilty tricking people. She'd disliked it as a child when someone would approach her with "Take a card, any card." Whereas Beatrice appeared to enjoy putting things over, having the essential stupidity of mankind revealed.

"She sounds like a lesbian," said Ibert, whom Rachel ran into one day on campus. "I'd look out."

"Even if it were true," said Rachel, "she's not going to jump me, for God's sake; I can handle her."

"The whole idea of a team. . . . That sounds ominous."

"It's a way to earn some money. . . . Better than typing." He had been getting her some typing jobs connected with his department.

"Better in what sense?"

"More involving. . . . Look, on my own, what can I do? I'm not going to join the circus."

"Why not?"

"Because it's a fantastically hard life. . . . There are no women clowns. They're regarded as freaks. . . . Anyway, it's not a sophisticated thing. Maybe in European circuses in the old days it was. But you know what the circus is today. It's huge. No one sees you; no one notices you."

She went to his apartment to pick up some papers for typing and demonstrated her prowess by juggling with four tangerines and a tennis ball.

"Very clever." He was watching her ironically. "No, you really are quite adept." He tossed her another tangerine, but she missed it.

"You can't do that many."

"*Pourquoi pas?*"

"There's a law of balances."

He served her coffee and cognac; it was after dinner, but she had had no dinner, having come straight home after class.

"You know who you should meet," he said, "my brother."

"Who's he?"

"No, you won't meet him. . . . He's in Paris. But if you ever go there. He's an excellent mime. . . . Oh, he doesn't use it much now. He's become a singer, fairly good, but he used to be quite entertaining . . . quite poignant."

"Is your whole family over there?"

"He is my whole family. . . . My parents are no longer living." His face got that stiff look which said she should not ask any more.

"I'll tell you the trouble with you, Rachel," he said a few minutes later. They were standing at the door, and she had her coat on, ready to leave.

"No, don't. . . . Tell me what's *isn't* wrong with me."

"No, I mean this. . . . You come and say, 'Look at me: I've married a black . . . I'm studying to be a clown,' expecting everyone to get horrified or excited. . . . But there's nothing wrong with those things. A little eccentric, maybe. But that's all. . . . So you're disappointed and you think, 'Why did I bother doing them?' and you move on to something else."

"Now, shit, you," Rachel said. "I'm not *that* frivolous. . . . God, you're like Beatrice."

"I hope not," he said dryly.

"You ought to meet her. You'd make a perfect pair."

"Be a clown," he said, "but take it seriously. It's an honorable profession."

She was angry, but laughing, perhaps nervously. "So does *your* life depend on teaching French?"

"Yes! Or in doing something equivalent. I want to lead a certain life. I must work."

Rachel sighed. "Someday you'll see me in the main ring at Barnum and Bailey and you'll say—"

"You're not *serious*, Rachel."

But she discovered, which pleased her, that she was good at clowning. Not at all of it. But even the things she wasn't good at, the physical exercises, she worked hard at. She wanted to master those physical skills. The hell with Ibert! He should see her, stumbling around on her stilts. Had he ever worked so hard on his fucking French poetry? She would show them. Edward, too. And the makeup intrigued her. At making herself up, at applying rouge, eye shadow and the like, she'd never been very adept. But this had another purpose, and she found herself able to be much more intrigued by it. It was more like painting a canvas; only the canvas was your face. And then, regular makeup had always seemed based on a knowledge of your own potential beauty, about which she had doubts, whereas this was more simply a disguise. A few times she went home on the subway with some of the makeup still on, and she didn't even feel embarrassed or awkward when people stared at her or smiled. It was almost a kind of protection.

"I'm studying to be a clown!" she told Julie and Dan, who called her one night unexpectedly, having evidently got the number from her parents.

They were at different ends of the extension. "You're fooling," was Julie's immediate, not amused response.

Dan said, "They didn't mention it."

To her parents she had been vaguer, only stressing the idea Beatrice had mentioned which she wasn't sure would ever be a reality, of forming a team and entertaining at children's birthday parties. "I'm getting pretty good," she said. "You should see me. I can ride a unicycle even."

"We're calling because we wondered if you might come down and visit us," Julie said, as though to say: enough of this nonsense.

Rachel was riled. "I'm fairly busy now. It's a six-week course, you know."

"Well, surely you have weekends."

"Yes, I could come."

"It's just—we'd like to see you," Dan said. "It's been so long, Rach. . . . Come on down."

"You won't try to improve my soul or give me lectures," Rachel made him promise.

"Never!"

With him at least, if not with Julie, she felt she could make light of everything.

"Okay, maybe I'll come. . . . Is any special weekend good?"

He named a few dates.

"I'll write and tell you. . . . Let me see how my schedule shapes up."

As far as her "schedule" went, she knew she must go to Philadelphia too and get her things. "Must" was not quite accurate. She could have requested that Edward send them in a big parcel, but she wanted to go. She had left so hurriedly, almost with the illusion that with her disappearance the whole structure would cease to exist, like those houses in fairy stories.

Meanwhile, there was Beatrice who was indefatigable about her plans for their future. Still, it was nice to think of having a future! Beatrice seemed to make the whole clown thing something dignified. Certainly she took it more seriously than half the people Rachel had ever known took what they were doing. Why? How had Beatrice got here? Why, at thirty-four, was she careening around a bare gym on wooden stilts while a small woman in spectacles barked criticisms at her? Well, there was a marriage somewhere, over long ago. Usually Rachel plunged in and asked personal questions about anything, but Beatrice had a kind of slipperiness, an evasiveness. Her pale, catlike face looked half-retreating, half-hostile. And at this moment Rachel felt she could hardly risk Beatrice's displeasure. If this "team" worked out, it would make her training seem worthwhile, at least on a small scale. If it didn't, the whole thing might seem just another exercise in futility or, as Ibert had said, a desire to seem eccentric for the sake of shocking or surprising people.

Anyway, she admired Beatrice. Primarily because she quickly

learned, from talking to some of the men in the class, that Beatrice aroused just that kind of instinctive, almost animal-like uneasiness and hostility that she herself would have liked to arouse.
Oh, true, there was her crowd-pleaser side. But she also, perhaps
more than that, would have liked to be the sort who genuinely
didn't give a damn, who was hated and who could hate back
with a pure, vengeful spite. Beatrice was, not to put too fine a
point on it, a castrater. And Rachel had always had ambitions of
wanting to be a castrating woman. She had always wanted to
have that power to make the killing remark, the statement that
would be so piercing, so true, so malevolent, and yet, as Beatrice
did it, so gently put that the protagonist would stagger back,
reeling, not yet certain what had happened, only aware later
that some vital organ had been permanently put out of commis-
sion. And the thing that made Beatrice more impressive was that
her castrating had a kind of general application. Of course, men
could be castrating, too—it was, after all, basically a psychic
phenomenon, not a physical one. And Beatrice, though she was
perhaps more vicious with men, would certainly have attacked
other women or children or crippled little old ladies. Rachel had
felt the knife plunging into her own side often enough not to
feel immune. It seemed instinctive; where Beatrice had learned
the trick, why, she would never know. If, after witnessing or
even enduring an especially devastating attack, you asked her
why, she would look blank, as though she hadn't the vaguest
idea what you were talking about; surely you must be mad.
Even that purity of self-deception Rachel admired, seeing it as
necessary for the carrying out of any great action.

"Beatrice, would you like to come to Washington with me?
I'm going to visit my brother and his wife."

"Why should I want to do that?"

"You might like Julie. . . . You and she have something in
common."

Did they? Sometimes Rachel felt she brought people together
just for the ironic pleasure of seeing them tangle with each other
while she watched from the sidelines. And she would have liked

an orchestra seat to a confrontation between Julie and Beatrice, both with wills of steel, but otherwise utterly incompatible, Julie as bourgeois and "stable" as Beatrice was eccentric and bohemian.

"I don't like the South," Beatrice said disdainfully.

"Where are you from?"

"Iowa . . . But we moved East when I was a child."

Beatrice in Iowa? Among fields of corn and scarecrows? Rachel suspected a carefully concealed background of unquestionable middle-classness.

"I don't really want to see them alone," Rachel confessed. "I guess it's partly that. . . . I came here to get away from family. Of course, Dan isn't like that, but still—"

"People's lives are tragedies," Beatrice said unexpectedly, flatly, "of one kind or another."

Rachel had seen that when she had something depressing or grim to relate, Beatrice's whole manner changed. She could be capable of such total compassion, you were left breathless and tried, desperately, to think of other sad things, other reasons you were an object of pity. If I had leukemia, she would be the first one at the hospital, Rachel thought. But she didn't hate Beatrice for this. She must think of herself as wounded, too. Which made the comparison to Julie who was so whole, so solid, absurd. What had she been thinking of?

"At a party I went to last night," Beatrice said, "a woman appeared naked."

"Why?" Rachel wanted to know.

"I don't know. . . . It was weird. I didn't like it. Everyone else seemed to know her. Her body wasn't good, even. . . . I locked myself in the bathroom, finally."

She's trying to say something, Rachel thought, but wasn't sure what. She recalled what Ibert had said about Beatrice being a lesbian.

"Why did you lock yourself in the bathroom, Beatrice?"

"Physical ugliness makes me sick! People have a responsibility to their bodies! . . . Anyway, I don't mind nudity, I don't mean that. But it has to have a setting. Here they did it to laugh at her. You could tell. She didn't mind. She thought of herself as laughable. But that's decadent. If you don't have pride in your body, you don't have pride in anything."

Beatrice's religion of the body struck Rachel as odd; no one she'd ever known had cared so much about it or at least had been willing to be so verbal on the subject. At home she stared at herself in the full-length mirror, pleased to see a possible lessening of flab, but unable to see anything holy.

She would go to Washington by herself.

Chapter Two

THE accent of the taxi driver who took her to Dan and Julie's house was almost incomprehensible. Rachel always had this feeling in the South; it was a different country. You felt you needed a guidebook, like in Europe. She had never traveled South farther than Washington. Edward had had no desire to. Well, why should he? Except that she had had a mild, almost perverse curiosity to meet an actual bigot, someone who would gawk at them. Was it just that boastfulness Ibert had spoken of? Wanting to seem "somebody," if only because you could find someone who would hate you for the wrong reasons. Which, of course, was so much easier than someone who hated you for the right reasons. To be refused at a hotel! Well, anyway, they'd never done it. Even Washington—they'd always, not for reasons of deliberate avoidance, had Dan and Julie visit them in Philadelphia.

When she arrived, Dan came to the door. "Julie's out," he said. "Her classes don't end till five."

"Classes?"

"She's in law school now. Didn't Mom show you the letter?"

"Oh, gosh, she might have, but I was kind of up in the air when I was home. I know I saw it, I just don't—"

"Yup, she's going full steam ahead. . . . Well, you know Julie." He seemed to have a kind of pride in her. Rachel only hoped he wouldn't be one of those men interviewed in the New York *Times* who, when his wife was appointed to some big deal job, smiled and looked vague and anonymous while the wife was being questioned on her views on art, religion, and the latest hems. You could say, that was his fate. Maybe it was oedipal. Mom had always been involved in politics, but not in the way Julie was where you felt she might make some impact.

"How's your own work?" She let him take her coat and followed him into the living room.

"Oh, okay . . . nothing special."

He was always self-deprecating, so it was hard to tell whether what he said was the truth or just a cover-up. The fact was that in the beginning he had done more civil rights work and now was with a large firm where she had the feeling he was partly swallowed up. Not that he would ever be fired, but he didn't seem the slick, pushy lawyer type whom you imagined making a name for himself in Washington.

"I'm sorry about Edward, Rach." He was talking with his back to her, a habit of his.

"Ya, well. . . ."

"Mom said she thought—"

"Don't quote me that crap, please!"

"Sure." He grinned. Then he looked at her quizzically. "I think Edward was a snob in parts. . . . Did he mind our being Jewish?"

Rachel grimaced. "I don't think he. . . . No, I mean, he liked it. He used to say—all that crap about Jewish vitality. . . . Anyway, Jews and blacks, the two great outcasts."

"Ya, only two great outcasts usually don't get along that well."

"Maybe. . . . Look, I'd love to feel it was something that simple."

"That's not simple."

"Put it this way. Julie's not Jewish. So if you got divorced and someone started to say, was it that, wouldn't you feel—"

"I feel all these things add up."

In some ways, she was glad he was throwing it all at her before Julie arrived. She would never have wanted to discuss it in front of her. But at the same time she was tired from the train and wanted, mostly, to have a drink and not think of Edward. "How about making me a vodka sour?" she said. "No, I agree. Things do add up. . . . But if Edward wants to screw around, it isn't because I am or am not Jewish."

"Why is it then?"

"Why does anyone?" Since he looked blank and somewhat evasive, she went on, "Look, I've given this a certain amount of thought, now that you ask. . . . I mean, you could say it's sexual. But I really don't feel I was such a failure in that department. I'll never qualify as playgirl of the Western world, but I'm not frigid. I mean, my orgasms can beat up anybody's orgasms!"

He laughed. "I doubt that's the point."

"Well, what is?"

Again he looked away. "I don't think men find . . . someone primarily for sexual reasons."

"Ya?"

"I don't think it's a physical thing, it—"

She took the vodka sour and gulped at it. "Okay, so now I know what you *don't* think it is. . . . How about saying what it *is!*"

"She made him feel better."

This answer was so lame and so sheepishly offered that Rachel grimaced. "Ya, and what else is new?"

Dan laughed. He pulled at his eyebrows, a nervous habit he had. "I don't know, Rach. . . . Look, I don't know Edward that well. Maybe he's just a bastard. Maybe he enjoys making you suffer."

"*That's* what I want to hear!" She looked around the apartment. "You have a lot more artwork than when I was here last."

"Ya, well . . . it's mostly from Julie's father. He collects it."

"Rather handy."

"It is and it isn't. . . . I feel we should collect our own."

"But it's expensive."

"True." He looked uncomfortable. "Uh—I need to check something in the kitchen."

"Sure. . . . Go ahead."

"On nights Julie works late, I cook. . . . I like to."

He seemed a little defensive, so Rachel said quickly, "I do too. . . . It's relaxing if you've just been sitting thinking all day."

"I wish I could say that was true of me." He peered into a large blue bowl. "This is something I invented. You marinate the pork chops in gin for half an hour."

"Sounds good."

"I like just tossing things in."

Rachel watched as he carefully selected a few spices from the shelf. And here we have the modern marriage. Reversal of Roles Ltd. Look, let him cook, will you? I'm letting him. Anyway, I thought you approved of that. I do, in a way.

"What does Julie intend to do once she's finished?"

He was sniffing at a spice bottle. "Oh . . . she hasn't worked it out that much yet. . . . Something in politics."

"Does she still do much?"

"Well, not now. . . . Ever since McCarthy faded out of the picture, she kind of lost interest. . . . Oh, she still sees him, but she doesn't seem to think there's much hope in it."

"I guess not." Rachel picked up a fork and poked at the chops. "Do you have your own butcher?"

"My what?"

"No, I just. . . . This man I was staying with in New York used to go to a wonderful butcher and—"

"What man?" He looked sly and, at the same time, a little disapproving, like her mother.

"Oh, no, nothing like that. . . . He was just. . . . Maybe I mentioned him, I knew him around the time Stef and I were going together. He teaches French at Columbia. Jacques Ibert."

"I don't remember."

"No, he just let me stay at his place a few days. . . . He's not interested in women."

"A *Frenchman* not interested in women?"

"It happens."

Julie came home at six thirty. She gave Rachel a quick kiss. "Hi, sweetie! Sorry I wasn't here to meet you."

She wasn't pretty. She was short and too chunky, but more than that, she didn't seem to give much of a damn about her appearance. She wasn't messy—she wore pants a lot, chicly tailored ones—but her hair was tied straight back in a bun, and she never wore a trace of makeup. At times she reminded Rachel of those old prints you saw of people like Rosa Luxemburg—Julie's face could get that severe, hair parted in the middle, I will go to my death on the altar of an ideal expression, which was intriguing, almost a substitute for good looks. She was a funny mixture. Rather standoffish with people, but indulging in baby talk with her poodle, Whimsey. At the same time she could drink almost anyone under the table without showing the least signs of inebriation, a talent Rachel admired no end, and she played poker like a fiend; you would have thought both her parents had been riverboat gamblers and she'd been raised with a poker chip for a pacifier.

"You know, it's incredible," she said as they slid into their seats for dinner and Dan brought forth the inebriated pork chops. "This guy who teaches this course—where did they find him? I mean, *I* know more about corporate law than he does!"

"You know a fair amount, though," Dan said.

She ignored this. "I happen to know a woman applied for that job and they turned her down, so you figure, well, they must have someone great. And then they dredge up this joker!"

Julie was a great women's lib supporter.

"The chops are good," Rachel said.

"Ya, they are." Julie grinned. "I always said—he'd make a great wife for somebody if he ever wanted."

Gulp. But no one seemed embarrassed. Well, there are hostilities and hostilities. Besides, she was jealous of Julie and probably took Dan's side too quickly.

"I guess Mom is the only one in our family who *doesn't* like to cook," Rachel said.

"Well, she's pretty good at pies and stuff," Dan said loyally.

"What are your parents *up* to these days?" Julie said. "You were just there, weren't you?"

"Oh, the same. . . . Mom's taking a course in weaving."

Julie shook her head. "That's really criminal. . . . A woman her age with her training could be doing so much!"

"So look, she worked all her life, let her enjoy herself," Dan said mildly.

"I'll let her!" She downed a glass of wine and poured herself another. "Look, I'm not going to run anyone's life for them. . . . How's clowning?"

Rachel started. "Oh . . . I like it."

"What are you—are you really serious, Rach? I mean, you wear wigs and crazy makeup and all that?"

"It's fun."

Julie shook her head. "I'm glad the progress of the world doesn't depend on your family."

Dan looked at her.

Rachel said, "This is a good wine."

Dan said, "It's from Julie's father. He sends it by the case."

"I liked that Pouilly Fuissé better," Julie said. "It was drier."

Dan poured himself another glass. "Well, to my untutored palate . . ."

Julie said, "Dan thinks we bum too much off my father . . . artwork and wine and all that. . . . I say, what has the bastard ever done in life except make money, so why shouldn't we spend it?"

"You'll notice there's a certain discrepancy with Julie's supposedly liberal ideals here," said Dan.

"Consistency is the last refuge of a something." Julie shrugged. "I'm a pragmatist."

"That you certainly are."

After supper Julie closeted herself in the study to go over some notes. Dan sat down to read the paper and put on some music. A marriage is a marriage is a marriage. Rachel had always firmly believed that people did not marry for any of the reasons they thought—because the other person was sexy, beautiful, smart, had a good sense of humor—but that there was some irrational underpinning which had nothing to do with surface motives. She had always felt in her own case that she had decided to marry Edward after seeing him cut his toenails. Instead of hacking them off as she did in great clumps and pieces, he cut ten perfect half-moons, which he then scooped up neatly in the palm of his hand and deposited in the wastebasket. And this gesture, so trivial, had seemed—still did seem—to imply a whole world of order and reason from which she was excluded, of which she knew scarcely anything, but which, by way of him, she might derive some vicarious pleasure. So—Dan and Julie, Quentin and Jacques, her parents, the world!

Dan helped her fix up the studio couch bed in the study after Julie had retired. It was an unfurnished room, mainly consisting of the couch and two desks, one heaped with books and papers (Julie's), the other neat as a pin with a few letters weighed down by a glass paperweight. "It's nice that you can have a guest room," she said, tugging at one end of the sheet.

"Ya, well, of course, once we have children. . . ."

"Oh, are you planning—"

He looked sheepish. "*I'd* like to . . . but we're not planning really."

"I see," she said but didn't.

They claimed they had no intention of fixing her up, nothing so crude. But to make a foursome had invited a fellow student of Julie's, someone named Oliver Regin, who would accompany them out to dinner and to the theater.

Oliver Regin was the sort of lawyer whom Rachel imagined Dan ought to be—not slick exactly, but on the make. He was short with wiry hair and a flat, almost Mongoloid face. Not her type, but someone with a lot of energy to burn. At the theater, while she was standing with him in the lobby—Julie and Dan had decided to stay in their seats—she said, "You know Julie from—"

"I introduced Dan to his mistress."

She smiled at him. It was so noisy in the lobby that she thought she'd either misunderstood or that he was finishing a joke or reference he had made earlier.

"I was sleeping with her for a while, but she—well, we're friends."

Was this the point to feel triumphant—Julie, the all-powerful, is finally getting hers—or to feel: ye gods, even Dan! In any case, there was a nasty, gloating quality to the way Oliver Regin delivered this bit of news which made her just say stiffly, "Why don't we go back? It's so noisy here."

He grinned at her and patted her shoulder. "She's a nice girl, don't worry."

Why should she worry? Dan had every motive, Julie might not care or might be sleeping around, too. So, who was worrying? But when she went down with Dan to get the Sunday *Times* after they'd returned, she said, "I don't like Oliver Regin."

"Oh." He looked uneasy. "I don't mind him. You have to get used to him. He's not that crude, really, as he seems. . . . He's very kind."

She frowned. "He said you were having an affair."

The expression on Dan's face was almost terror, immediately muted to a frowning "Oh, did he say that?"

"Are you?"

For a long time he didn't say anything. He had that way of suddenly going deaf on you. "I've been . . . seeing this woman," he said very slowly.

"Ya, well, I—"

"I believe you would find her a very sympathetic person, Rachel. . . . Maybe you would like to meet her. . . . She's—she's divorced also. She's an ornithologist."

"Birds?"

"Yes, she. . . ."

"But listen, Dan, how about Julie? Does she know?"

"Julie." He looked very thoughtful. "Well, you see . . . Julie and I so seldom sleep together that. . . ."

He spoke very slowly and in such a detached way that Rachel couldn't help saying wryly, "That you're fulfilling a physical need?"

He said, "I never knew anything about birds before . . . I was never interested in them. But you'd be amazed at how—"

"You sit around talking about *birds* all the time?"

"We do, yes. . . ."

"But she slept with Oliver Regin!"

"Yes, well, Oliver likes to think that."

"Likes to . . . Dan!"

"I very much doubt. . . . He says certain things. . . . Actually, Vernice is quite grateful to Oliver for certain things he once did, but there was never any. . . . Would you like to *meet* Vernice?"

Rachel sighed. "Dan, I don't know, I—"

"Vernice is someone Julie wouldn't understand," he said but in that flat, unemotional way. "They wouldn't be friends."

"I shouldn't think so."

"It's curious," he went on. "I've given this considerable thought. . . . They're very different types."

"Well, wouldn't it be more curious if they weren't?"

"Vernice . . . well, sometimes she reminds me of you, Rach."

"In that—"

"You know, her parents were killed in a concentration camp."

"No, I didn't, but—in what way does she—"

"Oh, like you? . . . Well, it's hard to say. She's a little bit uncertain of what she wants, she. . . ."

"Unlike Julie."

"I admire Julie a great deal." He sniffed. "Jesus, this damn hay fever!"

"I thought it was asthma."

"Oh, it's everything rolled into one. . . . You name it, I have it!" He blew his nose. "You and Vernice would have a lot in common; I wish you could meet her."

"I'd feel awkward."

"No, no, you shouldn't feel that." He looked at her, concerned. "Our relationship is not predominantly sexual."

"Well, I'm glad to hear it. . . . Or, I mean, I'm not. I—"

"You asked about Edward earlier, Rachel. . . . It may well be this is a parallel case."

"Dan, Mary, Mother of Jesus! Edward is not sitting around talking about fucking birds!"

"The birds are just a symbol," he said, getting a better grip on the paper. "You mustn't concentrate on the birds."

"I'm not concentrating on the birds!"

"Tomorrow we'll have tea with Vernice," he said, considering. "Julie goes to the library all afternoon Sundays."

"How did she get a name like—"

"Vernice is Southern," he said. "She's from Virginia. She talks very slowly. You have to get used to it. She's not stupid."

"No, well, I wouldn't imagine—"

They were at the door now, which relieved Rachel since Julie was standing just inside drinking a glass of milk and munching on a cookie. Rachel mumbled something about being tired and fled to the study.

She was rather hoping Dan would have forgotten about his offer, but on the nose of three, when Julie had departed, he came over, beaming, and said, "Vernice says we should pick up some cream for the tea. . . . She likes cream in her tea."

And of course, or maybe not of course, Vernice was not pretty. If you have been casting for a play the roles of (1) abandoned wife and (2) mistress, Vernice would surely have won out over Julie for the first part. She was thin with soft brownish hair hanging around her face, features that were best described as nondescript. She looked to Rachel rather like a bird with her thin arms and legs and her quiet, piping voice. And so? An oasis of calm? Yes, but there were oases and oases. There were a great many birds around the small apartment, birds in cages, stuffed birds, prints of birds in old, faded antique frames.

"Owls are my favorite," Vernice said. "Of course, I love night creatures in general."

She seemed genuinely naïve—or couldn't you say that of anyone?—with a smile that came slowly and gave a brief incandescence to her face. They sleep together? Rachel wondered. Maybe it was oedipal, maybe she just couldn't imagine Dan engaged in *legal* sex, to say nothing of illegal, but to imagine these two vague, repressed people actually getting to the point of removing their clothes! Did they do it behind screens? Did Vernice have long old-fashioned nightgowns with lace trailing on the floor? Oh, it *was* a perfect revenge! Julie would die if she met Vernice—or would she perhaps feel totally unthreatened since there was so little similarity?

Vernice poured tea from a china teapot with blue flowers on it. Dan sat watching her, smiling protectively as though he were the mother and Rachel the gentleman caller who had just stopped in unexpectedly.

"I like wombats," said Rachel. "Are they night creatures?" The word "creature" struck her as a little arcane, but she used it anyway.

"No, they're *not*," Vernice said, a little disapprovingly.

"You work in the Smithsonian Dan said?" said Rachel, stirring her tea.

"Oh, yes! I've worked there for years. It's a lovely place. . . . I'm very fond of old institutions," she said. "That's why I chose Washington partly. They've preserved so much of it. New York always seems to be being torn down!"

"Yes, well, I guess in the North there's less respect for landmarks," Rachel said. She wished Dan would say something.

"Dan and I have thought of traveling to Cambodia," Vernice said. "We'd love to see Angkor Wat."

Dan said, "Yes, well, Julie may want to go to summer school this year." He said her name quite calmly, as though she were the sister.

"I'm so impressed by what Dan says of Julie!" Vernice suddenly exclaimed. "She sounds like a person with so much energy! I just have none! Well, I have low blood pressure; that accounts for it partly, I guess. I'm always fainting in supermarkets and things like that!" She poured some more tea. "Last time it happened this very nice man just flung me over his shoulder like a side of beef and took me down to the basement for a glass of water. I was so grateful."

"You should be careful, darling," Dan said.

"Oh, I am. . . . Anyway, fainting isn't anything. I almost like it. You get this funny roaring in your ears, like the ocean. Did you ever—"

"No," Rachel said. "It sounds—"

"Yes, it is. Surprisingly it is." She cleared her throat. "I apologize for the heat," she said. "Well, Dan knows all this, I have such problems with the heat here. If you turn the radiator *off*, it's as cold as ice, and otherwise it's roasting! From heaven to hell, you could say."

"If your idea of heaven is freezing your toes off," said Dan.

Rachel stared from one of them to the other as they exchanged a little smile. Now here we have two people who have engaged in what used to be known as sexual congress. I mean, this fellow, this Dan, this brother, this husband, this asthma-ridden creature, has actually inserted his penis into the vagina of this wisteria blossom with her stuffed owls and painted teapots. This has taken place with some intensity of feeling, disobeying certain rules laid down by law. These people. . . . No, it was too incomprehensible. The mind *did* boggle, that was all there was to it. Maybe they just meet and have tea.

As she walked home with Dan, Rachel said, "Do you want to marry Vernice?"

He looked vague. "Oh—well, no. . . . She doesn't want to get married, anyway. Well, she is rather delicate. . . . And she was married, and it wasn't a very fortunate experience. I gather the man was rather—"

"A cad?"

"Precisely. . . . And she's one of these people who feels those things very keenly. . . . I mean, she doesn't hate men, but she's wary. . . ."

"Yes . . ." Rachel said. She sneezed. God, all she needed was to become asthmatic, too.

"Vernice is not really delicate," he said suddenly. "She's very sensitive, of course, but she's really very strong. I often think she's a stronger person than Julie in her own way. She has a very definite sense of who she is."

"Ya, well, that is rare these days," Rachel said.

"Julie feels she has to prove herself—and she will. No question of that. Julie will have an impact someday. I feel sure of it."

"Dan, listen—do you *hate* Julie?"

He looked startled. "What do you mean? No, of course not!"

"But I mean, you're—I don't know, you're attacking her indirectly. She would die if she knew!"

He smiled. "No, she wouldn't. Don't be silly. . . . Julie wouldn't die over something like this. I think she'd find it admirable." He gave his sly little smile. "I think she'd be pleased to think I'm capable. . . . Of course, I won't tell her. But I think she'd be pleased in a certain sense."

At five the deceived wife returned from the library with her books and a bag of pastrami sandwiches she'd picked up on the way. They ate in the kitchen just before Rachel had to catch the train back to New York.

"Dan may come to New York in a few months," Julie said. "Did he mention it? There's a conference there at Columbia."

"Oh, well, great," Rachel said. "You can stay with me. . . . That is, I think you can, if you can produce a statement saying you're definitely my brother. The lady who rents me this room—"

Julie slathered mustard all over a slice of rye bread. "I hardly think Dan would qualify as the immoral lover type."

Rachel gulped. Well, maybe she deserves it, being so smug. Dan looked neither embarrassed nor pleased. He just said, "Do you want my other half, Julie? It's a little fatty for me."

"See! Look at him! Then he'll sell me to market for a bigger price!" She took the sandwich. "If you have a metabolism like mine, everything turns to fat anyway. So you might as well start out with the genuine article."

"When Rachel was little, she liked to eat just the fat off ham," Dan said. "She used to throw away the ham part."

"I don't remember that," Rachel said.

"Don't you?" he said fondly. He sneezed.

Julie said, "Do you think asthma is due to sexual repression, Rachel? I wish I knew in Dan's case." She spoke as though he were either not present or a child too small to understand.

"I don't—" Rachel said, a little flustered.

"And what if it were?" Dan said with his sly little smile. "What would you do then?"

"I'd rape you more often, of course!"

Rachel said. "I think I should—"

They both leaped up. Dan said, "So I'll write when I'm coming, Rach."

"Yes, do. . . . Thanks so much, Julie. I'm glad I came!"

And I'm glad to get away! she thought, settling back in the taxi they had called for her. God, one's own life was enough without trying to understand other people's! Especially one's relatives.

At home she found the postcard. It said simply: "Will be in N.Y. Wednesday. Will call at your place at 4. Call me if this isn't convenient. Edward."

She turned the card around, almost as though the feel of it, something in its texture or weight, might reveal its intentions. But nothing. Just Edward's very neat, small handwriting—he was one of those people who could definitely have written the Lord's Prayer on the head of a pin or anywhere else you might fancy.

The day he was due to arrive she sprained her ankle falling off the unicycle. She loved the unicycle and rather prided herself that she'd learned it so quickly and well. Even the teacher who was not impressed with her other physical achievements had praised her. But of course, the to-be-predicted fall had come, and she had limped off to the doctor's office to be bandaged and advised to stay off it for a week at least and to take baths with her foot out of the tub. She tried to envision this and decided it would be easier simply not to take baths.

The same morning—possibly this had contributed to the cocky, slaphappy mood that had led to her fall—she took a Dexamyl Spansule. At college she had grown to love these pills but lately had stopped taking them so often. However, today it seemed imperative that she be in a gay, self-confident mood when Edward arrived. She would wear a red dress and perfume; she would talk and have a veritable list of topics with which to entertain him. She would play the clown! She would be funny, she would be. . . . Oh, hell, let her just live through it.

He had said he would arrive at four. He arrived at four. Edward was one of those people who were almost constitutionally incapable of arriving late. He seemed to have some built-in awareness of time, almost like a sixth sense. In the same way when she used to call Weather and then ask him to guess the temperature and humidity, he would rarely be more than five degrees off. With statistics, also, from something as improbable as how many flowered hats were sold in Iowa in 1919 to how many men fell on Flanders Field in 1917, he would always think a minute, as though there *were* a way of calculating such things, and then come up with an answer not far removed from the real one. So, he was an *idiot savant*, so what?

He knocked on her door. She went to open it. It had crossed her mind that if it were possible, she might have met him at Ibert's apartment, telling Ibert to go out for a few hours. Someplace impersonal. Her own room was so pitiful it would be so clear at a glance that she was far from living high off the hog. Did it matter? Well, yes, in a way.

She said, stammered, "Hi. . . . You're when you said you'd be."

"Yes." He looked at her.

She had not seen him for three months. And this is Edward.

He is not handsome. No, even she would say he was getting too fat. Not fat, he was tall enough—over six feet—to carry it off, but there was an incipient paunch there, no doubt of it. Which she didn't like. She liked *thin* men. Nor did she go all woozy in the knees at the sight of any black male of mating age. I mean, Jesus, she saw a hundred of them every day on the streets of New York and had no reaction at all. So you could rule out those two primary reasons why she felt, seeing him again, that like Vernice, she might have to be slung over someone's back like a slab of beef and revived with smelling salts in the basement of a supermarket.

"I was away when your card came," she said. "I—Julie and Dan. They said to. I hadn't seen them, so I—"

The main thing—she saw this now, having not anticipated it—was to keep a grasp on syntax. There was this alarming feeling that English was not her native tongue but a jangle of strange grammatical constructions which she hadn't quite mastered. Verbs came after nouns. Nouns were. . . .

"How are they doing?" Since she hadn't offered to take his coat, he removed it and draped it over the armchair. Then he sat down in the armchair.

"They're—oh, well, Julie's in law school. Did Mother—I thought—you spoke to her in. . . . Yes, she likes it, it's very, she finds it stimulating. She thinks. . . . Dan is fine."

"Good."

"He's having an affair with this funny girl! God, it's weird. Her name's Vernice. She's—she—it's something with birds. Some kind of. . . ." What was she saying? Please, be quiet. Why had she taken the Dexamyl? Her heart was beating too fast to go on beating. In a minute she would clearly have a heart attack, and then all her problems would be solved.

"I wouldn't have expected that of Dan," Edward said calmly. He took out a cigar and lit it. He smoked about ten of these a day.

"Why not?" She heard herself sounding belligerent. "I mean,

why shouldn't he, if he wants? He *wants* to! I mean, he *likes* this girl; she's very sweet; it's not sexual; it's not what you think."

"I don't think anything," Edward said, "since I never met her."

She stared at him. He was smoking his cigar. She had a momentary sensation of *déjà vu*, as though they were at home in their apartment after dinner, just talking. And for a second this feeling became so real that she forgot exactly where she was and had a moment of terror, as though a thread had been cut. Oh, no, not now—breakdowns later, she could handle all that when she was alone, by herself. And then as suddenly the thread was tied again, and she was where she was and Edward was sitting there because he had written her a postcard saying he would be sitting there. . . .

He said, "I brought you a copy of my paper. . . . It just came out." He opened his pigskin briefcase and withdrew a small printed sheaf. Not having a table to set it down on, he handed it to her.

"Thank you," she said. "Actually I saw it. I—no, wait a minute, I didn't really. I was in the library at Berkeley it was, and I looked for it, but they didn't have it yet. They had . . . the old issue."

"Yes, it just came out," he said.

"Yes," Rachel said. She smiled. "Um—do you want a drink, Edward? You know, like I have some things, not so much, but—would you like bourbon? I could—"

"I would like a little bourbon," he said thoughtfully.

"With ice or—"

"Yes, ice would be fine." He cleared his throat.

"I'll—it's—the kitchen is out in the hall. We—I'll be back in a second." She rushed off and down the hall, hoping there would be ice since she always forgot to refill the ice tray. In the kitchen a pot of something smelling vaguely burned was simmering or not simmering on the stove. Rachel grabbed a glass, rinsed it with hot water, hurled a few shattered hunks of ice in it, and rushed back to her room. The bourbon was in the closet, still unopened.

He smiled when he saw how much she'd given him. "A generous portion."

"Oh. . . . Is it too much? . . . I never know. You can—do you want to pour it—"

"Aren't you going to have anything?"

"Me? Oh. . . . Well, I guess." She hated straight bourbon but poured some in a plastic cup she had in the closet. Then she spilled it on her dress. She looked down with dismay.

"Have you been sick?" Edward said, frowning, not even mentioning the spilling. "You look a little—"

"No, I'm fine. I'm eating all these health foods now. Beatrice, this girl I met, thinks if you do—oh, shit, look! What should I do? My dress is soaked!"

"You can take it off."

She was going to cry. "I don't know if I . . . should." She stared at the soiled dress as though at a stain a puppy had made on the rug.

Edward stood up. Without touching her, just standing about one foot from where she was, he said, very gently, "Shall I take you to bed?"

He said it so softly, as though she really were ill and had to be taken care of, and for a moment she thought he was referring to her foot, which was in a bandage from her sprain. When they had first gone to bed together, he had used that expression, "take you to bed," and she remembered being struck at the time at how old-fashioned and almost courtly it seemed. Now, in the same spirit, he carried her to the bed, lowered the shades so the room was cast in half darkness, and removed her bourbon-stained dress.

She was crying. All through their lovemaking tears kept running and running down her cheeks as though they came from some secret source of which she knew nothing. And even as she felt some sexual excitement, even at the end, it was as though the orgasm were part of her tears, something flowing out of her without her will. Afterward his hand fell lightly on her bandaged leg. "What happened?"

"Oh, I—fell off a unicycle. I was—it's part of this course. . . . I'm going to be a clown." She sniffed. Oh, God, what were they *doing* here? Why? Had she no more will than an earthworm? For our next trick we will try jumping out the window and seeing if we can fly.

"Does it hurt?" he said.

Edward! I'm dying! "Oh, well, no, it's—they put this bandage on, it's—" I have leukemia, now will you feel sorry for me, you pig! They've broken every bone in my body, do you like that? She lay back and stared at the ceiling. He was going to say it was all a most god-awful and wretched mistake, that his lady astronomer was frigid as a heap of ice cubes, that he had finally come to his fucking senses and realized, finally realized in a blinding flash of. . . .

"I want to get married to Magda," Edward said.

Because of the fantasies that had been coursing hectically through her head, she had the momentary feeling he meant that they should be remarried and so said, "But we're not divorced yet."

"When we are."

When *who* is *what?* When what is—"We've been living together," Edward said, "Magda and I and we—"

He'd picked up the wrong script, that was all. It was just a mistake. "But listen, why? Are you in love with her?" She sat up so suddenly her leg wrenched in pain.

He was silent a moment. He had that trick or maybe just a habit of speech of waiting just long enough so you wondered if he had heard. "She respects me as a person," he said.

Edward—Jesus! Respects you! And what didn't I do? God, was she supposed to have washed his feet in hot water and lemon juice every night, shined his shoes? What did he want? "*I* respect you," she muttered.

He laughed. "You don't respect anybody, Rachel. . . . You once said that. I think it's true."

"But then—don't you see—it's nothing against *you!* I mean, it just shows I'm like that! So it doesn't matter."

He shook his head. Then he happened to glance at the wall above the bed where she had scotch-taped up photos of Che (dead, looking like Christ), Mao, Malcolm X, and Norman Mailer. "I see you still have all your heroes," he said ironically.

Rachel cringed. "Well, do—what do you want? Should I put up pictures of Nixon? Or Billy Graham?"

"You respect *them.*" He touched the wall.

"But they're dead! Mostly."

He would not look at her. "Rachel, look, you will never—I don't say it's your fault—respect me or care about my work. You never did. You never followed what I was doing. You never—"

"But God, Edward, I'm not an astronomer! You know I can't follow all that! I—"

"It's not a matter of following. You never cared about it." His mouth was bitter. "You have contempt for it. . . . All you wanted was for me to be a Malcolm."

Struck by a hint of truth in this, she hesitated for a second. "Well, no, it's not that—"

"I'm not, never *was,* never will *be,* don't *want* to be. . . . And Magda—"

"Oh, shit on her!" Rachel said violently. She clutched her head. "Oh, Christ, I feel sick, Edward, I feel so lousy, I took this Dexamyl before you came. I have such a *headache!* My heart is beating like a drum. . . . What's *wrong* with me?"

"You always get like that when you take them," he said calmly. "Why do you do it?"

"I wanted to be cheerful! I wanted to be gay! . . . I feel like my head's going to roll off. . . . Listen, Edward, I don't care about her! I mean, say you want to screw her. At least be honest."

"Is it easier to reduce everything to that level?"

"Everything *is* at that level. . . . The rest is a lie. Men are such liars! They never, they won't. . . . I bet she came over in fifty-six," she said suddenly, bitterly.

"What does it matter?"

"Those people were *fascists*. . . . God, Edward, that wasn't a real revolution! That's a lot of crap!"

"Well, *I* don't give a damn."

"Well, you *should*. Would you sleep with a *Nazi?*"

"Magda is not a Nazi."

"Those people were—they were duped. . . . Look, lots of them were anti-Semites, lots of them—"

He shook his head. "Why won't you take people as they are? I don't even care if she's Hungarian, much less what year she happened to have come over. When we're together—"

"Don't tell me about that!"

He looked startled. "About what?"

"I don't want to hear all that sexual crap about what you do with her!"

"Look, I hadn't the slightest intention—"

"I mean, I can sleep with people, too! Only I happen to have more taste than to pick some fascist pig who just happens to have a degree in astronomy!"

Edward began getting dressed.

Rachel was silent. Her heart was no longer beating so fast, but the Dexamyl had left her with an overwhelming feeling of nausea. "I wish there were some way I could throw up," she said, but mildly, absently, abandoning the argument in midstream.

"Tickle your throat," he suggested.

She nodded. From nowhere tears began rolling down her cheeks again.

Edward put his hand on her shoulder. "I'd like you to be happy," he said.

Rachel brought down her fist on the bed. "God, Edward— why are you such a filthy, filthy hypocrite? Why? Say you want me to die! Say you think I'm a rotten, neurotic, stinking Jew!"

"You want everything to be easy for you."

"What do you mean?"

"If I say those things, according to your script, then you feel great, right? Justified as hell. I have two choices: Either I'm Malcolm or I'm a 'bourgeois black sellout with decaying morals.' "

"I don't use clichés like that."

"You said Magda was a fascist pig."

She was silent. "Well, she probably is," she muttered.

Edward was dressed. He went and sat down in his chair again and picked up his glass of bourbon. He even relit his cigar. Rachel, in her half-slip and no bra, lay on the bed watching him.

"So why did you sleep with me, then?" she said.

"Because I wanted to."

"Why did you want to?"

He didn't reply. Then he said, "You've been sleeping around, haven't you?"

She smiled. "Does it matter? . . . Ya, I have six black lovers and six white ones and three mulattoes, now that you ask."

He said, "Your mother mentioned some—"

"Oh, let her screw herself!"

"I like your mother, Rachel."

"Well, she loves you. . . . So go service her. She'd be off her head with joy."

He flicked an ash off the cigar. "I don't want you to cheapen yourself," he said.

"Thanks."

She felt very removed, as though they were both dead, both ghosts discussing something that had happened in another century, hundreds of years ago.

"Say one honest thing, Edward," Rachel said suddenly.

"What do you want me to say?"

"Say you don't want me to sleep with people because you have a male crappy feeling that you can do it and I can't and it makes you mad to think—"

"Baby, don't start in about men."

"Men are the enemy, Edward. They are! You get it all mixed up. They have the power."

He smiled.

"Seriously. . . . I don't hate you for being black or screwing around. . . . It's just because you're a man, that's all."

"At least you're being honest."

"No, it's true. . . . Listen, I'd be a lesbian tomorrow, but women are so cruddy. I mean, who needs them? Otherwise I'd join women's lib."

"You should. . . . You'd be a great leader."

"So, what does this—does she cook for you? All kinds of stuff with paprika? That kind of thing? Pancakes for dessert?"

"She cooks."

"No wonder you're getting so fat. . . . Maybe she wants you to die young so she can collect the family estate."

After a pause Edward said gently, "I'm sorry you're so bitter, Rachel."

And at that she jumped up and began punching him wildly, saying, "You're *not* sorry! You're glad! Say you're glad, Edward! Say it, say it!"

He moved backward, as though frightened. She didn't know if he thought she wanted to sleep with him again. She had not intended a sexual assault, but the spasm of desire that ran through her involuntarily made her jump back, too.

"My lawyer will get in touch with you," he said stiffly.

"Yes . . . okay," she said. She crossed her hands over her breasts. "Thank you for bringing the paper."

He left his cigar still burning in the ashtray.

She lay on the bed for an hour. This was how people became catatonics. You lay and you lay, and anything you thought of, eating, moving, talking, seemed the same, not worth doing, not worth thinking of. Was it self-protective that her mind seemed unable to focus on anything that had happened? Snatches of things he had said, things she had said flitted through her mind, but disconnected, like cartoon balloons. And what had she meant? And what had he meant? Usually she would have regretted having said what she had or not having said other things, but now all she could think of to regret was having gone to bed with him so easily, not having done it, but having done it not knowing, still thinking he had left Magda. To have done it in some pure cold spirit of spite would have been different! A triumph of sorts.

Edward is Edward is Edward. Will never be Eddie or Ed. Will always smoke ten cigars a day. Will never lose his temper. But she had wanted that! Yes, of course, it was part of the contradiction. Say she had married Edward to rebel, to shock people, to be "original" as Ibert claimed, though you hardly even call it original anymore. But say also that she had wanted the opposite—wanted that security, even if it was based on fear or denial which was such a part of his nature, wanted that feeling he exuded of knowing what he wanted, of having made choices and feeling settled with them. How could he say she had wanted him to be a Malcolm? She had wanted him to feel a struggle, to be dissatisfied, sure, maybe to be like her. But had she really cast him as leader of the revolution, even in her mind, even in moments of insanity? She could have picked a black militant (or a white one, for that matter), and she'd picked instead a town house in Philadelphia with all the trimmings and intercourse three times a week and dinner parties and a father-in-law who played squash at the Princeton Club every Saturday afternoon and a mother-in-law who tinted her hair. Say she wanted to be an outsider, sneering at the mob, but say, too, she wanted to be safe inside on a rainy night and wanted thick steaks and good wine and knowing Monday what Tuesday would bring. Say Edward was black, but say, too, he was more white than she would ever be. Say he had gone to Princeton and been chosen for six of the best eating clubs and she had gone to Berkeley and waited on tables. Say she hated the Establishment but that she had taken a big bite in its hide with her crooked, unorthodontized teeth and was hanging on, waiting for it to shake her off. There were choices. There were communes and the East Village and the Peace Corps. There were lots of choices and she had made hers and he was right, what was she doing with dead Che sleeping like a saint on her wall? Pick J. Edgar Hoover, if you want to be honest, pick Quisling, pick all the great slimy compromisers, not the ones with shining eyes who died young.

Finally she got up and wended her way to V and T's, where, despite sorrow and the uncalculable tide of events, she wolfed down a medium mushroom and sausage pizza and a bottle of beer.

Chapter Three

HER leg refused to heal. She did all the things the doctor had said, tried to stay off it (as though that were possible, unless you were some sort of migratory bird), soaked it, didn't soak it. But at the end of two weeks she was still hobbling and, more relevant, would probably not be able to graduate as a clown. Everything at the school was physical: the yoga, the stilt walking, the tumbling. For the first week they allowed her to sit and watch or take part just in some minimal way. But by the end of the second week the director of the school called her aside and explained gently that this simply would not do; she could be free to stay but could not, it would violate all the rules, be allowed to get a certificate saying she had completed the course. Of course, as he pointed out, she could get a partial certificate and then come back as soon as her leg healed and simply finish those courses she had left incomplete. She would not have to start over from the beginning. Rachel accepted this judgment as fair and just, but a great weight seemed to settle over her. When would she ever finish? Why were things like this always happening to her? Did other people sprain their legs? No, of course not.

Beatrice was undaunted. She still felt her original scheme of their forming a "team" would be valid. "No one asks to see those papers," she said, "unless you're joining the circus or something. You want the training, the skills. Well, you have those. You'll be okay."

It was clear Beatrice intended to carry most of the show anyway; Rachel could see she was going to be a minor adjunct. "That's great of you, Beatrice," she said gratefully. "You think we really can do it, huh?"

Beatrice looked at her. "Of course we can. . . . Listen, I heard of something ten days from now. . . . My sister called. . . . Some couple in the suburbs, Long Island someplace, they've got this twelve-year-old kid, a boy, and it's his thirteenth birthday. She told them all about us. They're interested."

This was wonderful. So soon a real engagement, their career beginning. Rachel felt her spirits lighten. This would show Edward. Someday when she would be a great clown and he would be roaring his fat head off in the front row of the orchestra, she'd spit right in his eye! Spit? Where was her sense of violence? Something more potent than that! To Beatrice she said nothing of Edward. Why should she? First of all, Beatrice was down on men in general, and the few times Rachel had mentioned anything or tried, discreetly, to bid for sympathy, Beatrice had said things like, "Yeah, don't let them kick you around, baby." Which was not quite to the point somehow. Rachel felt maybe it was a matter of pride. She didn't want to be part of some great swarming mass of ill-treated womanhood. She was a special case, right? Different! Special! Yeah, man.

The deal in Huntington was arranged. Saturday, two o'clock, November 20. They were to arrive an hour early, bringing costumes, equipment, etc. For a feverish week Rachel went to Beatrice's pad every evening to "practice." Beatrice decided everything—the costumes they were to wear, what they were to say. She was at once stage manager, director, main star. But Rachel didn't mind. Usually she would have resented having someone else wield all the authority, but here it was a help. Beatrice was so much more confident, took it all so much more seriously than she ever could have. She had theories, a whole philosophy, by God. They could have been going to the White House for a state dinner for the gravity with which she regarded it.

They went out by train. There was talk of renting a cab, but this seemed too expensive. And so, Beatrice with the suitcases and their costumes, Rachel with the white mice, rabbit, and other equipment, sat gloomily on the Long Island train, watching the rain pour down outside the window as Huntington drew closer. They took a cab to the house.

The couple was named Violet and Martin Rugoff, their son, Lamont. But it was a black maid who came to the door, all done up like a black maid in a Hollywood comedy of thirty years earlier in frilled white hat, apron, uniform. "Are you the entertainers?" she inquired haughtily, eyeing them a little suspiciously as they dripped all over the front door mat.

"Yes, we are," said Beatrice crisply. Even dripping, she could, with her six-foot posture, tinted pink sunglasses, and sweeping black cape, manage not to be intimidated by anyone. Rachel slunk in the background, hoping to be taken for a deaf-mute.

"You can dress inside," the maid said. "I believe Mrs. Rugoff will appear shortly."

Mrs. Rugoff did not appear shortly. They sank down in giant pale-blue brocade chairs and waited.

"I hate it when people have money and don't know how to spend it," Rachel said, looking around at the decor.

Beatrice made a face at her: Are you going to crap us up so early in the game?

"Listen, can mice catch colds?" Rachel wanted to know a moment later. "They seem awfully lethargic. And it's so damp."

"They just have to live through today," Beatrice said darkly.

"Maybe I should get them a little lettuce or stuff from the kitchen."

"Well, let's wait for what's-her-name to show, okay? Just cool it."

Rachel sneezed. "Cool it? I'm going to get pneumonia in a minute. I thought they'd offer us hot rum toddies or something."

"Look, you're hired help, dear, so forget all that." Beatrice sniffed. "God, where is the golden lady?"

"What if it was next Saturday?"

"Well, Bessie seemed to expect us." She indicated the direction whence the maid had disappeared.

"Is that her name?"

"It always is."

At that moment a man appeared in the doorway. "I'm Martin Rugoff," he said, smiling genially. Martin Rugoff was short and a little heavy, balding with a huge, dark handlebar mustache, the contours of which gave his face a slightly mournful, basset-hound look. He was dressed in a dark-green sports shirt and a white tie with giant maroon polka dots on it. "Mrs. Rugoff is a little detained," he said placatingly, as though this were a not uncommon event. "But I think you can . . . why don't you go change inside? We'll have the—the children's room ought to be best, we thought. If you like—"

They trooped after him to look at the children's room. It was the size of an average apartment house lobby, the walls crammed with toys, small jungle gyms, gaily painted posters, the wall a vivid grass-green indoor-outdoor carpet. "I think this will be adequate," Beatrice said after a pause.

"Yes, well, we thought . . . you arrange it however you think best." He smiled again. "You know, we're so pleased you girls could come. It's such terrible weather. I'm sorry you had to—"

"No, we didn't mind," Rachel said, trying to set him at his ease; he seemed so nervous though it was his own house.

"So! Well, that's about it. . . . The bathroom is in here. . . . And you can change right here since Lamont is over visiting a friend. . . . We wanted to get him out of the way till the big event."

"Yes, that's always wise," Beatrice said. She set down her suitcase as Martin Rugoff sidled out of the room.

Rachel uncovered the mice, who appeared to be okay. Then she went off to explore a little. A few minutes later she came back. Beatrice was going over the magic tricks, spreading everything out on the table.

"Hey, dig the bathroom!" Rachel said. "Did you see it?"

"No, what's so special about it?" Beatrice looked bemused.

"It's a ballroom. . . . Jesus, it's bigger than my whole room! It's all in black marble with gold spigots and the tub! Wow, there's this round tub. It's, like, six feet in diameter, bigger, maybe nine feet. . . . Do you think I could take a bath, Bea?"

"Rachel, will you take it easy? No, you cannot take a bath. . . . Will you get in your fucking costume?"

"I've always wanted to take a bath in a round tub," Rachel said mournfully.

"Maybe after the show if you're good."

"They could put a harpsichord in there," Rachel said. "That's what *I'd* do."

"You'd put a what? I thought you didn't play any instrument."

"I don't, but it's just the place for a harpsichord. Didn't you always have this fantasy of taking a bath in a huge, round tub with faint harpsichord music tinkling in the background while someone handed you a huge platter of perfectly ripe nectarines?"

"Frankly, no," Beatrice said. She was smoothing greenish paint onto her face. "Rachel, listen—"

Rachel sat down. A minute later she popped up. "God, I'm starved!" she exploded.

"Are you out of your mind? You just had lunch before we came."

"Listen, I'll never last," Rachel moaned. "Seriously. I have this fantastic hunger. My stomach is like a drum."

"Rachel, Jesus!"

"Bea, look, I'll tell you what—let me just nip into the kitchen and grab a bite. Violet isn't here yet; the mice need some carrots. So does Geronimo. Look at the poor creature; his ears are all folded over."

"Well, beat it back here in a hurry, that's all I have to say!"

"I *will!*"

Rachel raced down the hall and looked frantically around for the kitchen. The house was absolutely quiet, but it was so big there might have been an orgy going on in the next room and you'd never have known.

Bessie was sitting in the kitchen shelling peas at a huge butcher block table. Rachel said plaintively, "Umm . . . Could we—the thing is, our rabbit needs a little . . . stuff."

"What *kind* of stuff?" Bessie squinted at her.

"Oh, anything, he has a small appetite." Rachel opened the refrigerator door. In one bin she found half a head of iceberg lettuce and a bunch of carrots. "Could I take these?" Then she spied a Persian melon, cut in quarters. "How about this melon?" she said. "Is anyone—"

"You take whatever you need, honey," Bessie said, suddenly surprisingly agreeable.

"Ya, well, maybe a little melon." Rachel took a bag and threw in her spoils. She also made off with a container of cottage cheese, a box of Fig Newtons, and a quart of milk. The bell rang. "Oops, must be the cake," Bessie said. "They had it ordered, you know . . . I can't do that kind of thing, that kind of fancy cake . . . I told Mrs. Rugoff, I said—"

At that moment a small dark-haired woman in a beige leather mini dress stalked into the kitchen. "Bessie, that's the cake! Aren't you going to answer it?"

"Yes, ma'am, I was just—"

Violet Rugoff glared at Rachel. Rachel muttered, "I'm, uh, one of the entertainers."

"Well, hadn't you better get ready? It *starts* at three." She had big, rather beautiful dark eyes, smeared around with eye shadow and dark hair tumbled below her shoulders.

Rachel smiled obsequiously. "Ya, well, our rabbit. . . . He's part of the act and we had to. . . ." She backed out of the room. "We'll be ready in a sec," she said.

Beatrice was already in her costume. The problem with Beatrice, one Beatrice herself seemed to recognize, was that she could be a little scary with her height and her manner. She was dressed in a flowing gown imprinted with large silver stars and had a pointed, medieval-type hat. Her skin was pale greenish, and she had artificial nails, painted silver, attached to her real ones. She had eradicated her eyebrows and painted others high up which gave her a startled, imperious expression. As a foil to this, Rachel was to be fat and padded out in a floppy pink and blue costume with a pink wig that was made from an old dish mop. Beatrice was to do the magic tricks which would form the major part of the show. Rachel would bungle around, tumbling, playing the fool, pretending not to understand what was going on, messing up some of the tricks.

"She's out there," Rachel said, opening the bag.

"Who?"

"The lady of the manor."

"Oh. . . . What's she like?"

"Kind of sexy and neurotic-looking."

"Yeah, she's in group therapy, Sally said. They all are out here, in something or other."

Rachel began munching on a piece of melon. "Oh, Beatrice!" she said.

"What?"

"This melon. . . . It's fabulous. . . . Have a piece."

"Now?" Beatrice looked at her as though she were crazy. "Rachel, if you don't get into that fucking costume in five minutes!"

Rachel began getting into her costume, still munching on the melon. "This is no ordinary melon, Beatrice. Seriously. This is, like, the Platonic essence of melon. I can't describe it, it—"

"Don't describe it. Just shut up and get busy." She was moving the table and arranging her magic hat. Rachel was to bring in the mice in the middle and let some of them loose. Until then they would be kept in the bathroom along with the spare equipment.

"I've never had a melon like this," Rachel was saying as Martin Rugoff entered the room.

"Well, Lamont is here!" he said brightly.

"Will the children come straight in?" Beatrice said.

"Well, well, I think. . . . We'll open the presents and then

. . . your show and then the cake, well, Mrs. Rugoff has it all planned."

At that moment Violet Rugoff stalked into the room. She gave only a perfunctory glance at the table with the magic equipment, then turned to her husband and said, "Where are the twins?"

"The twins?" He looked bewildered. "I thought you—"

"Oh, Jesus, Martin! I told you. . . . Oh, I shouldn't have let Margaret go for the ice cream. . . . They're probably crawling all over creation! God knows what they're into!"

"I thought I saw them—"

"Well, go get them, will you! Leash them up or toss them in the pen or something! That's all I need right now." She looked at Beatrice. "We'll do the presents first," she said. "Would you like to wait in the bathroom?"

"How will we know when to come out?" Rachel said.

Beatrice gave her a dirty look. Violet Rugoff said, "Someone will come and get you."

They sat on the edge of the round tub. Rachel put some finishing touches on her makeup with a small sable brush. "Hey, who are the twins?" she said. "I thought there was only one."

"One what?"

"Child . . . Lamont, I thought his name was."

"So, who said it was a child? . . . I thought they meant dogs."

"Dogs?"

"Well, she said: leash them up."

"Ya, but she said pen . . . I thought playpen, you know. . . . Oh, God, I have this terrible fantasy."

"What?"

"There is no child. . . . There are no twins. . . . They're both crazy. . . . It's like some weird Albee play where for years they've been. . . ."

"Rachel, for Christ's sake, my sister has seen the fucking child. Her son plays with him. He exists."

"Well, that's something, anyway. . . . Are you nervous, Beatrice? You look kind of strange."

"I'm supposed to look kind of strange. . . . No, I feel okay," Beatrice sat down on the toilet and morosely lit a cigarette. "Don't tell me I gave up smoking," she said.

The great moment arrived. There was a knock at the door, a whispered hiss, and a moment later Beatrice, as though to the manner born, swept out in her green gown, Rachel tripping after her.

And it was all easy! Beatrice was wonderful. Rachel, who had to stand and watch her a good deal of the time, was flabbergasted at her cool. She did all the tricks impeccably, she made small talk, ad libbed. Once Rachel got so fascinated she forgot to do her own piece, but none of the children seemed to notice. In fact, Rachel felt terribly warmed because they seemed to love her. She hammed it up outrageously, fell, stumbled, did somersaults into the crowd, and everyone giggled. There was just one mishap. At one point Rachel was supposed to do a mock operation on the rabbit. In fact, the real rabbit was discreetly slipped into his box beneath the table and a fake rabbit was laid out on the table. Beatrice presumably opened up his stomach, and Rachel began pulling out a variety of objects—flowers, scarves, jelly beans, and, at the end, a bunch of little white mice, which were to be allowed to scamper around among the children while Rachel pretended to be in great consternation about getting them back in their box. In fact, she *was* in great consternation because the mice, perhaps owing to the large crowd—there must have been thirty children—took off like bats out of hell, and Rachel had no idea where they had gone. There were genuine screams of fear—it seemed some little girls were terrified of mice—and a moment of panic ensued while the hunt for the errant mice went on. In the end two were still missing, but no one seemed to realize it so Rachel, grinning, perspiring, pretended everything was all right.

At the end of the show the children gathered around to look at the rabbit while Beatrice let them play with some of the equipment. Rachel went into the black marble bathroom to wash her face with cold water. As she was coming out, Martin Rugoff suddenly came over and said, "Well, that was just swell! Wonderful! You two girls are really talented."

Rachel smiled self-deprecatingly.

"Listen, come on in for a drink, how about it? You look like you need one."

She trotted obediently after him into the living room. Now about forty people were drinking, eating, chatting, smoking. While the birthday had been taking place, a cocktail party for the parents had been going on. Now the two events began to dovetail as smeary children in party hats rushed in, clutching jelly beans, to regale their elders with the wonders of the day. Little Lamont, the hero, stood to one side, holding a huge boat. Rachel always felt that children of very rich parents were either the type you hated or pitied. Lamont was the type you pitied. He was too thin with his mother's huge dark eyes, and he looked —more a trait of his father, perhaps—as though he would have liked nothing better than to fade unobtrusively into the background. Seeing Rachel, he said, "I liked . . . your rabbit."

"Yes, he's nice, isn't he?" Rachel said.

"Are you a man or a woman?" he wanted to know.

"I'm a woman," Rachel said.

But in fact, she felt more a kind of neuter being, suspended, at least for the time she was encased in her clown costume, from any of the requirements of male-female interactions. It was nice. Usually in a gathering like this, a cocktail party with such a plethora of elegant, group-therapized suburbanites, she would have felt either acutely hostile, uncomfortable, or both. But now, in her guise as clown, she sat comfortably on the end of the couch and felt quite at ease, as though whether she talked or did not talk to anyone was a matter of no import. In front of her on the cocktail table was a giant mound of tartare steak. For a second she had a fantasy of being alone and falling on it like a dog—she loved raw meat—but instead she decorously lathered a slice of melba toast as thick as seemed seemly and crunched into it. A hand appeared, Martin Rugoff's, handing her a gin and tonic. She drank it down as though it were water. He sat beside her on the couch.

"Listen, I want to ask you something. . . . Maybe this seems too personal. . . . But how did a girl like you happen to get into doing this? I mean, it's fascinating, but odd, don't you think . . . being a clown . . . at your age, well not your age, but the whole—"

"Well, actually . . . I'm, I'm also, I'm really a zoologist," Rachel found herself saying. Why? What was wrong with clown? I'm really vice-president of AT and T; I'm really a high-priced Jewish call girl.

"I see. . . . You just do this." He smiled, bemused. "It must be a great satisfaction to make people laugh," he said. "You feel you're really getting through to people, really communicating. . . . I used to want to run away to the circus and be a clown."

"Ya, well, it has its merits." Rachel reached forward and prepared another helping of tartare steak for herself. "What do *you* do?" she said, she hoped not hostilely.

"Oh, I'm—I manage a chain of delicatessens. . . . My father does, really. . . . But I manage a few of them in the Bronx and Queens."

She smiled. "You have great food in this house," she said.

"My wife is always dieting," Martin Rugoff said sadly. "I don't think she needs to, do you? She hasn't gained a pound since we were married. . . . But she says she *feels* fat."

"Martin!"

He looked up, then turned to Rachel. "Well, I guess. . . . Oh, they're bringing in the twins," he said.

The twins turned out to be human, after all: two nine-month-old babies, both dressed in purple and white stretch suits. Their nanny or maid or whatever, a redoubtable lady in white, set them down on the floor and they began crawling among the guests, clutching at the hors d'oeuvres and being cooed at by adults. Rachel suddenly remembered the mice. She went over to

Beatrice, who was regally nibbling on fondue and looking as though the whole party were in her honor.

"Beatrice!" she hissed.

"What?"

"The mice. . . . There're still two of them missing."

Beatrice smiled. "Oh, forget it. . . . They'll turn up."

"They'll turn up shitting all over Mrs. Rugoff's best divan or something."

Gradually the party dispersed. Rachel went in with Beatrice to pack their gear. "Someone offered to give us a ride back," Beatrice said.

"Oh, great."

Rachel was tired and glad, because of the presence of the unknown couple who gave them the lift, not to have to talk. She left her costume on, flung her coat over it, and dozed most of the way in the back seat while Beatrice made small talk with the couple.

The next day Beatrice called. "Well, we're in business!" she said.

"We are?"

"Yup. . . . Some couple called this morning and asked if we could come out to Scarsdale in two weeks. . . . And somebody else said they thought they'd be interested, but weren't sure."

"That's good, Bea. . . . You were wonderful."

"Yes, I think I . . . I was rather pleased," was the most Beatrice would say.

And so they began, going to other people's houses and performing for assorted children. The Rugoffs had been a good dry run. Many of the couples were less wealthy and had less elaborate parties, but there were no disasters, and after each performance someone inevitably came over and mentioned they might need someone or knew someone who might need someone. Rachel was content; she even wrote her parents, mentioning the clowning in more detail than she had before, feeling that now it had a status and a *raison d'être*.

* * *

One day she received the first official papers about the separation agreement. Subsequently she went to see Edward's lawyer. She was sure at a glance that he was a friend of Edward's father, that sort of middle-aged, successful New York black with frizzled, grayish hair, very urbane, soft-spoken. He seemed surprised and a little suspicious when she said she wanted no alimony. She was surprised herself. But alimony had always seemed to her to smack of such a nasty image—grasping little ladies in minks trying to make bond slaves out of former husbands, an intricate, acceptable form of medieval torture: I will never be happy; *you* will never be happy. Yes, it was at odds with her revenge motif, her desire to be a Napoleon, to wield power. But this seemed power on such a petty level. You could see, rather, committing murder, setting off a bomb.

"You have professional training which will enable you to support yourself, I take it?" Mr. Trevor said, squinting at her from behind his mahogany desk.

"Ya, well, I. . . . Yes, I do," Rachel said.

"Because you understand that such an agreement is binding. If you change your mind later, the whole matter can become much more complicated. I don't intend to question your motives. I just wish to make sure you are in full grasp. . . ."

"No, I'm in full grasp," Rachel muttered, wishing this were ever true.

He sat back, evidently ready to believe her, at least for the moment. "Well, it's a great pleasure to have things resolved so easily," he said. "You know, it could always be this way, but people are so. . . ."

"Yes," Rachel agreed hastily.

"There's such bitterness, you wouldn't believe it."

"I can imagine."

"Of course, you're lucky." He paused just long enough for Rachel to wonder: me? "You have no children," he went on smoothly.

"Ya, well, I guess in a sense that is—"

"It all stems from that," he said. "Believe me. Everything. You have children and you have a terrible mess."

"Still, I guess they have their advantages," she said wistfully.

"Children? Oh, of course! Well, I love children," he said a little indignantly. "I have four myself. I have three grandchildren. No, there's no question that children. . . . I just meant in the professional sense and then . . . yes, that's a different matter."

"Do you know Edward's family?" she said suddenly.

"Oh, yes, yes, I've known them for years." He smiled. "A wonderful family. . . . My daughter, Margaret, my youngest, she and Alison attended the same school for years."

Of course, he was being paid to be genial, and maybe he really was in the sense that she was being so little trouble. Damn, she *wanted* to be trouble. Would they just be divorced like that, so unctuously, so smoothly, with no one to stand by and scream or shout or accuse? No witnesses and secret papers and semen-stained sheets? No nastiness?

After that day she became obsessed with the idea of going to Philadelphia. For one thing, she had a perfect right. Look over her things etc. No, but she wanted to go to, as she thought of it, "commit an act of desecration." She liked that phrase. It had a kind of full way of rolling off the tongue. An act of desecration. No alimony. That was too petty, too small. Something wilder, more revolutionary. A bomb maybe. Or a fire. When she would go, she decided to leave to the inspiration of the moment. A day would come, and she would know: This was the day.

The same day in early December, several hours after she had left the lawyer's office, she met Martin Rugoff. She was in Horn and Hardart, reaching for a glass of water to go with her dish of creamed spinach and codfish cakes, when she looked up and saw his mournful face. He was grappling with the napkin container that seemed to be stuck, but when he saw her, his face lit up. A half hour later he had insisted on taking her to a quiet pub to tell her something terrible that had happened.

Rachel felt two ways about terrible things that had happened to other people. Usually she would have liked to think of herself as compassionate as the next man or woman, but her own troubles had left her a little cynical, a little annoyed, actually, when anyone else began to weep and wail. On the other hand, there was something consoling about being needed, even as a wailing wall, to that extent. Martin Rugoff talked of suicide, he talked of the decline of the delicatessen business, but the main thing was that his wife, his Violet, had left him, was at that very moment in Tampa, Florida, with her boyfriend, a maker of underground movies. "And she took the twins!" he exclaimed.

"The—"

"Sebastian and Flora. . . . You met them at the party, didn't you? They're beautiful. Oh, they're fat, wonderful, *beautiful* babies! She took them! Just like that."

"Is that legal?" Rachel wondered aloud.

He threw up his hands. "Legal, schmegal. You tell me what's legal. She did it so it's legal. . . . Women have all the fucking rights in this country. It's a fact." He sighed deeply. "But listen, you know, the fact is, I did such a stupid thing. I really ought to kill myself. I never heard of such a stupid thing."

"What was that?"

He shook his head. "You sure you want to hear all this crap? No, really, for this I could kill myself. . . . Well, I had an affair."

"Ya?"

"Ya, well, you think so what, right? He had an affair, big deal, it wasn't even an affair really, that's the irony of it. I slept with this girl, woman, whatever you want to call her, three times all together. . . . But the trouble is, well, it's a long story. Vi and I are in group therapy and—"

"Yes, I know," Rachel said.

"You know?" He looked at her suspiciously.

"Ya, well, Beatrice said her sister said—"

"Beatrice? Your friend? The tall, skinny—"

"Right. . . . Her sister."

"*I* see. . . . Well, so anyway, Vi used to be in the group, but she stopped. Had enough for a while, and I started. It's a great thing. I love it. It's the best show in town, let's face it. Lots of talented people. Do you know we have this guy who's the fastest guy in the world?"

"At what?" Rachel wanted to know.

"At running. . . . No, that's his problem, I guess. He's not so fast at anything else."

"Ya, that does sound bad," Rachel said.

He frowned. "So where was I? Ya, well, this girl. She's in the group. Just a typical neurotic. I can't defend it. An attractive girl. That's about it. Screwed up as the devil. I mean, you'd think I'd know better. Why pick someone out of the group? It's bound to get back, right? . . . Maybe I wanted it to get back? I don't know . . . I mean, look, in my own defense, I'll say this, this girl was pretty hot for me. Or pretended to be. How can you ever tell?"

"I don't know," Rachel said.

"Some men I guess can tell. I'm what I suppose is in some ways a pushover. But that's another story. So, to make a long story short, we screw a few times, call it quits, and then, whammo, this kid tries to kill herself. . . . Now, I mean, like I knew this girl wasn't in such hot shape, but who is?"

"Nobody," Rachel offered.

"Right! You talk about death, you want to kill yourself, you can't face the coming day, it's par for the course, right? Maybe I was being cynical. I figured she's trying to be profound, make an impression, you know. . . . But the thing is, she did this right from the beginning. It wasn't like I said this is it and then—"

"No, I get it," Rachel said.

"You get the picture? . . . So, it gets back to Violet through this woman, oh, it's some complicated mess. Let's just say it gets back to Violet."

"And that was why she left you?" Rachel said, wanting someone to weave the threads together.

His face suddenly looked blank, as though she were someone who'd asked him the time on a day he'd forgotten his watch. "Is that why she left me?"

"I don't know . . . I was just asking you."

He pondered. "Well, you've got to know that I'm Vi's third husband. So you figure right there she has some problems with men, right? I mean, the first one you can't count she was pretty young, in college, and the second, well, you can't really count either because her mother was dying and she'd always wanted her to marry a dentist from the Bronx so she did, so in a way I'm the only one who really counts and you could say it's like she's only been married once, who's counting? But let's face it, in a court of law, she's on her third marriage, and that doesn't sound so good. . . . She's a very strange woman, a very sensitive woman. . . . What'd you think of her? Did you form any impression?"

"She seemed high-keyed," said Rachel.

"Yeah, well, she's that all right. She's a pretty good-looking woman, I think; maybe I'm not objective—"

"No, I thought so," Rachel concurred.

"Not *fat*," he said.

"No, not fat."

"I don't know where she gets this idea she's fat. . . . Anyway, she finds out about this girl, and she's devastated. Naturally, now this is typical of Vi, she says she doesn't care about what I did, just about this poor girl, how could I be so heartless?" He shook his head. "Do you like that? The one thing I *wasn't* responsible for—that she hangs me for. I'm a murderer—the girl didn't die, by the way, she's as right as a trivet—but still, I'm a murderer. . . . Then, whammo, off to Palm Springs or wherever with this joker, leaving Lamont, I mean I like Lamont but it's *her* kid for Christ sake from her first marriage and the twins are mine, so you'd figure, wouldn't you, if she takes anyone, she'd take Lamont . . . I don't know. Do you understand women?"

Rachel wondered for a moment if he still thought of her as

the neutral figure, the Clown, from the party, but he added, "They say it takes one to know one. . . . Oh, who knows?" He paid for their drinks, and they stepped outside into the chilly February twilight. Rachel blinked to adjust her eyes after the darkness. Martin Rugoff was silent for a long time. Then suddenly he said, "Listen, I'm going to say something weird. I just want to tell you first, so if you think it's weird, don't be offended . . . I just wondered—you don't feel like coming home and spending the weekend with me. . . . The thing is, like, I'm dying in this big house. It's twelve rooms, and I'm dying, I'm going crazy, I just want company, that's it, no sexual stuff. I admit I'm horny, but I'm an adult man, so they say. If you want to sit around knitting all weekend, you can. No rape scenes or anything. You call the punches. I mean this."

Rachel smiled. "I don't knit."

"How about it?"

"Well, how about Lamont? Won't he mind?"

"Lamont? He'll love it. He loved you! He wants to marry you! He'll go wild."

"No, but I mean, won't it be awkward—for you? Bringing somebody home and—"

"Honey, euh, no, you're sweet, sure, it'll be awkward, but, like, it's awkward that his Mommy up and left with a cross-eyed Hungarian carphead, isn't it?"

"Is he really Hungarian?" Rachel said.

"Yeah, well, some mixture, you know those Eastern European bastards."

"That's a remarkable coincidence," she said.

"Yeah, well, there're Hungarians floating around all over the place. Stick a pin in—you want to come?"

"Sure," Rachel said.

"I'm not an impulsive man," he said as he started the car. "I mean, you're probably getting this impression I do crazy things all day long, sleep with chicks, invite people home, believe me, nothing could be further . . . I've done nothing! You'd have to look hard, really search, to find someone who's done *less* than me. It would take some looking, believe me. I'm the Jewish Walter Mitty. It's all in the head, you know? If you could be arrested for what you're thinking, I'd spend my life in jail. But as far as action goes, forget it. . . . How about you, are you a doer? I mean, do you do things like this much?"

"Not *precisely* like this," Rachel qualified cautiously.

That answer seemed to satisfy him. "I can't say I'm going to be a great companion this weekend. I want you to know that, too. Like, now I'm talking a blue streak, you probably think, well, at least, he's a talker, it'll be a good show, but the fact is half the time I'm morose as hell. You have to scream at me to get me to open my mouth. That's what Vi says. She ought to know, I guess." He turned onto the parkway. "I like Lamont, he's a nice kid. Don't get me wrong about what I said before. Any other time I'd love having him around. Even now we have a pretty good time—he plays chess, he cooks, he's not bad to have around. It's just. . . ."

They ate supper in the kitchen. Lamont was evidently spending the night with a friend. Rugoff made salami and eggs. "I can offer you endive or romaine," he said when it came to the salad.

"Fancy stuff," said Rachel.

"Ya, well, Vi was always dieting, as I've said, so we have enough rabbit food around here to feed a whole. . . . Did you say romaine? I have a fair hand with blue cheese dressing, if we have blue cheese, we used to, I don't know *what* we have around here anymore."

After dinner Rachel asked if she could take a bath in the black marble bathroom.

"Sure, honey, it's all yours. . . . Bath, shower, whatever you feel like." As she was undressing in the bathroom, he said, "Do you mind if I watch you take your bath? I love watching people take baths. I used to bathe the twins every night. I won't pull any funny stuff, I just want to watch. . . . But say no, if it bugs you."

"No, stay, that's okay." She piled her clothes on the floor.

"Do you want some Bubble Club?" he said thoughtfully, watching her. "The twins used to love that."

"Sure," Rachel said. She filled the tub close to overflowing. Martin Rugoff squirted in some pink liquid Bubble Club. Rachel climbed in and sank back. "I love this tub," she said.

He smiled. "Ya, it's a great tub, isn't it?" He sat back. "I'm glad you like it."

There was a moment's pause.

Then Martin Rugoff said, "Say, how would you feel if I took a bath with you? Feel free to say no. I won't just jump in or anything. I mean, don't feel any obligation."

"No, jump in," Rachel said, "sure."

He began undressing. "It's ironical. . . . You know, I got this tub, I won't even tell you what it cost, because I thought how great it would be if Vi and I could take baths together, you know? The average tub, you're lucky if you can fit in yourself —this one, you could have an orgy, not that I'd ever know. . . . But Vi didn't like me to get in with her. . . . You want to know why?"

"Why?" Rachel said. His body, she observed, was in better shape than she'd expected.

"Well, once, when we were just married, you know how you confess all these crazy things, things you never told anyone before?" He dipped a toe in. "Hey—do you really like it this hot?"

"Ya, is it *too* hot?"

"No, I'll get used to it, I guess." He eased himself into the suds. "Well, I once told her that when I was a kid, I used to pee in the tub. In fact, that I still do occasionally. Not a remarkable fact. I don't know how we got around to the topic, frankly, but, anyway, ever since then, whenever I'd try to get in the tub with her, she'd be looking at me like I was some kind of untrained dog. You know, she liked her tub with bath oils and perfumes and stuff. I told her—look, I don't pee in your tub, it's not like I *always* pee, but she'd never believe me, she always thought, whammo, while she wasn't looking, I might give a squirt."

Rachel began to wash her arms. "*I* pee in the tub," she said.

"Do you? Terrific! Hey, what a bond! Huh? Like, who needs Dostoevsky, right?"

"It's easier than getting out to do it," Rachel said.

"And you get just as clean, that's a fact," Martin Rugoff said. He squinted at her. "You know, I think one of your breasts is bigger than the other one, is that true?"

"A little," Rachel said. "I had this curvature of the spine when I was little. It's more that it sticks out more."

He nodded sagely. "I don't mind it. I wouldn't have mentioned it otherwise. I like little defects in nice-looking women. . . . Like Vi had this what-do-you-call-it, a birthmark on her left thigh—she hated it! Always talked about having it removed. 'Why?' I'd say. 'It makes you unique.' 'Who needs to be unique?' she'd say. 'I want to be pretty.' Isn't it funny? All the pretty women, they never think they're pretty. That's been my experience anyway. The dogs—*they* have self-confidence. I don't know why that should be so. . . . Would you like me to wash your back?"

"Okay," Rachel said, turning around.

He soaped up a long boar bristle brush. "Is that too rough?"

"No, it feels great."

"I see what you mean about the curvature," he said. "I mean, I probably wouldn't have noticed it if you hadn't mentioned it."

"It doesn't bother me," Rachel said. "It doesn't hurt or anything."

"One thing—I hope you won't mind my saying this, you could stand to gain a little weight. . . . Not much. . . . Just a pound here or there. That's what I think. Of course, I may be of the old school. You know, like, Mia Farrow isn't my dish, exactly."

Afterward he dried her off carefully with an enormous purple beach towel. Rachel sighed. "I've always had a fantasy about this," she said.

He looked so totally delighted she hadn't the heart to say that her fantasy had been of taking a bubble bath in a round tub, so she just added, "That was a lovely bath."

There was talk of where she should sleep—in the guest room, the downstairs couch, until Rachel said, "Oh, I'll sleep here." She smiled sheepishly. "Actually, I'm a bit horny myself," she said.

Martin Rugoff smiled. "Well." He almost blushed. "I guess that's convenient, isn't it?"

Rachel crawled into the bed. "You should have a round bed, too."

"I've thought of it," he said. "Only I always wondered—wouldn't you roll out?"

"I don't know," Rachel said. "You've got a point, though."

In the morning they had Nova Scotia salmon and Sara Lee croissants and waffles made by Lamont.

"These are great waffles," Rachel said. She was in one of Violet's bathrobes and what she imagined were called mules.

"I add a little Grand Marnier," Lamont said. "That's my secret."

"That's a good secret," she said. She was relieved. He seemed, if anything, delighted to see her; there was no awkwardness.

"I told you," Rugoff said, "he's a great cook. . . . You ought to taste his shrimp gumbo."

"I make a good chicken archduke," Lamont said thoughtfully, spreading cream cheese on a croissant. "Dad, you know, I hate to say it, but—"

"Say it, say it," said Rugoff. He winked at Rachel. "Frankness—that's what we want from the younger generation, right?"

"This salmon isn't exactly the best you've ever gotten," Lamont said.

"No?" Rugoff sniffed at a piece inquiringly. "Well, I'll speak to Bernie. Jesus knows, it ought to be good at those prices."

"It tastes good to me," Rachel said.

"Oh, it's good," Lamont said. "It just lacks a certain—"

"He's the expert," Rugoff said.

It was a relaxed weekend. Rachel played chess with Lamont a few times, but he was so obviously superior to her that even when he tried to let her win a few games, she lost. Saturday night the three of them went to the movies, and afterward she had another bath in the round tub. Sunday evening, as she was about to go back to the city, Lamont took her aside.

"You know, it's really good you came out," he said. "I was getting a little worried about Dad."

"Oh. . . . Gee, well—"

"You know, he's really been thrown for a loop by this. You may not be able to tell. He's been in really bad shape."

"Yes, well, it must be. . . . You must miss her, too, I guess."

"Mother?" He looked thoughtful. Then he grinned. "Well, it's a lot quieter since she left. Maybe it's *too* quiet. . . . No, what bothers me with Mother is I'm not all that sure she's going to be happy."

"You don't think so?"

"No, well, you see, Mother's—well, she's romantic, you know? She acts on impulse. Sometimes that's good, but she gets taken advantage of. . . . Personally, I think she made one big mistake."

"What was that?" Rachel wanted to know.

"Well, it was her leaving group. I think she wasn't ready for it . . . I mean, she *thought* she was, but I don't think she was. *That's* where everything started."

"I see," Rachel said, hoping she did.

He cleared his throat and looked a little embarrassed. "I hope you don't mind my discussing these family things in your presence."

"No, I'm . . . really interested," Rachel said.

He shook her hand. "I hope you'll come out again. . . . You've done Dad a world of good. I hope you don't mind my saying so. He needs a woman around. I think that's one of his problems."

"I suppose most men do," Rachel said.

"Do they?" He got his thoughtful look. "I suppose so."

In the car on the way back Rugoff said, "So, how do you like Lamont? He's a sweetheart, isn't he?"

"Yes, I like him," Rachel said. "He seems very . . . aware of things."

Rugoff raised his eyebrows. "Let me tell you. . . . That kid knows more than either of us will ever hope to know about people, about bugs—just ask him about butterflies sometime."

"I will," Rachel said.

As he was dropping her off at her apartment, he said, "How about next weekend? Are you game?"

"Sure," Rachel said. "Why not?"

"That's the spirit." He grinned. "I'll stock up on Bubble Club."

Chapter Four

A ND thus began her affair with Martin Rugoff. She usually
drove out with him on Thursday night or, later, when the
weather was nice, he lent her a motor scooter he had bought but
never used and she drove out on that, staying until Sunday or
Monday. It was her first affair with an "older man." Sometimes
she pondered why it had taken her until this advanced age to go
through such an archetypal experience. But frankly, she had
never liked "older men." Maybe her father was too much there,
too solid and present for her to want to search for a substitute in
some grossly oedipal way. Also, it struck her that to have a
penchant for older men you had to want either to be babied or
to be maternal, neither of which she basically did. Then, too,
she'd always assumed women went for older men because they
were suaver, richer, more established, and she had always considered herself too competitive to enjoy a relationship with
someone so much above her. She didn't *want* to look up to
anyone. At least someone of her own age would be going
through the same struggles, anxieties. But with Martin Rugoff
these doubts were waved aside, primarily because she felt she
could have a comfortable time with him and they would not fall
in love. Probably one day Violet would come rushing home and
she would depart, none the worse for wear. Meanwhile, she did
her typing during the week and her performances with Beatrice
whenever they came up.

She had not intended to tell Beatrice about Rugoff, but in the end she had to because Beatrice often had to get in touch with her at the last moment. Her reaction was predictable.

"You mean that wretched little man with the mustache?"

"Well, for one thing, he's half a foot taller than me. . . . He is a bit wretched, true, not in the pejorative sense, and he does have a mustache."

"I can't *believe* it," Beatrice said. "Are you promiscuous, Rachel? That's terrible!"

"Bea, Jesus!" It was amazing, Beatrice, the freethinker, the women's lib expert, with this hidden cache of Midwest morality. You can take the girl out of the. . . . "He's a very sweet man," Rachel said. "I really like him. We have fun together."

"It's sick," Beatrice said. "And that house in the suburbs—"

"Suddenly you're a Marxist? I'm not marrying him, for God's sake. . . . Should I be sitting at home masturbating with an unripe banana? Find me a better solution and I'll take it."

How would Beatrice have been happier? If Martin Rugoff were taller? If he lived in the East Village? If he was a civil rights lawyer? If he were a woman? The hell with it! Rachel thought. From then on, whenever Beatrice referred sarcastically to "Marty," she just shrugged and said he was fine, thanks. What did Beatrice do for sex, anyway? Maybe the remark about the unripe banana had been cruel, but still, she wasn't unattractive. Granted fifty, maybe sixty percent of men would be too short for her and a few more scared off by her manner, but some men liked challenges. It was her problem, but Rachel couldn't repress a certain curiosity. You didn't see Beatrice as an old maid, that was for sure.

One evening, on an impulse, she invited Ibert and Quentin, who was back from Prague, out for dinner at Rugoff's house. She and Lamont spent the afternoon making beef Wellington. He was better at crust than she was, but she was better at rolling it up and shaping it. They spent a considerable time picking the wine.

"Dad has all these superb vintages," Lamont said, showing her the wine racks in the butler's pantry, "but some of them he's saved *too* long. I think we'll find there's too much sediment."

Rachel took out one bottle. "Hey! A Château Rothschild!"

"Yes, but it's just a Mouton," he said. He put it back. "That wasn't a very good year."

Lamont still slept with a light on in his room, and he wore pajamas with bears on them and collected stamps. Half the time he looked like the small, frail, timorous thirteen-year-old that he really was; the other half Rachel felt as though he were her uncle or some much older, wiser, benevolent relative.

They set the table, waiting for the guests and for Rugoff, who was still at work.

"Mother called up last night," Lamont said while they were putting out the silverware.

"Oh, gee . . . how is she?"

"Not very good, I don't think. . . . She sounded somewhat hysterical."

"Did you talk to her?"

"A little. . . . I wanted to keep Dad off the phone as long as possible, frankly. After he talks to her, he's a wreck. I saw him crying the other night. He tried to pretend it was just a cold, but his eyes were all red."

"The poor sweetheart," Rachel said, pulling out another wine.

"Mother used to say she felt his behavior was extremely infantile. Sometimes I'm inclined to think she's right." He took the bottle from her. "We need something a little lighter," he said. "That one is too robust, I think we'll find."

Rachel had told Rugoff and Lamont that Quentin and Ibert were lovers, just to forestall any awkward speculations.

"Oh, that's okay," Rugoff had said. "We're men of the world, aren't we?"

Lamont shrugged as though: of course.

"They aren't the type that'll show up in tapered purple pants or anything," Rugoff said a moment later.

Rachel shook her head. "No more than you would. No, Ibert

would die . . . I mean, it's not that kind of. . . . You'll like him I think."

To Ibert, to make the situation seem more French and acceptable, she said she was now the mistress of an older man who had a lovely house in the country and wouldn't he and Quentin like to join them for dinner? He had always claimed this should be her true profession, anyway. She decided to really vamp it up in one of Violet's burgundy velvet gowns, her hair, which was growing longer, loose, lots of eye shadow. She would be witty and pour wine in large crystal goblets and act as though having a salon and entertaining intellectual men were what she had been trained for since birth. Bessie, with whom Rachel had established a certain working relationship, made a peach mousse for dessert.

The meal was fantastic. Lamont, a dish towel wrapped around his waist, outdid himself with the hors d'oeuvres. The beef Wellington was a masterpiece. Even Ibert was impressed by the wine. Sitting there, in the candlelight, Rachel felt as though she were onstage in the last act of *Don Giovanni*. Let Edward see her now! At least her morals were decaying in style, if you could even say they were. Actually, maybe they were improving with age.

After dinner Rugoff got out his flute, and the talk turned to music. Rachel had known he played, but had never realized it was so serious. Quentin, who played the oboe, was very impressed by Rugoff's flute. "Is it a Haynes?"

Rugoff smiled. "I wish it were. . . . No, it has a nice tone, though, don't you think?" And suddenly he began a Mozart flute quintet, running through several bars by himself. They all sat spellbound. He played as though he were singing so that the notes seemed to hang in the air, a bird whistling by himself in some dark, utterly deserted forest. Staring at him, Rachel was amazed.

"That was very fine," Ibert said when he was done. "You know Jean Pierre Rampal, of course?"

"Well." Rugoff smiled. "I think I have every recording he ever made." He put one on the phonograph.

Quentin and Ibert sat back, sipping their cognac, and all of them listened. Rachel felt they were all getting on so well she was a little superfluous. In her red velvet gown she tripped into the kitchen to help Lamont with the dishes.

"Ya, Dad's pretty good," he said when she commented on Rugoff's playing. "He surprises you sometimes."

That night, perhaps in the same spirit, he surprised her by suddenly being very ardent when they made love and she had a fantasy that he was imagining her body as that golden flute that he had never quite been able to afford. And perhaps similarly inspired by the analogy, she felt her body to be a very expensive, beautifully put-together instrument which, upon occasion, could certainly have a remarkable tone. He said, "I liked your friends, Rachel."

She murmured something.

He said, "I feel happy right now. . . . The hell with Violet."

But in the dark of the night he suddenly wanted to know all about Edward and why she had left him. Whatever she said, she could see he had some mental image of Edward as a woolly-haired, dashiki-wearing revolutionary—the facts of his life, his being an astronomer, the town house, all were brushed aside as so much ephemera. Moreover, he rather admired her for this, as though she had spent three years in the den of a lion and come out unscathed.

"No, it wasn't like that, really," she said.

"Ya, well, marriage is always. . . ." He sighed. "Do you think marriage is dead?"

Rachel yawned. She felt inordinately sleepy. "Gee, I don't know, Martin. . . . Probably, it's—"

There was a noise from Lamont's room. It sounded like someone saying, "What? What?" very loudly. Rachel ran in. He was sitting up in bed, his hair tousled, trying to turn on the bed light. Until his thirteenth birthday he had slept with it on and then had tried giving it up, substituting a light in the hall, but Rugoff had said it wasn't working.

"What's wrong?" she said.

"There were those tigers," he said. He frowned, squinting at her, trying to recover himself.

She was relieved in a way that he could have nightmares about tigers. She said, "I guess they went away."

"I guess."

"Do you want something to eat?"

"Maybe some chocolate milk."

It seemed his gourmet tastes fell away under stress. Rachel mixed some instant cocoa with milk and brought it to him in a white mug. He said, "Is Dad sleeping?"

"I think so."

"Tell him to take his blood pressure pill. . . . He always forgets. I was going to remind him last night."

"I'll tell him."

She tucked him back in and left the bed light on. "Might as well."

"That doesn't strike you as overly infantile?"

She shrugged. "I don't know. I mean, I always had one myself."

In bed Rugoff was asleep, snoring lightly. He didn't wake when she crept in beside him. She was glad; she wasn't in the mood for more talk about the life or death of marriage.

That Tuesday, just a few days into 1972, she decided to go to Philadelphia. She had had the train schedule in her purse for months and knew it almost by heart—anyway, they ran quite frequently. She decided on an eleven o'clock train, arriving at twelve thirty. Edward was almost never home in the middle of the day in the middle of the week. On the train she debated what her "act of desecration" would be. Fire seemed the most likely. The trouble was she recalled long conversations with Edward and his parents about fireproofing, and the gist of it, that she remembered, was that the house was in pretty good shape. Of course, you could light a fire from the inside, and even if the house didn't burn down, certain property would at least be damaged. She thought with a certain satisfaction of watching the draperies and wall-to-wall carpets which had been so carefully selected by his older sister, Rita, an interior decorator, slowly smolder. That should have been done long ago, in any case. But did things keep burning once they started? There must be some scientific principle at work there, but could you just light a match to something and expect it to take from there? Or did you need to do special things with kerosene-soaked rags and heaps of kindling? If only she'd been a girl scout! All those girl-hood years gone to waste. A bomb would be easier. But bombs —how did you get them? Again, probably you had to make them, and then what if they exploded while you were still there? Oh, she should have gone to a school for arsonists, for under-ground guerrillas, not for clowns!

The house looked the same, not that it could be expected to look any other way. It was on a side street and, on a quiet day, had the look of one of those Currier and Ives prints of a century ago. There was even an eccentric old lady with two Afghan hounds who sometimes walked them in the courtyard, adding to the illusion of otherworldly elegance.

Her key still worked. Well, sure. It would be beneath Edward to change the lock. If one has to stoop to something as petty as that. . . . She would show him. Trust humanity, will you, you bugger? Oh, my God, was today Agnes' day? This wasn't going to be like one of those silly Hollywood movies where you were fouled up on some tiny, irrelevant detail. What *was* her day? Of course, her day might have been changed, but Rachel imagined not. It would be more like Edward to have things go on just as they had before. Someone still had to clean the house, didn't they? Unless old Magda, but no, lady astronomers didn't stoop to anything as gross as vacuuming. I don't know, now that you mention it. Never having. . . . Well, the hell with it. Here she was. Onward! *Avanti, popolo!*

Silence. With all those wall-to-wall carpets, of course, sounds tended to be muffled, but she thought the house had a silent air to it. Jesus, her heart! She hadn't even taken a Dexamyl! Take it easy, will you?

Everything was the same. It was all so horribly, eerily the

same, like a waxworks museum. She almost expected to see small waxen images of herself and Edward sitting in the living room, he with his cigar burning in the green malachite turtle ashtray, she . . .

She went into the bedroom. Aha. Aha, what? Yes, really, what had she expected? Semen-stained sheets? Crumpled love notes? Blood on the bathroom floor? Actually, the bed was made. "We've been living together," he'd said or something to that effect. Could that have meant at her place? Rachel stood in front of the dressing table. A frightening sense of immobility seemed to have seized her. She felt as though she were in a pit of quicksand, sinking, sinking. . . . Set off a bomb? She'd be lucky to get out of this lousy place in one piece mentally. Not that she'd entered it in one piece mentally, but. . . . She pulled open a bureau drawer. Her underwear. Still there. Still crumpled up, not folded. This was *her* house. She lived here. "I've kept her room exactly the same since her death." Yes, and this is my first wife on top of the bookcase. Hey, *there* was an idea. That would give Edward a scare. Perch up there and then, very silently, when he came home to go to sleep, say. . . . Should she take her things? She swung open the closet door. Rows of dresses hanging there, that old canvas bag she'd been meaning to have cleaned. She stared at the things. They seemed so tangible, more real than she was. Objects had such a life of their own. They were more real than people, more solid.

Suddenly exhausted, as though she had run all the way from New York instead of having come by train, she sprawled out on the king-size double bed, covered now, as always, with its white fur throw. *Was* the white in this fucking house symbolic? Oh come on, there're a hundred, a thousand upper-middle-class apartments in Philadelphia, Boston, New York with the same off-white wall-to-wall carpets, the same white vinyl couches, plexiglass tables, stainless steel *étagères*. All chosen, in this instance, by Rita. You couldn't have helped pick the furnishings? Well, it had been laziness, partly. They had simply taken over a brownstone owned by his parents. And what did she, whose parents had lived all their lives with the same Salvation Army bureaus that jutted out too far, creaky beds and cardboard storage boxes, know of "interior decoration" and lamps and rugs? Such decisions, so she'd thought at the time, intimidated, offended her.

Anyway, white isn't just the opposite of black, fathead. It's a clear display of affluence, you know, like money— M-O-N-E-Y. Because it can get dirty so fast. It's showing you don't care. Just as her parents always picked dark green and brown for everything, clothes included, so even after twenty years the ingrained dirt wouldn't show.

Stroking the soft fur, Rachel suddenly began thinking of the letter she had left for Edward when she'd departed so precipitously for Berkeley. "You have denied your Blackness and by denying that have denied your Self. You are a Hollow Man." Jesus, what had all those capitalized nouns been for? Had she thought she was writing German? "I am leaving our white apartment with its white walls and white carpets because I am not white enough. Not in that sense. . . . Your detachment, your arrogance are all white." And hadn't there been something to the effect of "I'm not saying you have to wear an Afro or eat soul food. Those are clichés. But. . . ." God, at the time that letter had struck her as a masterpiece. She'd felt like retyping it and sending it to the New York *Times*. Now, with the intervening months, she wondered if there had been one honest word in it.

What was all this black-white garbage? Hadn't she, a poor girl, married a rich man, the oldest, most monotonous of love stories, done for all the trivial, crass reasons but somehow condoned by society from Cinderella on up (or down). Hadn't she simply wanted the elegance, the luxury, Edward's family embodied but which she would have rejected as "disgusting" had it come in a white model? In black she could enjoy it, even while pretending to disown it, to complain about it. Give me back my bed of nails! Yeah, man.

Christ, why not admit it? She'd lived in the same tiny room with her brother till they both went away to college, for God's sake. Who wouldn't want luxury? And it wasn't *just* the luxury, it was the something, the coolness and detachment, that seemed to go with it. Everyone in her family *cared* so much. There were so many Communists, suicides, crazy, alcoholic brothers, people for whom life was too real, blinding, frightening. Edward's parents would die in their sleep. Whatever rejections they had suffered as blacks had been integrated into a stony wall of politeness. The world has its faults. Poor world. *Her* family, had they ever been turned away as Jews from a hotel, would have moaned, beat their breasts, alternated between self-castigation—"we must somehow have deserved it"—and virulent abuse. Edward's family in a similar situation would walk away with a slight smile.

"I don't *care* if it's phony! I don't *care* if it's 'skin deep.' Let it be!"

Or was all that irrelevant, too? Had she left him just because he had been sleeping with a pale-skinned, blond, blue-eyed Catholic Hungarian lady astronomer with a size 38 bust—yes, Edward, your computer did its homework well. It *did* pick that woman, girl, who in all ways represented a rejection of me and all I care about. Good show, old fellow.

Thinking of Magda stirred the old anger again. Rachel sat straight up in bed. The fur suddenly seemed repugnant, not soothing, decadent. Like wet chewing gum on a bus seat. She went to the study. It was Edward's study, really, but there was a corner she used for her own books, papers, etc. All her things were still there, including what she was looking for, the black india ink and small sable brush with which she had liked to practice calligraphy. She unscrewed the top of the bottle of ink; it was still good, not dried up. She wet the brush in her mouth to make its tip more pointed. Where to start? Right here, perhaps. Where else? Going over to Edward's desk, she opened up the vinyl-covered pad with ETC. printed on top of it and wrote in small, perfect letters "fuck you" on the first page.

After that it was easy. She took her time, slowly circling the apartment, brush in one hand, container of black india ink in the other. She wrote it in the kitchen on the side of the stove, on a plastic bowl in the refrigerator containing some leftover meat, on the canister filled with sugar. In the living room she wrote it on one side of a cream-colored lamp shade, underneath an ashtray, right next to a large Andy Warhol painting, on the leg of the baby grand piano. In the bedroom she wrote it across the front of one of Edward's shirts, on the windowsill, on a light bulb that someone had unscrewed and left on a chair. In the bathroom she wrote it on the hot-water faucet, over the outlet for Edward's electric shaver, and on the lavender plastic Kleenex box holder. In the front hall she wrote it in the corner of one of a series of giant white ceramic tiles, on the leaf of a plastic rose standing in a glass vase, and on the doorknob. Leaving the apartment, she wrote it on the front steps and on the plastic watering can which Edward used to water the begonias in the summer. Rachel felt pleased, calm, happy, fulfilled. The thought of all those small, delicate, beautifully printed "fuck you's" proliferating around the apartment was a nice thought. They were so tiny maybe Edward wouldn't see them at first. He'd be having wretched, stuffy tea with Magda as hostess for some people in his department and suddenly someone, maybe Spiegelman, who was the acting head, would move the ashtray, look down and. . . .

Rachel sighed. She was ravenous, and munching on a marzipan pig she'd been saving in her bag helped. She bit off the ears, the head. Edward had had his say about her fondness for marzipan goodies, especially in colored animal forms. Up yours, Edward, she thought, and swallowed the pig's rear end, tail and all, her mouth moist with the wonderful, almondy sweetness. Yes, the trip had been worth it, after all.

At home there was a note from Beatrice saying she should call. She did, and on the phone Beatrice sounded subdued and soft-spoken, said she wondered if Rachel could come for dinner. Hanging up, agreeing to arrive in half an hour, Rachel felt puzzled, particularly by Beatrice's tone. Lately they had not been getting on too well. It was partly the affair with Rugoff, of which Beatrice disapproved. Then, too, Rachel had shown up at a picketing of City Hall to protest unfair abortion laws in her clown costume. The picketing was sponsored by one of Beatrice's women's lib groups, and when she had caught sight of Rachel, she was furious. "What's wrong with you? This is a serious thing."

"I know," Rachel had said. "I just thought—"

"God, you have no sense of proportion," Beatrice said. "Is this a time to clown? When *lives* are at stake?"

"I know, Bea." Rachel had hung her head in its big, floppy pink wig. "I'm sorry."

Reflecting on it, she had no idea if she'd just done it to get Beatrice's goat. In fact, she was in perfect sympathy with the aims proposed by the group. But ever since then Beatrice had been even chillier than ever, scarcely speaking when they had one of their interminable rides out to Huntington or Scarsdale or Leonia. Now, over health food spaghetti, Beatrice confessed that she had been having an affair.

"*Mazel tov,*" said Rachel, wishing Beatrice had the sense to serve wine, even Gallo.

Beatrice looked away. "It's not as simple as that."

The following tale emerged. The person in question who had won Beatrice's stony heart was a fairly famous woman sculptress who, Rachel gathered, was giving her a hard time. Beatrice went on about agonized evenings, drugs, odd people in the wings, and all the while Rachel, chewing on the grainy pasta, could only feel one thing: a terrible sense of disappointment. For what surprised her was not this conclusive evidence that Beatrice was a lesbian, but that, amazingly, she seemed to be a total masochist in relation to her lady love. Beatrice! The castrater par excellence. The sadist, the maker of devastating remarks, was groveling, was considering suicide, was feeling herself a nonentity! Was there no hope for womankind? Are we all drips and grovelers under the skin? Better if Beatrice had confessed a murder or the rape of a thirteen-year-old child.

"Gee, it sounds like you've been having a tough time," Rachel said, trying to conceal her real feelings. "She sounds like kind of a bastard."

"She's not!" Suddenly Beatrice was the old Beatrice again, fiery and fierce. "She's a remarkable person. You should meet her, Rachel. She's the most brilliant person I've ever met! It's me, it's all me."

"Ya, well. . . ."

"Knowing her has changed my life," Beatrice said.

She went on, clearing away the spaghetti plates. No salad? Oh Beatrice, you deserve to suffer. Of the essentials, of why one woman would choose another woman, of what exactly they did and how and why Rachel could only form a vague picture. It must be oral—a lot of kissing? No, but it's the emotional thing. She wants to be trampled on. *Wants* it. Oh, Beatrice, how could you, you've ruined my image of you.

But from then on Rachel found that she could regard Beatrice as probably she should have all along, just a person, an ordinary person to boot. No more cringing or feeling inadequate. If Beatrice made nasty remarks about Rugoff, Rachel just shrugged them off. You have your unripe banana, I have mine. To each his own.

Rugoff lay in the sun porch, his shirt off, while Rachel pummeled him along his backbone. "Oh, great," he moaned. "Jesus, that feels wonderful."

His skin was as white as cream of wheat, but he insisted on lapping up whatever he could of the sun. To Rachel's steady pounding he said, "Rach, tell me—give me your honest opinion, huh?"

"Sure."

"What is the thing with Violet? Is it that she left me? Is it a pride thing? . . . Jesus, she called again last night. Now why? What has she got to say? Just want to stick the needles in?"

"A little of that, probably."

"Not a word about Lamont. . . . How do you like that? Her own kid. She had him when she was eighteen."

"Maybe that's why."

"I mean, let's face it, Violet has suffered. . . . She hasn't had an easy life."

"Yeah," Rachel said.

"You're not so sympathetic, eh? No, but it's true. She's an insecure person. Anxieties! My God, you wouldn't believe some of the things—she won't fly, she won't this, she won't that. . . . Do you know, when we were first married, I had to buy her clothes for her. She wouldn't enter a clothes store, that's the truth. She was afraid of what the salesladies would say. Can you imagine? Here's this beautiful girl—how do you explain it?"

Rachel shrugged. She lay down on her stomach. "You do me," she said.

She pulled off her shirt and lay on the towel while he massaged her. "Do you know what I really feel badly about?" he said.

"What?"

"I don't even miss the twins anymore. . . . I used to dream about them every night, especially Flora. . . . Now I hardly remember them. It's crazy, but when I think of them, I see these two babies, but, like, it could be any two babies. I feel like they were never here or born or anything. . . . Oh, and that childbirth! That course we took with all the breathing! I thought *I* had those babies. By the time they wheeled Vi away into the delivery room, believe me, *I* was ready for an anesthetic. . . . And now—"

She was silent. He rubbed her. "I'm sorry, Rach. You're mad, huh? All this old crud. . . . No, I ought to stop talking about it. It's just salt in the wounds, right? The hell with it. . . . I just have to tell you this one thing. Here's the supreme irony. I'm eating in Childs the other day, and who walks in but the redhead, you know, the girl from the group who I. . . . Looking terrific! Dyed her hair, something, all I know is here's this kid supposed to be at death's door because of me, she comes over, starts talking, no hard feelings, nothing. Listen, I'll tell you—it struck me I could have taken her home. I didn't want to, I'm not crazy, but if I had been— She didn't consider me responsible at all. How do you like that? And Vi still talks about that girl like I'd strangled her with my bare hands. . . . I don't want to make you jealous. . . . Hey, what are you, crying? Sweetie, what is it? Jesus, I'm a baboon. Oh, no." He sat her up and began patting her shoulders.

Rachel said, "No, it's nothing to do with. . . . I'm just—"

"No, I'm an insensitive son of a bitch. How do you like that? I can't shut up for one second about all this garbage, this—"

"Marty, I swear, it has nothing—" And it didn't. Yet she could tell as the tears spilled endlessly down and splashed on her breasts that he was flattered, touched, that these tears might be for him. He put his hands over her breasts. "Look at these poor little fellows," he said. "They're so pale."

"They don't get enough sun," Rachel said, laughing and sniffing.

"They don't get enough attention. Look at the poor darlings. Neglected—"

It was Lamont's afternoon at his analyst so they went inside and made love in the living room on the guanaco rug which had a wonderful smell of leaves and animals and dust. And Rachel thought maybe she was happy. Rugoff was right—did you have to be beaten to feel you were alive? The hell with that! Live! Love!

He played her the flute piece she liked best of all, and she lay, nude, on the soft, furry rug, her breasts feeling still tingling from the spring sun. I'm a bird in a forest, the hell with being human. I'm a lady bug crawling through a deep, deep pile of. . . .

The door swung open from outside. Knowing it was Lamont, she raced into the bedroom while Rugoff, immersed in the melody, played on.

* * *

Ibert and Quentin invited her to tea. They were planning a long trip to the Far East. She felt envious as they spread maps on the table, debated hotels.

"Somehow India doesn't interest me," Ibert said thoughtfully. "All that poverty. . . . They seem such a disorganized people."

Quentin smiled at Rachel. "Isn't that typical? The French. Organization above everything. . . . How about their art, their—"

"It's all mysticism," Ibert said, not at all disconcerted. "No, I'm sure it fulfills a purpose for them, no question of that. . . . But all those children begging on the streets, all those unclean cows wandering—"

"Jacques, you have the most incredibly stereotyped notions," Quentin said. Again, half to Rachel, he said, "Isn't it amazing, a man with his erudition—"

"I said I'd go, didn't I?" Ibert said. "No, I want to go. . . . It's just, I don't have that pull." He made a gesture as though something were being forcibly drawn from his body.

"Where I'd like to go," Rachel said, a little uncomfortable at this sparring between them, "is China."

"Hong Kong?" Ibert handed her a teacup with a look of distaste on his face.

"No, Red China—I've always wanted to go. I should think it would be terribly exciting."

"Exciting?" He grimaced. "My dear, those revolutionary countries are the dullest thing in the world. Lots of dronelike little people, all dressed in baggy clothes—"

She laughed. "You're so superficial!"

"Superficial! Eating bowls of rice every day!"

"But how about the spirit? The revolutionary ardor?"

"Nonsense." He stirred his tea. "That's all propaganda, Rachel. . . . No, I'm amazed, both of you really—" he said, nodding to Quentin. "You accept these superficial ideas."

"You're the one who's superficial," Rachel said. "My God, look at the French with their sauces and their couture—what could be more—"

"On the contrary, that's life," Ibert said firmly.

"You can't argue with him," Quentin said.

"I guess it's great to believe in your own culture so strongly," said Rachel, half-ironically.

"It's not a question of believing in one's culture," Ibert began, but Quentin interrupted.

"Now, Jacques, you must admit it. It's precisely that. . . . Just a kind of chauvinism at bottom. . . . But I agree with Rachel. I wish I could feel that way about America."

"No one feels that way about America," Rachel said.

"Oh, some people do," said Ibert.

"Just wild-eyed Western Senators and people like that," put in Quentin. "Yes, Rachel and I are people without a country, Jacques. A fact you, with your comfortable insularity, can't quite appreciate."

Rachel felt as though she were being bounced back and forth like a tennis ball in their sallies. She was reminded for a moment of Julie and Dan. And wondered fleetingly which, if either, of them was unfaithful and how that worked out.

"We both, by the way, just to elevate the conversation slightly," said Ibert, "liked your friend very much."

"I thought you would," Rachel said, smiling.

Ibert turned to Quentin. "You say I never have any influence in the world," he said. "Well, it so happens, Rachel can testify, in this very room, a few months ago, I was telling her her true destiny was to be a woman of the modern age, take on lovers, forget all this nonsense about marriage, babies, all that middle-class claptrap, and you see—"

"Yes, I did just what you said," Rachel said. "Wasn't that good of me?"

"It was very good, my dear. . . . Wasn't I right?"

He was teasing her; still she couldn't help looking a little sad as she said, "I wish everything *were* just the way you said. So simple."

"You aren't falling in love?"

"No, not that."

"I must admit," he went on, again to Quentin, "that at first hand I thought—here, the typical Jew, the businessman, couldn't she have picked someone more prepossessing—"

"Jacques, you are really too much," Quentin said.

"It's okay," said Rachel.

"No, but then," Ibert went on, unruffled, "I saw that underneath, here was a man of some quality, of some distinction—"

"His flute *was* remarkable," Quentin said.

"Yes, all Quentin could talk about was what a fine *instrument* the man possessed." He looked at him archly. "I have rarely heard such a superior tone," he mimicked.

"It was a beautiful tone," Quentin said calmly.

"Yes, well, no doubt it was, it was, I acknowledged it, but above and beyond that, the man, as I say, had a certain—"

"*Je ne sais quoi*," suggested Rachel.

"You see, you both enjoy teasing me. . . . Well, I accept it. I accept my role, the butt of all—"

"He really is a sorry specimen, isn't he?" Quentin said.

"Terrible," said Rachel. "How about some more tea, folks? Can you spare some?"

"I felt," Ibert went on, "in this man's relation to you a very nice sense of courtesy, of romantic refinement, of gentle sensuality—in short, a man who knows how to treat women as they should be treated."

"Gosh, I wish Marty could hear you," Rachel said. "He'd love it."

"He has suffered," Ibert went on, lost in these musings, "that much is clear. Here we have a man whom life, women have not treated kindly, but who—*here* is what is important—has triumphed over these sufferings, has acquired a gentleness, a superiority—"

"You see, he's really talking about himself," Quentin said.

"I know," said Rachel.

Ibert shook his head. "You two! Such merciless skepticism. I've never seen the like."

"But is one lover enough?" Rachel said teasingly. "I thought you'd require at least three or four."

He looked taken aback. "Did I counsel promiscuity? Not at all."

"I see," she said.

"You know, Rachel is also a clown," Ibert said to Quentin. "You don't want to show him your juggling, my dear?"

"Sure. . . . Give me a couple of oranges."

While Ibert disappeared for the oranges, she said to Quentin, "I can never tell how much he's just making fun of me."

"That's his manner," Quentin said.

"Does it bother you?"

"At times. . . . Not very much anymore. . . . Jacques is really very kindhearted."

"Is he?" She was touched that he would even say that.

"Absolutely. . . . Though he would cut your throat if you said it in his presence."

"He would what?" Ibert said, returning with a bowl of tangerines. "Are these all right? I seem to be out of—"

"Perfect," Rachel said. She took a couple and began tossing them rhythmically in the air, feeling, with their eyes upon her, that supreme sense of self-confidence which she felt so rarely these days. She would not drop them, she had the rhythm, the balance in her bones, and she felt she could have sat all day in that dim apartment with the two of them watching her and the maps in disarray on the floor, on the table.

Going home later, she reflected on how comfortable their lives together seemed to be. Sparring, yes, but not in a *Who's Afraid of Virginia Woolf*ish way. They seemed to really like each other, to have "worked things out." Not like Beatrice and her lady sculptress with all that agony and masochism. So maybe. . . . So maybe, what? It didn't really clear things up for her any, no matter what conclusions she decided to draw about it.

I want order in my life, Rachel found herself thinking as she entered her apartment. Peace and order. So go to the Far East and look at Buddhas. You go and come back and tell me about it. She went to her desk and sat down to finish her typing.

Chapter Five

IN the middle of January Violet came back. The following
Thursday, as Rachel was typing away, ready to leave on the
motor scooter in half an hour, a call came from Rugoff. His
voice was low, almost a whisper.

"Listen, sweetheart . . . I'm not home. I'm at a phone
booth—"

"So talk louder. I can hardly hear you."

"Listen, it's terrible. I don't know what to say," he said. "Vi is
back. She came back last night."

"For good?"

"I don't know. Look, I know nothing. She's hardly talking to
anybody but Bessie. . . . It's terrible. . . . But you better
not—"

"Of course I won't!"

"Honey, I feel so badly . . . I want to keep you out of this."

"I *am* out of it."

"She just arrived . . . Lamont and I were watching the Late
Show, and the door opens, just like that. . . . She has the twins
with her. . . . Oh, I can't describe it. No calls first, nothing."

"Marty, don't explain. Really. I understand."

"I want to see you," he said. "Let me call you Monday."

"Sure."

"Don't be upset, sweetheart, okay? Promise me."

"I won't. . . . Listen, you don't be either. . . . You sound
awful."

"Sure, sure. . . . Okay, be good, puss."

Well, she had expected it. So what else was new? She was used to rugs being pulled out from under her. But didn't you have to admire Violet? Why can't I be like that? Driving people crazy. The grand gesture. You will, dear. Give yourself time.

But she felt sad. What was she going to do with herself? She had been looking forward. . . . Look at all the typing you'll get done. More money. Big deal. Sunday afternoon as she was sitting at the window, gazing out, the phone rang again.

"Sweetheart?"

" 'Tis I."

"Listen, do you think—I've got to ask you this tremendous favor?"

"Sure."

"Well, could Lamont and I come and stay with you tonight? Or, like maybe for a week or so?"

"With me?"

"Ya, well, just for tonight . . . I mean, we can go to a hotel, it's just—"

"No, you can come here. Sure. It's just—I just have the two beds."

"No, we have sleeping bags, that's okay."

"Well, what about Violet, is she still there?"

"Yes, she's—listen, I can't go into it now. . . . So we'll come, right? Maybe all go out and eat, huh? How about it?"

"Fine. What time will you be here?"

"Give us an hour."

"You have an hour."

"We'll see you, puss."

They arrived on her doorstep looking like something out of a Chaplin comedy, both bedraggled, unshaven—even Lamont somehow looked unshaved. If they had been wrapped in a blanket, you would have had to take them in.

"So here we are!"

They had the sleeping bag and two suitcases, both carried by Rugoff. Lamont had a large cardboard carton under one arm. "I brought my butterfly collection," he said. "Is that okay?"

"It's great. . . . Just what I need around here. So where do we eat?"

Rugoff smiled. "That's what I like—you're always hungry, Rach."

"What do you mean, hungry? I'm starving."

They went to a steak house, where she alone ate anything. Lamont toyed with a tuna fish sandwich and Rugoff had three steins of beer. "So, kid," he said later when they were both in pajamas—Lamont was sleeping on the extra bed—they were both out in the hall, not very private, but everyone's door was closed, and it was the only place Lamont wouldn't hear them. "We have been through the mill. Let me tell you. If I thought I knew before what. . . . You know what she calls this? A trial separation. 'From who?' I wanted to know. From carphead? Like, I'm only her husband, right? Not a separation from *me*. I said, how've you been? Talk to my lawyer about it, she says. Now look, couldn't she have gone to a hotel? I mean, if she can't even tell me how she is, I wasn't being personal, just how are you, if that is such an invasion of her rights or whatever, so why come home? What for?"

Rachel cleared her throat. "It's the same old story."

"But why?" His voice rose to a wail. "*Why* is she like that?"

Suddenly a door opened, and a plump girl in a bathrobe walked past them to the kitchen. Rugoff glared at her. "Who's that?"

"I don't know," Rachel said. "Some girl."

He looked around. "What is this? Who are all these people?"

"They live here, that's all."

"But so where's your privacy?"

"Who can afford privacy? Look, it's cheap. . . . If I want privacy, I go to my room."

He sighed. "I don't know. . . ."

Rachel bristled. "Look, go to a hotel if. . . ."

He put his hand on her shoulder. "No, don't be silly, honey. . . . So where was I—Vi? So you think it's the same old story, huh?"

"Of course it is!" Rachel said impatiently.

He spread open his hands. "If only I knew why she was like that! If only I knew!"

"Marty, listen, for Christ's sake, what difference would it make if you knew? So what if her grandmother hung her by her left toe for three years as a child? What would you know if you knew that? She is what she is."

"There has to be a reason."

"Why was Hitler Hitler?"

He sighed more deeply. "Oh, God! You're right, I guess. . . ."

"No, what's stupid," Rachel said, "is being surprised. I mean, naïveté up to a point is okay, but what do you expect? She'll do her thing—"

"And her thing is sticking pins, right?"

"Right. So don't be surprised when you look down and see blood on the carpet."

He grinned. "Ya, no, you're right, you're, you're right. . . . But she walked in the door so meekly, so quietly. . . . And the twins. They're so tan, little butterballs. Poor little Flora. You should have seen her. When she saw me, she leaned over and started making this sound—they don't really talk yet. Jesus, I thought she'd have a heart attack. Can you imagine? A little baby like that with such deep feelings? It's amazing."

"No, it is sweet," Rachel said crabbily.

"Right away she's giving orders, telling Bessie what to do, shorten her hems, make this pie, calling people. Like we're not there, like we don't exist. Hardly greets Lamont. . . . You think underneath she's suffering?"

"No," Rachel said.

"No? Not even a little? . . . Yeah, you're right. Why should she? Meanwhile, carphead is calling up every five minutes pleading, cursing—that man is such a buffoon, so crass! I mean, I know I'm not objective, but you'd think Charles Boyer, someone smooth, slick, even a little oily, but this guy! He could be in the Mafia."

"Maybe he is."

"Believe me, if they took Hungarians, he'd be in."

The girl walked back from the kitchen again.

"She's too fat," Rugoff whispered. "What's she eating at this time of night for?"

"Marty, ssh!"

"God, I hate fat women! Why should a woman be fat?" He squeezed her shoulder. "At least Lamont is sleeping. . . . Honey, I wish we had some privacy. Maybe he'll go to a movie tomorrow, what do you think?"

"Alone?"

"Maybe he has some friend." He looked mournful. "No, you're right, we've got to be nice to him."

They tiptoed back to Rachel's room. She pulled the curtains across. Rugoff whispered, "Could I get in bed with you just a second?"

"Better not, maybe."

"Ya. Well. . . ." He kissed her absently. "I don't know, Rach. . . . You say life has to be this way. . . ."

"Did I say that?"

"I don't know," he muttered, getting into his sleeping bag. "Sometimes it seems. . . ."

But he was asleep before he could finish the thought.

The next morning he went down to Chock Full o'Nuts and brought back coffee cake, coffee, milk, and juice in a paper bag.

"How did you sleep?" Rachel asked Lamont while Rugoff was still gone.

"Okay." He was still sitting up in bed. "I like your apartment, Rachel."

Rachel smiled. "It's not really an apartment even, just a room."

"It's nice. . . . That's what I'd like to do. . . . Have a room like this, all by myself."

"Maybe when you're older."

He went to the window. "You have a view and everything."

She said, "I wish there was another room. . . . There's not much privacy for you."

After a moment he said, "Dad and you probably might like to be alone. . . . I might go to a movie."

Euh! Was he up all through their conversation? Or was it just his usual observant nature? "We could all go . . . I don't want you going alone."

"Oh, that's okay . . . I can ask someone to take me in. . . . Some old lady."

"No, that's too seedy," Rachel said. "I don't trust old ladies."

Rugoff, coming back, said, "Don't trust who? Why?"

"I don't trust *nobody,*" Rachel said in a mock tough voice.

Biting into his coffee cake, Lamont said, "Hey, this is great! I like this!"

Rugoff looked suspiciously at his coffee. "Yeah, I guess. . . ."

"It's true, eating out of bags makes it taste different," Rachel said.

They sat in silence, munching. Rugoff said, "We can't impose on you all week, Rach. We know that."

"Oh, come on. . . . So what? Stay a month!"

Lamont's face lit up. "Gee, Dad, let's! That'll be terrific!"

"No, listen," Rugoff said. "None of that. . . . We have to be serious. . . . I mean, like, decisions have to be made. . . Why are we here? We have a house."

"I don't *like* our house," Lamont said.

"Like it, you like it. . . . So we'll find another house. . . . Maybe it *is* a little too big."

"Could you move the tub?" Rachel asked wistfully.

"Why not? No, that's the thing. Sell the house! Who needs it, it's a white elephant. . . . But selling a house is a big deal," he said suddenly, reversing. "You don't just *sell* a house." He looked at Rachel and Lamont as though expecting them to disagree. "I mean, there're market values. . . . You don't just sell it like that. It's a big decision. . . . I'm fond of that house, in a way. It has certain. . . ." He trailed off. Lamont and Rachel watched him with concern.

"Did you take your pill, Dad?" Lamont said suddenly.

"Oh, Jesus, no! I forgot!" He leaped up. "What would I do without him?"

"My brother has high blood pressure, too," Rachel said.

"Men always have something," Rugoff said from the bathroom. "How can they help it? It's women who are lucky."

"What do you mean, lucky?"

"They live longer, they—"

"So be one!" she said.

"That's all I need. I have enough problems, *bubela*." He yawned. "God, I'm dead."

"You just got up," Lamont pointed out.

"I know. . . . But I hardly slept. . . . Who's that joker who was practicing the recorder at three in the morning?" he asked Rachel.

"Recorder? Maybe Myron, I don't know."

"What a place this is. . . . What do your parents think of this?"

"They never saw it."

"A good thing. . . . Anyway, listen, I'm beat, kids. . . . You two go to the movies, okay? Go see whatever you like. . . . I'm going to nap."

Rachel and Lamont went to see the show at Radio City Music Hall. They stayed for the entire program, the clowns, the stage show, passing a large box of popcorn between them. It was a musical version of Charlie Brown.

"I don't think they really captured the spirit of the original," Lamont said as they staggered out into the late afternoon.

"They never do," Rachel said.

"I liked it, though," he added hastily.

On the bus on the way home he said, "You know I have what I think is not such a bad idea."

"Namely?"

"Well, I could stay here with you—and Dad could go back and straighten things out with Mom. . . ." Since Rachel said nothing, he went on, "The thing is, he should straighten things out, don't you think? Dad had this tendency to procrastinate, you might not have noticed."

"I've noticed," Rachel said.

"I mean, he says he worked it out in group, learning to face things and all that, but sometimes I'm not so sure. . . . Anyway, under stress he tends. . . ."

"Ya, well, we all do," Rachel said.

"So the thing is this," he said. "Here's how I have it figured. I go to school next week anyway. . . . Well, there's this guy in my class who lives in Manhattan. I can come in with him and take the bus here. We can eat out or I could cook—"

Rachel sighed.

"It's a good plan!" he said. "I know it is."

"It is and it isn't," said Rachel.

"Dad won't go back, you mean."

"Among other things."

"You think I'm too young—"

"No, no, nobody's too young for anything. . . . Well, let's— let's see what he says."

When Lamont was asleep that night, Rugoff said, "Listen, I have this plan, Rach."

"What?"

"Maybe Lamont ought to go back and stay at the house, what do you think?"

"With Violet?"

"Ya! I mean, it's her child! It's her goddamn child! Now where's her sense of responsibility about that?"

"I don't know where it is, but it sure as hell hasn't shown its horny head very much."

"But would she just be mean to her own child? Ignore him? What? Aren't we underestimating the maternal—"

"There you go again!" Rachel said.

"Ya, no, you're right. . . . I guess he stays with us. . . . Oh, Christ, what are we supposed to do?"

"About what?"

"I can't sleep in the same room with you every night."

"Sure you can. . . . Listen, we'll work something out."

"Will we?" He looked disheartened.

They stayed with her for a week. Every night Rugoff called home, and every night Bessie answered and said, yes, Mrs. Rugoff was still there, everyone was doing just fine, thank you.

"What a turncoat!" Rugoff would say when he hung up. "When she left, you should have heard her! What a crummy mother Vi was, all this stuff. Now!"

After school Lamont would show up as Rachel was finishing her typing, and they would play chess till Rugoff came home from work. Then they would go out to eat, usually to one of the Chinese places along Broadway. "Let's make a rule," Lamont said, "that every night we order something we never had before." So they feasted on sea bass in brown sauce and other delicacies which Rugoff only picked at.

On Friday night when Rugoff called, there was no answer. He tried again later in the evening, and there was still no answer. Saturday morning he tried again. From then on throughout the weekend he kept rushing to the phone in the middle of whatever they were doing, like a man with a bad attack of cramps, occasionally saying, "Now, I'm not going to call for at least two more hours." By Sunday afternoon he was saying, "What do you think? Have they left?"

"It looks like it," Rachel said.

"They could have gone away for the weekend."

"Where?"

"Anywhere! How do I know where?" He frowned. "Listen, you know what I'm going to do? I'm going to drive out there. If she's there, I'll come back. If she's not, the two of you come out by train and I'll pick you up at the station."

Lamont and Rachel waited in her room, listening to the Beatles till Rugoff called. He sounded jubilant. "The coast is clear!"

"You're sure she's really gone?" Rachel said. "Not just—"

"No, all her stuff, everything's gone. . . . The place is a mess, but I swear to Jesus they're out of here. Listen, Bessie'll be in in the morning. We can ask her. . . . So what train will you take?"

"But, Marty, wait a sec, why should I come out? It's not the weekend."

"What does the weekend have to do with it?"

"Well, I go out weekends, remember? We have a schedule."

"Oh, the hell with that!"

"No, I've got to stick to it," she insisted. "I've got to have a life of my own."

"Rachel, Jesus, come out this one night, will you? I don't want to drive all the way in and then back and then—"

"Okay, we'll take"—she consulted the schedule—"the eight o five."

The house, he had been right, was a mess. Dirty bathtubs, food unwrapped, left lying on the kitchen counter, opened bottles of baby food.

"They must have whirled out of here in a hurry," Rugoff said. "And where was schmatzhead Bessie to clean up?"

"Marty, come on."

"Look, it's not some fleabag hotel. She could at least clean the place up." Seeing the look on Rachel's face, he said, "Okay, okay, I won't—"

He put Lamont to bed while she tried to make some perfunctory order out of the kitchen. He opened a few tins of sardines and some caviar, and for the first time in a week, she saw him eat ravenously, as though he'd just been let out of a concentration camp. In the bath he lay back and let her wash his hair. He kept sighing, "Jesus, Rach—"

"Don't."

"No, I won't."

In bed he fell on her like on the tin of sardines, with an ardor she found it not difficult to reciprocate, if only because of the enforced abstinence of the past week. Often, making love with him, she found it necessary to evoke ghosts of the past—Edward sometimes, imaginary men flitted by while she tried not to feel guilty about this. On the top of the hill, as she pictured it, was the orgasm, and she was on a bicycle, trying to get there. These imaginary figures were just to push her up, but when she was there, almost there, knew she wouldn't go suddenly rolling down again, she would dismiss them abruptly and allow herself the luxury of being in the actual situation. With him Rachel always felt herself to be a better lover than she had with Edward. Was it that she was less involved? Or that he always seemed so grateful, so touched, even, if she fellated him or devoted to his body even a reasonable amount of interest. She would think, I am making someone happy, and have a virtuous glow, as though she were helping an old lady across the street, none of which really prevented her from rather enjoying it herself.

"You know, for two people who aren't in love, I think we do pretty well," he said.

"*I* think we do," she said sleepily, turning over on her side.

"I mean, you take most marriages. Look at them! I'll take a bet we have a better time together than nine out of ten people on this block."

"We're not married," she pointed out.

"Ya." He grew thoughtful. "You think it's that?"

"Maybe partly."

"I don't think it's that," he said.

"Maybe it's not."

"I think we've both learned from bitter experience. . . . I think that's what it is. . . . Hell, why can't people learn things? Do they have to be slaves to the past? Do they have to be steeped in all these rotten old neurotic patterns that—"

"Yes," said Rachel.

"Sometimes I wonder . . ." he was saying as she finally did drop off to sleep.

Chapter Six

THE next weekend Rugoff took Rachel to one of his delicatessens. He had some business to transact, and Rachel wandered
around, inspecting rings of salami, bagels, inhaling the rich, mel-
lifluous odors of ripe cheese, wrinkly olives, crusty breads. Only
she felt, as she had all week, a little funny. A little funny could
be anything. Coming down with something. Getting over something. Just being tired. Emotional. God knows what it could be.
She hadn't given it a thought. But suddenly, sitting on a stool behind the counter, waiting for Rugoff to finish whatever he was
doing, the possibility came to her. She was staring somewhat
morosely at a tremendous round of Brie cheese, watching it
swell—it seemed to do it as she watched—out of its waxy cover.
Around her was a tremendous din of voices, orders, good-
natured cajolery. And in the midst of this, as though superim-
posed on that round of Brie, came the message in large black letters: You're pregnant, kid. I *am?* She stared, hypnotized, at the
Brie for a long time. It was like reading some newspaper
headline and trying to figure out the implications on world
events. She wasn't even sure what she felt, the idea seemed so peculiar. I've never met a purple cow, I never hope to meet one.
Well, dear, I have news for you. . . .

On the way home—Rugoff was driving her back to her place
since it was Sunday night—she was unusually silent. Rugoff, immersed in the details he had been discussing, didn't notice. "What
are they doing with those breads?" he said. "Did you see that?
They ought to be out front. Who said to put them in the back

with all that canned goods? . . . It's amazing. You know, you'd figure some things are so simple—no one could foul them up. You watch—someone fouls them up. . . . Hey, puss, what's up? Sleepy?"

They had made love earlier. He said this fondly. She tried to smile and said, "Ya, a little."

A minute later he was saying, "You know, for some reason Vi couldn't stand that guy—did you happen to notice him?—Arnold, the one who runs the store. It was the oddest thing. Just couldn't stand him. Used to say. . . ."

When she got home that evening, she sat in the chair looking out at the Columbia campus, and she could feel only one thing: pleasure. Where is your fucking reality principle, you goof? I mean, like, who needs this? Your life is so well organized you have to start looking for complications? The thing was, she wanted to call someone up and tell the good news. And yet there was no one who would regard it as good news. Which ought to indicate something. But for years I tried to get pregnant. So I'm retroactive, is that such a crime? That's the thing with you, dear. It's always a case of doing the right thing at the wrong time or the wrong thing at the. . . . Granted no one would find the news good, would most people find it *bad?* Rachel tried envisioning the people she knew, Julie, Rugoff, her parents. Surely no one would be conventionally shocked or horrified. No? Well, why should they, after all? They won't be, if you get rid of *it.* Then it'll be like a missed period, and what's a little blood among friends? But people are always having babies. Yes, and so? I could have it and. . . . Sweetie, why not save yourself a lot of time and energy and quit all this scheming? But I like it! I want to indulge myself. I'm feeling happy. Well, if you're feeling happy, there's something wrong with you. Did I deny that? This is at best an inconvenience, at worst a. . . . I'm going to call Edward and tell him. You do that, dear. No, really, I think he should know. Why? Christ, all that fussing with temperature charts and thermometers and doctors and tests. He *deserves* to know. But he doesn't *care,* you big goofy fool. He doesn't give a shit. Not even a little one. What do you mean? I mean, I mean. I mean what I mean. Let's face it. There is no one on the surface of this great round globe who is going to be made happy by this event. Like, *no* one. Okay, I accept that. You say you accept it. I ac*cept* it. No one, right? Right. So let's take it from there. No one? No one. How about Rugoff? He loves babies. Sweetie, he loves his *own* babies, he's *married*. You're not in *love* with him. I mean, I can give a thousand reasons why. . . . I can sell it. Jewish babies are worth a lot. Hey, great idea. Get pregnant every year and. . . . Let's settle one thing. As of now, this is a fantasy. So why discuss it? Go for a test, and then think about it. But I *know*. You know, you know a lot of things. Go for a test. I'll go for a test, did I say I wouldn't? Because everything else belongs under the category of Fruitless Speculation. Right? What would I do if. . . . Now that's a waste of time. So my time is so valuable I can't sit here for half an hour and. . . . It's not the time. You're getting yourself worked up. I'm *not* worked up. What do you mean "worked up"? I mean, sure, I have some emotional reaction, so what do you want? Is that what you call getting all worked up? Yes, it is. Well, goof off, then. . . . Hey, you know who'll think it's a gas? Beatrice. Very funny. Well, look, why can't I make jokes? Is that a crime? You want me to be so morbid. Should I feel like killing myself? I really feel very happy. So you've said. I'm glad to feel happy. Feeling happy is better than feeling sad. Under *some* circumstances. If you strangle someone and you feel happy. . . . Why do you pick these violent analogies? Who's strangled anyone? I'm just saying unto every situation, there is an appropriate response, and your response in this particular situation—to wit, happiness—is not appropriate.

For a week similar arguments went on in her mind, battles to and fro between imaginary combatants. No one ever seemed to win. It was usually a draw. The superego versus the id? Who knew. But by the end of the week, worn out from thinking about it, Rachel decided the least she could do was go for a pregnancy test. She knew a lab in New York—she had once gone to it when there had been a false alarm with Stef. It was in a small brownstone in the East Nineties. The white-clad secretary behind the desk asked her name with indifference. She gave her married name. When they asked the name of her doctor, she put down her father's name and her own present phone number. That way she could get the news directly. They took blood. Between blood and urine, blood seemed more emphatic. She went out with a small circular bandage in the crook of her arm, feeling that a little ritual bloodletting had a certain appropriateness under the circumstances. Perhaps under most circumstances when you came down to it. The next morning she sat in her room, trying to type, ears peeled for the phone. It rang twice, once with a wrong number. The third time, at ten thirty, a woman's voice, said, "Can I speak to Dr. Ovcharov, please?"

"Oh, I'm sorry, he's busy at the moment," Rachel said. "Could I possibly take a message?"

She *could* possibly take a message. The report on Mrs. R. Wittiker had been positive.

After she had hung up the phone, Rachel went back to her room. She had a sudden feeling she hadn't heard what the woman had said. She said *positive*, you dum-dum. You heard her. Did I hear her? I just don't trust my own ears. Well, you've trusted them up till now. No, not until the report arrived in the mail and she saw it before her very own eyes would she have that certainty, that absolute conviction, she decided. But what if you don't trust your own eyes? Come on, that's a totally different thing. It'll be there, I can peruse the piece of paper.

In two days the report came. Positive. Yes, there was that word, no mistaking it. No taking it for anything else. Eight very clearly typed letters.

So. Crack open the champagne. I can't afford champagne. Go crack open some root beer. Crack open your own head, dope. . . . Stop it. I'm still happy. I said I was. I am.

But now to tell somebody. Somehow she had to tell somebody. Maybe there were people who could bear these things in silence. Presumably even married women sometimes waited months to tell their husbands. Well, they were a different breed. Was there a purpose in her telling? No, not in any practical sense, but she wanted, very much, to have a reaction. Let it be horror, let it be rage, indignation, contempt. But the final proof that this had really happened would be someone, anyone, saying, "You mean you're really. . . ."

It would have to be Rugoff. Which was awkward in a sense since he might feel she was doing it to pressure him, but she felt she could get around that. Beatrice would be outraged or disgusted, her parents were certainly out for a while until she had digested the whole thing, Dan and Julie she would just as soon postpone, especially the idea of telling them together—telling just one and not the other would be either impossible or awkward. You could tell a doctor. I want a human response, not a medical one. Okay.

She had a performance to give with Beatrice that Saturday afternoon and didn't reach Rugoff's till seven in the evening. She plopped into a chair, her clown costume still on, and gratefully drank a giant whiskey sour which he prepared for her. Lamont was out.

"Hey, guess what?" she said with false heartiness, not knowing how to begin. "I have great news! I'm pregnant!"

She waited while he looked at her with disbelief. "That's not possible," he said very flatly.

"What do you mean? It sure as hell *is*, friend. Want to see the lab report?"

"But, Rach, you're on the pill!"

"I am? Who said that?"

"Aren't you?"

"No!"

"Well, what do you—what are those little pills you take every morning?"

"Those are vitamin C."

"Vitamin C! But you take them *every* morning!"

"I know. . . . That's how come I'm so healthy. You know? Haven't you noticed? I'm really in fantastically good health. You know I haven't gotten a cold all winter?"

"Terrific. . . . But listen, what *have* you been using then?"

"Nothing."

"Nothing? What do you mean, nothing?"

"I mean nothing. I mean, like I never have. . . . I have never used anything. Or I have always used nothing. Is that a double negative?"

"Well, what are you—dumb? You *can't* be dumb, honey. You're not."

"I'm not dumb. . . . I'm smart as a whip."

"So you have something against birth control or something?"

"No, not a whit of it. I love birth control. . . . It's just—well, the thing is, I won't bore you with my whole life story, but I tried for years to get pregnant, years, and finally this little doctor in Philadelphia told me I had a one in a million chance to get pregnant. So after that I figured—what the hell."

"Why should you have a one in a million chance?"

Rachel squirmed. "Can I have another drink? . . . Well, it's— I have a tipped uterus. You know, like evidently, I guess I don't really understand it, but it's like one of those pinball machines that's out of order and says tilt? All the sperm swim all the way up there, and then they just drift downstream again. They never make it."

"Evidently one did."

"Evidently. . . . But you wanted to know why I never—"

Rugoff looked disgusted. "God, what do these doctors know? They're crazy! I hate doctors!"

"Marty, listen—"

"If I told you the crud I've gotten from doctors. Take high blood pressure."

"Marty?"

"What?" He looked angry at being interrupted.

"No, it's just I want to say right from the start, I can see, like, you look a little anxious. So I want to say I'm not telling you so you should feel pressured to marry me or fork over three hundred dollars for an abortion or anything like that. You're absolutely in the clear morally, financially, everything. . . . I just felt like telling someone."

"Don't be silly, Rach," he said. "Of *course* I'm responsible."

"You're *not!*"

"So who is? Who else have you been sleeping with?"

"It's not a matter of that," she said. "So maybe the doctor in Philadelphia is responsible. . . . The point is, I don't want that aspect of it—"

"Listen, I have a very simple solution to the whole thing," he said. "I don't know why I didn't think of it before."

"Ya?"

"Well, you don't want to go through all this red tape stuff in New York. . . . Well, listen, frankly I swore never to tell anyone about this, but Vi's best friend, Carol Trampler, she once— oh, it was some business, I forget now what. I think it was, ya, she had this coil in only it came out or it didn't work. Something. Anyway, she got pregnant. She was married, but she had three kids, you know how it is. Anyway, we got the name of this guy in Puerto Rico—We could go there! You and I! We'll go together. Listen, why didn't I think of it right away?" He was excited. "It'll be a vacation. We'll go to Puerto Rico, we'll lie around on the sand for a week, two weeks. You'll go one afternoon. . . . This is a regular guy, it's not some seedy little back-room-type thing. This man has an office, he—"

"I want to have the baby."

She spoke so quietly that he just glared at her, as though he hadn't heard right. Finally he said, "Oh, come on, Rach, you're not that kind of girl."

"What kind of girl aren't I?"

"You know—the type that screws up their life for no reason."

"Well, that might be open to question, but in any case, it's irrelevant. I just want the baby."

"You just want the baby? What do you *want* with a baby?"

"I want what anyone wants with a baby. . . . I thought you liked babies."

"I *love* babies! No, I do, but, like—you're not married."

"But that doesn't matter."

"Of course it matters! Don't be naïve."

"I'm not being. Seriously, I can't think of one person I know who would give a damn if I had an illegitimate child. Not one. No one would care."

"Your parents would care."

"Leave my parents out of it."

"No, why should I? I like your parents. They sound like very nice people. . . . They'll die, Rach. You'll be killing them."

"Marty, you never met them. . . . They'll love it. Really. They'll be shocked a little at first, but look at it this way, it's their first grandbaby—think how happy they'll be!"

"They'll be miserable, they'll want to kill themselves."

"They won't. . . . Anyway, even if they would, *I* want the baby. I'm an adult, right?"

"But why do you? You keep saying I want the baby, I want the baby. So wait till you're married!"

"But the doctor said I have one chance in a million. So this is my one chance. I may never have another chance again."

"Maybe this just proves the doctor was wrong. . . . Maybe your uterus tipped back again."

"Maybe. . . . And maybe he was right and this is the one and only chance I'll ever have in my whole life. *Ever.*"

Rugoff shook his head. "I don't know. . . . I want another drink myself." He came back a few minutes later. "You know, I can't help feeling it's just the abortion thing. *All* women feel that. The guilt, the—"

"It's *not* that! Damn it, I believe in abortion."

"You may believe in it in the abstract, but when it hits home—"

"No, listen, Marty, you're so wrong about this. I would have an abortion every day in the week." Seeing he was looking at her with total suspicion, she laughed nervously. "I would! Now you're thinking—there she goes again. But I wouldn't feel the least guilt. Look, I believe women should have the right to strangle their newborn babies with their bare hands if they feel like it."

"Well, that's another story."

"Granted . . . I'm just saying I am not held back for one tiny instant by any feeling about abortion. . . . I just want this fucking baby. God, what's wrong? Do I seem so unmaternal? You think I'd be such a lousy mother? Women have babies every day! Old women, young women. Look at all these movie stars with illegitimate babies."

Rugoff raised his hand. "Precisely! They're movie stars. They can do anything, they're exempt. . . . How're you going to support this child, anyway?"

"Oh, I'll find a way. . . . That's no problem."

He shook his head again. "Rachel, you know you are the most incredible mixture of common sense and sheer, unadulterated—"

"Marty, listen, I just want to make one more stab at getting across what I feel. . . . Say you're me, okay?"

"Okay."

"So, like, say you were told you had one chance in a million—"

"Jesus, you keep quoting that crackpot doctor! What does he know? One in a million. These guys say anything. Rach, listen, Vi's brother is a gynecologist—a bigger phony you've never met. Those guys would say *anything*. So don't give me one in a million."

"So how do you explain that I never got pregnant before?"

"I told you. . . . Your uterus was tipped. Now it's not."

"So maybe it'll tip back again. . . . Anyway, why should I listen to you? No, I mean it's not personal, but look at the chance I'm taking. Maybe you're right. If so, great. Maybe you're not."

"Life is full of chances."

She closed her eyes. "Bull."

"Honey, I want you to be happy!" He came over and put his

hands over hers. "No, I do. . . . I mean, look at my life. I know I've screwed it up. Why should you screw up yours?"

"I have already."

"No, you haven't. . . . You're young. Here you'll have this baby saddled around your neck."

Rachel said nothing. "I'm going to cry," she announced.

"Cry," he said. "Do. No, you should have right from the start. Have a good cry."

Rachel found tears slithering down her cheeks. "I *do* want to be happy," she said. "Only I want the baby *too*."

He patted her shoulder. "Sweetheart."

"People get what they want in life. . . . Why not me? Why should I be exempt?"

"You *will* get what you want, honey."

"I can manage a baby. . . . Seriously—" She sniffed. "It's only temporary anyway. I'll marry again."

"Sure you will."

"Who would want to marry somebody who'd care if I had a child? Who *needs* that kind of person?"

He didn't speak, just kept patting her shoulder. "God, I feel so rotten."

"Marty, don't! Why? Don't be dumb."

"I'm responsible."

"Who says? Who says it's yours?"

He drew back. "Well, whose *is* it?"

She shrugged. "I don't know."

"You *have* to know."

"*Why* do I have to know?"

"Well, who have you been sleeping with?"

She hesitated. Besides the one time with Edward, since she had come to New York, she had slept with two people other than Rugoff, one a friend of her brother's who had been passing through the city, another, one of the clowns in training at her school. Neither had been experiences of exceptional quality sensually or in any other way. Normally she would have forgotten them, but now she said, "Just a few people here and there. . . .

Not recently, but the thing is I don't know when I conceived. My cycles are so weird anyway. Like, sometimes I never get a period, sometimes I get one every twenty-seven days. . . . But I mean, the point is, you needn't feel responsible on that ground."

"I didn't know you were sleeping around with all sorts of people, Rach." He looked hurt.

"I'm not! . . . No, these were, like, way back, a month or so ago. It's just—I really don't know what month I'm *in*. It could be the third month; it could be the first month."

He was still frowning and toying with his drink. "How many of these men *were* there?"

"Marty! Gee whillickers! Like, I just said it to make you happy. You don't have to feel responsible. You should feel *good* . . . There weren't all that many. You know. I was in New York, I was lonely. I mean, I'm not what would pejoratively be known as an easy lay, if that's what you're worried about. . . . Frankly, I think it's more my worry than yours, if I am. . . . Or was."

"It makes me feel crummy," he said.

Rachel sighed. "Oh, no! . . . Well, listen, if you want to feel crummy, feel crummy. . . . I mean, that's a right no one should deny anyone." But seeing him so forlorn, she kissed him. "No, don't! Come on, be happy! *I'm* happy."

"Are you? Really?"

"Ya, I am. It's really true. I've felt all glowing. I really feel wonderful."

"That *is* good, Rach," he said wistfully.

"I wish you could get pregnant. You'd see," she said. "It's just this great feeling. I feel useful. I feel—"

"What doctor will you go to?" he wanted to know.

"Oh, I'll find somebody," she said airily.

"Let me find somebody for you," he said. "I don't want you going to some rattled-up old lecher."

Rachel grinned. "Hey, that sounds like fun. I've never met a rattled-up old lecher."

"I mean it, Rach. . . . You've got to start taking care of yourself. You really do."

She became serious, too. "I'm going to. Really. I'm going to drink tons of milk and eat leafy stuff and all that. Get lots of rest. . . . I'll have the biggest, fattest baby you ever saw."

The doctor Rugoff recommended was a Herman Gottwillig with a big office on Park Avenue flooded with chic, well-manicured ladies with very neat pregnant bellies. He would probably be expensive, but, Rachel figured, why not? Be self-indulgent. Marty was right. This was no time for griminess. She'd have a private room, the works. Marty would pay, he wanted to, he could afford it easily. Hell, with an illegitimate child, bastard or bastardess, you needed better care, more kindly treatment. There was no one to shove pillows under you at night, no one to discuss names with. You needed the best. *I admire your philosophy, dear. It's just it doesn't sound very different from your usual. . . .*

Herman was a thin, sardonic fellow, graying at the temples. He seemed not at all impressed or even interested that Rachel wasn't married. Never asked who the husband might be. Just told her to strip, flung her on the scale, took her blood pressure, poked around in her innards for a while, and pronounced her in fine shape. Didn't he care? Sitting opposite him as he jotted little notes in his pad, Rachel felt slightly hurt. *Dear, this is typical. Why should he care? Why should you want him to? Should he storm up and down and denounce the younger generation? Look, he'll be getting his cut, what's it to him?* She recalled Ibert's saying—you always want people to be horrified at what you do or shocked. True? Yes, true, by God. She'd just been born in the wrong century. She wanted to be a martyr, an outcast, a pariah, and it was getting harder every day. Even if you were a leper these days, there'd probably be some nice resort in Palm Springs where you could lounge around and play golf, where they'd cure you with some new drug. You just couldn't win.

"I would say—we can never be perfectly accurate in these

matters as you know," he said, looking up, "that the birthdate will be August third."

Such precision! She admired that.

He handed her a sheet of paper. "Here you'll find certain guidelines that may be of use."

She folded it and put it in her purse. She remained staring at him, thinking there must be something else, something to make this meeting more dramatic or eventful, but he just said, "I'll see you in a month then. You can make an appointment with my nurse on the way out."

Treating herself to a chocolate malted at Schrafft's afterward, she perused his list. He'd got to be joking! Rub your breasts with cocoa butter every night? What *was* cocoa butter anyway? And why? It sounded so greasy. And unesthetic. Wouldn't the sheets get all smeared up? Who was supposed to rub them—you or someone else? Intercourse is permitted up to. . . . Well, that gave her quite a lot of time. Exercise, eight hours of sleep, raw vegetables. It sounded like girl scout camp. Rachel sighed, put the list back in her pocket, and drained the rest of her malted. August. It was now February. She felt her belly, but it seemed as flat as ever. When would she begin to show? At that point she would write her parents. They had threatened to come visit in the fall anyway. Should she tell Beatrice? She'd said she wanted reactions, but after the session with Rugoff, she felt she could well wait another few months for any more of the same. At the same time, she hated not telling. Face the fire. What'll she do? And who cares? You've made your stand. Anyway, who knows —Beatrice might be delighted, you couldn't tell. She waited for one evening when they were having a reasonably congenial meal down in the Village after a performance.

"Bea, want to hear something funny?"

"Sure, I like jokes," Beatrice said dryly.

"I'm going to be a Mom."

"A *who*?"

"In six months. . . . Swallow your spaghetti, dear. Yup. Saw the doctor, everything."

"You're not marrying that little—"

"Noo. . . . Not marrying anybody."

"So you—what are you—you're just in the third month! You don't have to have it."

"I know I don't *have* to have it. . . . I *want* to have it." Was this going to be the scene with Rugoff revisited?

Beatrice mopped up her marinara sauce. "If you give me some bull about the value of human life, even in the—"

"I will *not* give you any bull about the value of human life."

"So listen, sweetie, I know a million people you can go to. Not seedy types. Real doctors. Virginia knows this little man who—"

Rachel sighed. "Bea, I don't want a little man. I don't want a big man. I don't want any sort of man of any shape, size or color. I want to have the baby. . . . Everybody knows a little man," she grumbled.

"What are you going to do with a baby?" Beatrice wanted to know.

"I'll do with it whatever people do with babies."

"Are you having natural childbirth?"

"Dunno. Hadn't thought about it."

Suddenly Beatrice became vehement. "You *have* to!"

"If I have to, I will. . . . *Why* do I have to?"

"It's the only way. . . . Those drugs are terrible. They're terrible for the baby. They cause brain damage. Do you know that? Today I even was reading in the *Post* this study that said that any drugs, even these local anesthetics, are very, very harmful."

"So why do they give them?" Rachel wanted to know.

"Because they hate women! That's why!" Beatrice glared at the waiter, who was coming to refill their water glasses. "What do they care? Anything to shut them up. I've heard doctors say that."

"I thought drugs were to make it easier."

"Oh, crap! What's natural is always easier."

"Well, maybe you've got something there." Rachel always felt talking to Beatrice was like talking to a confirmed Marxist. Her views, on women, naturalness, everything, always seemed to dovetail into a program of such incredible smoothness. I want to be able to explain the world, too.

"Don't get all fat and slovenly," Beatrice went on. "That's disgusting. Just gain around fifteen pounds. Eat cottage cheese a lot. High protein."

"Gee, Bea, I got this list from my doctor—"

"Doctors know *nothing*," Beatrice said firmly. "Forget what he said. No, I'm telling you, Rachel, there's nothing more repellent than these dumb, fat cow women dragging themselves around. They're decaying! They're in a state of decay."

"I don't want to decay," Rachel said hastily.

"Don't. . . . But just remember you're the type that can if you don't watch out."

"What type is that?" Rachel said warily, not sure she really wanted to know.

"Well, *you* know what you're like," Beatrice said. "Sleeping with all these men, shuffling along—"

Rachel laughed nervously. "Beatrice! What's 'all these men'? I'm sure that statistically if you compare me—"

"I think this is actually an excellent idea," Beatrice said reflectively, ignoring her, "the more I think about it. It'll be a maturing experience for you. You'll have to do it yourself. You'll rise to the occasion."

Rachel grimaced. "I hope I will."

"You will. No, it's true, this may be a turning point for you, Rachel."

Oh, dear! Help! Can't I turn back? Rachel felt as though she'd just had a talk with her high school adviser on what her "future" would be. Couldn't you just *do* something these days? Why did everyone have to draw conclusions, make predictions, look at things from all angles? But in any case she couldn't help being pleased by this stamp of approval from Beatrice. Beatrice was, after all, a kind of parent substitute. And she said good, and that meant it *was* good. Of course it was good. Not that she'd ever thought otherwise, but it was fine to hear it reiterated.

She felt as though she were in bloom. She expanded, grew fat, puffed out her belly, and considered herself in very fine shape. It was easy to continue the performances with Bea—if anything, her pregnant state, up to a point, made her a more ideal clown. She had been uncertain if the tumbling might be harmful, but Beatrice scoffed at this, citing, as Rachel should have suspected she would, ballet dancer friends who had been flung from dancer to dancer in their seventh month, people who had played tennis up till the point of delivery, skied, mountain climbed, performed feats compared to which a little tumbling was a mere nothing. At night she lay in bed and felt the baby moving around restlessly, like someone on an uncomfortable mattress, unable to find a good position. At times it scared her—it was so inexorable. The baby was like a time bomb—it had to go off. It had to come out. And would she be good at giving birth? She had always felt herself the type who did not excel at natural functions. She would, she thought, die badly. Edward would die well. She had given some thought to that. She liked Beatrice's visions of natural childbirth but wondered if the peasant in her was really all that strong. Or the desire even to regard this as the peak of her life. Wasn't that a sort of male chauvinism? Of course, Beatrice would say no, she would say it was he, she, the woman, giving birth. *How* she happened to be there, why, who was responsible, were irrelevant. Well, mebbee.

She went to buy maternity clothes but found herself intimidated by rows of little salesladies who brought out "outfits" of the sort worn by the women in Herman's waiting room. They were the kind of clothes she would never wear normally. Why start now? For a couple of dollars she bought herself a bunch of dashikis and wore these with a black turtleneck and black slacks.

When she was in her seventh month—it was May by then, one of those too hot New York days, dusty, wretched—the doctor told her she was going to have twins.

"But they don't run in my family," she protested, as though he had just told her she had syphilis.

"That doesn't matter," he replied calmly. "Maybe they run in your . . . They don't have to, in any case. Sometimes they just happen."

He seemed so calm about the whole thing. What was it to him! "Are you sure?" she said. "I mean, I wonder if—"

"I heard two heartbeats," he said. "Would you like to hear them?"

"No, well, I believe you . . . but don't you think, it couldn't just be that it's one heart beating very fast? Maybe it has a heart murmur or—"

Herman smiled. "Don't you like twins, Miss Ovcharov?"

She smiled uncertainly. "Sure, I *guess* I do. I mean—"

"Most women are a little overwhelmed at first. And of course, in your . . . position, but I think you'll find it will all fall into line pretty quickly. . . . You might want to consider a baby nurse for the first few months."

I might want to consider suicide for the first few months, Rachel thought as she left his office. This couldn't be. It just couldn't. Since when did unmarried women have twins? They never did. She had never heard of it, never considered it possible. Look, nature doesn't care if you're married or not. But, but. . . . Twins were, well, a family. I mean, one baby, okay—you could carry it around, you could have it sleep in a bureau drawer, but twins! Twins evoked pictures in baby magazines of women feeding a row of hungry mouths and endorsing various brands of baby products. It meant diaper services and formulas and. . . . Well, what's the big deal? So does one. But somehow, she could not explain it, the difference between one and two was more than just one. Two was a family. Two was a whole big deal. Suddenly, after seven months of complete nonchalance, she got cold feet. What was she doing here? She knew nothing about babies! She'd never seen a baby, much less two babies. Was she out of her mind? Was this nature's way of playing some monstrous practical joke? She had never trusted nature. Two of them! What were they doing in there? No wonder there'd been so much movement when she lay down. They were probably fighting already, arguing about the most comfortable side of the uterus.

For the next few weeks she was plunged in gloom. Now look, I didn't ask for this. So what? Why? Wasn't it good enough that I said I could handle one? Why do people keep testing me? Is this like a pie-eating contest? Okay, you've eaten twenty, now let's—Only Rugoff, whom she finally, reluctantly, told, was delighted.

"That's *wonderful!*" he said. Lamont was away at summer camp. They now had the house to themselves on weekends. "Twins are just great!"

"*You* have them," Rachel grumbled.

"You're going to love them," he said. All day he went around beaming, as though she'd just told him he'd inherited a million dollars. That night he even proposed to her. "I've given this some thought," he said. "It isn't just out of the blue. It's not pity, believe me. You may think I'm some pushover in certain respects, but underneath I'm not."

"Hard as nails?" Rachel said.

"No, I am. . . . Really. I can look out for myself. . . . No, the thing is, I've thought of it. Look how well we get along! Look at all those miserable married couples!"

Rachel rolled over on her side to be more comfortable. The twins were playing leapfrog again. "Ya, only I don't quite see the connective there."

"We'll be happy!" he said. "Happier than *them*, anyway."

"Ya, but is happier than them, some abstract them, what one wants out of life?"

"I'm talking about chances," he said. "I'm talking about solid facts. . . . We get along extremely well."

"But we're not married. . . . Anyway, I'm not even divorced yet. I'm just separated."

"Eventually you'll be divorced. . . . So we were married? Would things be that different?"

"Yes!" Rachel said.

He looked taken aback by the vehemence of her reply. "Why?"

"Because they would. . . . Because I'd be demanding and mean and you'd be—some other thing."

"That always has to happen?"

"Yes."

"What are you going by?" he said. "Just bitter past experience, right?"

"Just common Jewish horse sense."

"Are there Jewish horses?" he said wryly. A moment later he said, "Look, I'm just trying to be practical, Rach. What are you going to *do* with twins? How can you handle them?"

"That's my problem."

"Ya, but I want to help."

"That's how you got into all these messes before," she reminded him, "wanting to help. . . . Let someone else sink for a change. You stay dry on the shore."

"I don't *want* to stay dry on the shore." He reached for the can of beer he'd set on the floor beside the bed. "I'm not being altruistic, you've got me all wrong. . . . I love twins. I'd have a ball. You wouldn't have to get up at night. I like all that. Even middle-of-the-night feedings and baths, the whole bit. . . . Think of the advantages for you."

"I'd save on a baby nurse," she said reflectively.

"Right . . . I've got experience. It's not like some Irish girl off the boat."

Rachel lay back and sighed. "Why can't I ever get traditional marriage proposals?" she said. "Why can't someone get down on their hands and knees—"

"Hands and knees! Knees aren't enough?"

"I meant knees . . . whatever they do."

"You want to know how I proposed to Vi?" He drained the rest of the beer.

"No," she said grumpily. "That's what I mean . . . I don't

want to spend the next twenty years of my life talking about **Vi.** I'm sick of her."

He scratched his head. "I'm sick of her too. . . . You're right, I should shut up about it."

"No, you shouldn't. . . . It's therapeutic for you. I just don't want to hear any more about the lady, that's all." After a few minutes of silence, she said, "Jesus, they're kicking like fiends."

"That's a good sign," Rugoff said, reaching over to feel her belly.

"Is it?"

"Definitely. . . . You don't want a sluggish baby."

"I don't?"

"These are going to be two little balls of fire," he said, smiling with some satisfaction.

Rachel said, "Listen, I'll think about your . . . thing, okay?"

"The marriage thing?"

"Ya, I mean, like, I don't have to decide now, do I?"

"No, not at all."

"Let's just play it by ear," she said.

But he was still paying attention only to the movements in her big belly. "Will you feel those buggers!" he said.

"I can feel them," Rachel said. "Don't worry."

She felt the time had come to call her parents and tell them. She'd expected, somehow, that she would meet some irrelevant friend of her mother's on a bus who would dash for a phone three seconds after seeing her. But the closest call had been a brief encounter with a friend of her father's, who appeared not to have noticed—that had been back in her fourth month and she was wearing a heavy winter coat, so she wasn't too worried. How could she tell them? Since she had put it off so long, it would be so easy to just put it off a little longer, till the baby was born—there she went! Babies! Plural, dear. Babies, then. But she wanted, somehow, to tell them. It was like making her last will and testament. If she went into labor without their knowing, she would feel guilty. And maybe it was a regressive thing. They would care anyhow, in that primeval way parents had to care, and at the moment that seemed like a good thing. She knew she had to start it off as a joke. Somehow no other way would do.

"Hey, folks," she said, after making small talk for a few minutes, "what would you say if someone said you were about to have *two* grandchildren in *two* months?"

"I'd say that person had a rather vivid imagination," her father said dryly.

"Well, guess again."

"Rachel, you're pregnant, aren't you?" her mother said.

"I am."

"I knew this had to happen," her mother said darkly.

"When is the baby due?" her father asked. As usual, conversations with the two of them were a counterpoint between reason (her father) and emotion (her mother).

"August third," she said. "Only, it's, like, babies, not baby. . . . It's going to be twins."

"*How* can it be twins?" her mother said indignantly. "No one in our family ever had twins."

"Well, he heard them."

"Who?"

"The doctor. . . . He heard two heartbeats."

"I hope you're going to a good man," her father said. "Who recommended him?"

"Oh, he's excellent, Dad. Really."

"What hospital is he connected with?"

"Mount Sinai."

"Yes, well, that should be—"

"But you know, like, I'm not married," she raced on, wanting to get all the refuse out of the way first. "Nor going to be."

"What about Edward?" her mother wanted to know.

"What *about* him?"

"Well, what does he think?"

"He doesn't know."

"Doesn't know! Why not?"

"Because it has nothing to do with him, that's why. We're divorced. He may be remarried by now. . . . What's it to him?"

"Remarried?"

"Ya, he was planning to when I last saw him. . . . It has nothing to do with him, Mom."

"Well, it has to do with *somebody*, doesn't it?"

"It has to do with *me!* I'm having it! . . . Them."

"I knew we should have gone East to see you," her mother said. "Wasn't I saying that the other night, Abe? I said I was sure we should have—"

"Mom, really, that wouldn't have changed the course of events very much."

"We always make the mistake of assuming you can handle yourself," her mother went on. "You know, I think this reaction to Dr. Spock has something to it. We give children all this responsibility, and what do they do with it?"

"Mom, don't blame Dr. Spock. Leave him out of it."

"I'm *not* blaming Dr. Spock. I'm saying—"

"I thought you'd be happy," she said, trying to smile, though they couldn't see her. "Like, here you are—two great big grandchildren! Just like you always said you wanted."

Her mother would only say, "How will you handle them, Rachel? You don't know anything about babies."

"So lots of people don't know anything about babies. . . . I'll learn."

"But do you have . . . equipment . . . I mean, have you bought a crib—cribs and—"

"I'll take care of all that."

"You see? Abe, are you still there?"

"I'm still here," came her father's voice.

"She hasn't even bought cribs yet," her mother said. "Oh my God, what are you living in—some hovel, oh, Abe, will you say something for God's sake! She's going to take these babies home to some place with roaches and—"

"Estelle, calm down," her father said.

"It's going to work out all right, Mom," Rachel said hastily. She had called for consolation?

"I'm going to have a nervous breakdown," her mother said. "Rachel, *why* do you do these things? *Why?*"

"Estelle—"

"Mom—"

There was a silence.

Her father's voice said, "Estelle?"

"I think she hung up," Rachel said.

Her father sighed. "Oh, dear," he said.

"It's going to be okay, Dad," Rachel said.

"No, I'm thinking about your mother," he said. "She's going to be in a state. . . . Do you want us to come and visit you?"

"If you feel like it . . . I mean, after they're born."

He cleared his throat. "I think we'll all adjust to this in time. . . . It's just a matter of. . . . You know your mother."

"I know my mother," Rachel said.

"The main thing is for you not to get excited. . . . You're taking good care of yourself? Lots of milk and so on?"

"Excellent! Really, I'm in fantastic shape, Dad."

"No, well, that's good. . . . Take care of yourself, darling."

So what had she expected? Hadn't it all been par for the course? Wouldn't she be the same if her only daughter—Oh hell, so what! Why all this stuff about roaches? Jesus! How about me!

Still, she was glad to have done it. Now it was over. Everyone who had to know knew. She could wait. There would be no more surprises anyway.

Chapter Seven

TWINS were said to be early, so for the last month Rachel stayed around Columbia. She had stopped doing performances with Beatrice anyway. She told Rugoff she would have to stop coming out even for weekends. He insisted that by driving fast he could get her to the hospital in time, but she didn't want to chance it. Someone she knew had given birth in a cab. Probably it would be fine, nothing to it, but she didn't want to give it a try. At home she practiced the breathing she had learned in her natural childbirth course. The course consisted only of women and was taught by a dykey-seeming unmarried nurse. As far as Rachel knew, everyone assumed she was married. But knowing she wasn't made her feel slightly alienated from the other jolly plump girls who practiced their breathing self-consciously but eagerly. After class she always escaped as quickly as she could, not wanting anyone to ask her for coffee or even to chat over trivia. It surprised her really, this streak of cowardice in herself. But who were these people? Why should they know about her private life. She felt a disbelief in the whole natural childbirth idea anyway. Systems never worked. That was one thing you could count on.

In July the campus was relatively quiet. Rachel took to sitting in the park under a tree, reading, treating herself to steaks as often as she felt like it and sleeping twelve or fourteen hours a night.

One day she was standing in front of Taylor's House of Paperback Books looking in the window at a giant poster of Mao.

She was wearing her usual pregnancy costume—the black turtleneck and slacks, the red and gold dashiki, and the Afro wig which she sometimes put on just for fun. While staring at the poster, she became aware that someone was staring at her. After a few moments of irresolution, she glanced up. It was Edward.

He was wearing a business suit, a new flashy red and green tie, and gold-rimmed glasses (his old ones had been tortoiseshell). Otherwise he looked exactly the same. "Hi," she said.

"Hi."

They stood staring at each other. Rachel's heart began thumping too fast. Don't let me give birth right here and now, it wouldn't be dignified, okay? Just that one last favor, and then you can let me die in childbirth or anything you like.

"How are you?" he said.

"I'm very well. . . . Fine."

Evidently he could not bring himself to mention her pregnant state, though his eyes kept riveting on her belly. "Would you . . . like to have a drink?"

"A—sure. Why not?" Walking beside him, she said, "Why are you here?"

"There's a conference. . . . I've just come for the last three days, really."

"Are you giving a paper?"

"No, just attending."

They went into a coffee shop where she ordered iced coffee with whipped cream on top. He was still staring at her as though she were Frankenstein risen from the grave. "You look different," she said, almost to help him out. "You have new glasses."

He touched them self-consciously. "Yes, do you like them?"

"I don't know." She squinted at him. "You look a little sinister, actually. . . . Sort of like someone in a Hitchcock movie you expect to see sitting across from you in a darkened train."

"That doesn't sound so good."

"It's probably a matter of getting used to them." His mistress must have fancy taste. She spooned up the whipped cream.

Edward cleared his throat. "I didn't know about . . . I hadn't heard that—"

She flushed. "Ya, well, I. . . ." She shrugged.

"Who's the lucky man?" he said.

She looked at him, for a moment not understanding. Was the heat slowing down her reflexes? Then, after a second, she said, "Oh . . . I don't know."

"That sounds typical," he said dryly.

Refusing to rise to the bait, she just said, "Well, you know . . . my cycles are so screwed up that. . . ." She glared at him. Edward, if you make one slighting remark, one, I will throw this drink in your goddamn face. Just because your life has been programmed from birth to death with nary a false move. You'll get yours someday, kid. Her whole body was so tensed up she had to forcibly make herself sit back.

"You're not planning to marry the father?" he said.

"I don't know who the father *is*," she said flatly.

"Don't you *care* who he is?"

"No, not really." She stared at him belligerently. "It's my baby. That's how I think of it. I'm going to have it. I've carried it around for nine months. I'm going to take care of it for the next twenty years. What does it matter who he is?"

"Most women would care."

"Oh, shit, Edward! What the hell do you know about most women?"

He stiffened.

"I mean, I'm not going around the city flinging paternity suits right and left," she went on. "That's not my style, somehow. . . . I could get married if I wanted. I don't feel like it."

"Rachel, I really didn't mean to—"

"Well, drop it then."

Damn it, why couldn't she be civilized and nice? Why couldn't they sit together and chat like an ex-husband and ex-wife in a Noel Coward play, making nostalgic, enigmatic remarks? Why was it that in Edward's presence her physical self which usually like a good child sat in its room and played quietly suddenly became a monster, threatening to throw plates against the wall?

"How is life in Philadelphia?" she said after a long pause, trying to regain her composure.

"Fine. . . . Ali's getting married so there's a lot of. . . ." He looked away.

Ali was his younger sister, flirtatious, pretty, a model. She had been "engaged" to someone or other almost the entire three years Rachel and Edward had been married.

Rachel recalled her decorations on the furniture and wondered how much effort and cleaning polish had been expended in removing them . . . But he would not mention Magda. Okay. So why should he? She would blabber on about everything, and he would say nothing. That's why she always lost at poker. "Do you like the man she's marrying?" she said.

Edward was looking at her, but so lost in thought he evidently didn't hear. Where was he? After a moment he regained himself. "Oh . . . he's a nice guy."

"Rita must be jealous."

He allowed himself a slow smile. "She hasn't been too easy to be around lately." He said, "Your hair looks different. . . . Is that a new style?"

Rachel smiled. "No, it's a wig . . . Can't you tell?" Impulsively she yanked it off her head and thrust it at him. "It only cost thirty dollars."

He touched it diffidently, as though she had just presented him with a muddy puppy. "Yes, it's very . . . I think I prefer your real hair."

"Ya, well, I just wear it for fun . . . now and then."

It struck her that this must be the most excruciating cup of coffee, iced or regular, she had ever consumed. Should she start practicing her natural childbirth breathing just for distraction?

Edward said, "How have you been feeling . . . I mean, during your. . . ."

God, he couldn't bring himself to refer to it! Was this the Victorian age? Should she have been closeted in a murky room for nine months? "I've felt fine, really good," she said. "Well, you know, I always wanted a baby."

"I remember," he said.

Softly, for a moment forgetting her anger, she said, "I was so surprised that it could happen . . . I guess it bowled me over in a way . . . after what that doctor had said."

"I always thought someday it would happen," Edward said thoughtfully.

"Did you?" She considered this fact. "I guess I didn't. . . . I suppose I'm more of a pessimist about these things."

"Yes, you are."

Everything each of them said seemed to her to come out very slowly, like the news issuing from those machines in Times Square, almost letter by letter. She managed to divert the conversation to the conference he was attending. With relief he seized on this and expanded at some length on the papers he had heard, those he was planning to hear. She understood not a word of it and had the feeling he knew she didn't and that neither of them cared. Finally he rose, and they went to the exit.

The light outside seemed glaring after the cool dark coffeehouse. Rachel squinted, feeling as though she'd been hit on the head with a sledgehammer. They walked slowly to the corner. Then, as they were almost there and she was considering what an appropriate exit line might be, Edward said, not even looking at her, "Could *I* be the father?"

Rachel stared at him. For that second he turned to face her, and the expression on his face was one she could scarcely believe. She had never seen it before. She said, "Well . . . sure, I guess you could. I mean, there was that time we. . . ."

"Yes, I was thinking of that."

He said nothing more. At the corner they parted gravely, shook hands, and Edward walked off without even saying good-bye, still with that absorbed or stunned look. Rachel went up to her room and lay down at once on the bed. She felt weak, physically exhausted, as though she'd got no sleep all week. In front of her, like a giant poster for toothpaste, was Edward's face as he had said, "Could *I* be the father?"

You had to know Edward's face to interpret that expression, but somehow, if nothing else, she felt she knew Edward's face, and that expression said one thing: He cared. He *cared* who the father was. He wanted to *be* the father. My God! For some reason, odd as it was, until this precise moment, she had never given a moment's thought to who the father really was. She had not been joking when she had said she regarded it as her baby. Maybe it was egotism. But she had felt as though the baby were just there, like an immaculate conception; *her* baby. If she had ever thought of it at all, it was to assume that the father was probably Darell Woodbridge II, the friend of Dan's with whom she had slept with so little passion or interest that snowy February night. Why Darell Woodbridge II? Just because he was the least relevant person and it was her theory about life that the least relevant thing was usually the thing that happened. Not the most horrible, but the most insignificant. And what could be more fitting than that her child, her children, should have inherited genes from a man whose name she had trouble remembering, whom she had never especially liked, much less fancied herself in love with. You couldn't deny that it had a certain inevitable quality about it. She had even toyed with or mentally referred to the child as Darell III. Must everything be a joke? Well, why not? Maybe that was her protection, who knew? But lying there on the bed, she realized suddenly, angrily, that she wanted Edward to be the father of those twins. Damn it. Why hadn't she thought of this earlier? What good would *thinking* of it earlier have done? But she felt as though in some mystical way it would have done some good. You couldn't suddenly at the last minute put in a plea for who the father could or should be. It would seem too frivolous, too ill considered. Whereas God or nature or whoever planned these things might certainly have been touched if right from the start she had requested this father rather than that. Oh, bull! *He wanted to be the father*. This fact, this amazing, unique fact, was something she could not get out of her head for one second in the next twenty-four hours. Why? What was it to him? Sheer gross pride? He'd always wanted a child, so even now. . . . Oh, Edward, God damn you! If it hadn't been for this, she could have sidled through the child-birth, not caring what came out of her. Oh, sure, she had worried about deformities, conjured images of blind children, children with clubfeet, cleft palates, but apart from that she had not thought to worry. Whether it or they were boys or girls she really didn't care. And now to have to care! Who needed this? Was God, if he existed, a sadist? Why this final, gratuitous torment? Hadn't she been good? She was having the baby; she was on the side of birth, life, not death. So where was her reward? Why must there always *be* a reward? Not *always*. But why this final turn of the screw? She had never felt she believed in a malevolent universe, but maybe she was going to end up having no choice. . . . And why should he *care?* He could have plenty of babies! Hell, his sperm were fine, healthy as little pups. It was her. *He* had nothing to worry about. Was it all those years of trying, the fact that now, finally, the possibility of success was too tempting to be ignored, no matter what the circumstances? How could you figure Edward out? Cold when you expected him to be warm, warm when you expected him to be—so, he's a human being, so go sue him. Damn, damn it to hell!

The next evening he called her from Philadelphia. Just called to "find out how she was doing." Well, she was doing fine. How *should* she be doing? They chatted, their conversation having that peculiar mixture of distance and intimacy that had prevailed in the coffeehouse. On the one hand, the immense stiffness, like two blind people on a tightrope; on the other hand, the fact that couldn't be ignored that there was scarcely a nuance of feeling, a fact, trivial or of consequence, that they did not know about each other. Speaking to him, she knew which chair he was probably sitting in, knew in what position he had crossed his legs, and this knowledge, gratuitous, prosaic, was, at the same time, the only important reality.

For the next two weeks he called her every few days. And it was always the same. Nothing special. Just wondered how she was. Had her doctor said anything special? What, *what* did he have in mind? Edward, you're wasting a lot of phone money if Darell III comes popping out with two heads. Was that even primarily what he had in mind? If only she had X-ray eyes! She wanted to know in advance, to be spared all this crap, this suspense.

Then, precisely two weeks to the day that she had met him, she went into labor. It was the middle of the night, three something, and she had gotten up to pee. Getting back in bed, she heard a small pop as though a balloon had burst and realized that the sheet beneath her was wet. She started to get up again, still groggy, when her whole body, like a well-trained lion at the crack of some anonymous whip, doubled over and began to shake like a leaf. She lay back while the contraction swept over her. What was she supposed to do? Pant? Breathe? But what stage was she in? And why was it hurting so much? They had said pain was all in the mind, that knowing what was going to happen would banish fear and thus pain. Hell! This *hurt!* This was unfair. She staggered to the phone, called her doctor. His answering service said he would call her back. Where was he? Out at some party in Mamaroneck? Why wasn't the blasted man home in bed where he should be instead of gallivanting around town? Two minutes later he called her back.

Rachel was standing right beside the phone, leaning against the wall, eyes closed, trying to live through another contraction.

"How fast are they coming?" he wanted to know.

"About every two minutes."

"Well, get over to the hospital right away. . . . I'll see you there."

But she had been told that in first labors the doctors had you sit at home for hours, sometimes days. Get right over there? Sweet Jesus, how? In a daze she pulled a dress, she had no idea which one, off a hanger and over her head and grabbed the suitcase she had packed a few weeks earlier. In the elevator—luckily she was alone—she had another contraction. I'm not going to live through this, Rachel thought with surprise. I'm going to die. Will you get out of the elevator? You're not going to die. Outside, it was cool and dark, the unearthly quiet of predawn. She got a cab right away. Either the driver didn't notice she was pregnant or didn't care. She sank back in the seat, almost unconscious. At the hospital the same black and white cat that had sat there during her natural childbirth classes was quietly licking its paws. She pushed blindly through the revolving door.

After that everything sped up even faster, like a movie tape unwinding from its spool. She found herself in a room with a huge clock on the wall with hands that seemed to jerk forward spasmodically, devouring half hours, then nibbling delicately on minutes. Herman appeared, squeezed her belly, said something, and disappeared. They gave her a shot of Demerol. The Demerol was wonderful. The pains came back, got worse, but at a distance, like a mad dog held on a leash. Only at the end, just before they wheeled her into the delivery room, did she have the feeling, the conviction, she was going to burst. The babies seemed to be straining out of her like cannonballs, and she imagined herself splattering in a million gory pieces on the floor and wall, like something out of a Mickey Spillane mystery.

"Wake up, Rachel!" Herman yelled. "Your baby's being born! This is once in a lifetime!"

Rachel tried to open her eyes, but they were dragged down by lead. "I can't, I'm too sleepy," she moaned and passed out.

When she awoke, she was all by herself in a very quiet room. What had happened? She touched her belly. It was flat. But where was everybody? Where were the nurses? She felt frightened. A second later the same nurse, a young Irish Catholic girl, who had given her the Demerol, walked briskly into the room and began kneading her belly back and forth, as though it were an old grapefruit. Blood ran out between her legs.

"What happened?" she said.

"Oh, it was fine. . . . Two little girls."

"But where are they?"

"They're upstairs. . . . You'll see them at feeding time."

At feeding time! What *was* this? She'd gone through this whole thing just to have the babies snatched away? It seemed ominous. Was this some indirect way of telling her there was something wrong?

What color were they? You couldn't very well ask that, could you? It would seem rude. What sex, okay. I want to know what color they were, damn it! You'll know, you'll know.

They came and wheeled her onto the elevator. It was morning. Eight o'clock. It was over. She had lived. She had done it. The nurse who was wheeling her exchanged a few words with one of the orderlies on the floor. Both of them bored. Just another night. Nothing special. But for some reason their boredom, the very ordinariness of it to them, intensified her own feeling of slaphappy excitement. Lying there, being wheeled down the wall like a slab of beef for that day's lunch, she thought: I'll never be happier than this.

She ate the biggest breakfast she had ever eaten in her life—hot oatmeal with cream and sugar, eggs, danish, coffee. She felt she could have had ten more babies, a hundred more. Was this the aftereffect of the Demerol? She had been expecting to feel some letdown, and instead this manic exuberance took her aback.

At ten they brought the babies in. One of them was sleeping in the bassinet. "We fed her so you'd just have the one to do," the nurse explained, setting a bottle of sugar water on the bedside table.

Rachel sat up and took the bundle that was shoved at her. The babies were black.

She took her time about calling Edward. First she called her parents, then Rugoff, then Beatrice. She chatted with everyone, gave a blow-by-blow description of the labor, and to no one did she mention anything of the babies' color. Why should she? What was it to them? But calling Edward, she allowed herself the luxury of a small, satisfied smile. Power! For this one moment of her life she had power of the kind she had always wanted, and she was determined to relish it to the hilt.

He answered the phone after one ring. "Hello?"

"It's me! So I had two girls!" She could not, though she had wanted to keep cool, keep the excitement out of her voice.

"That's wonderful," he said without a trace of hesitation. "How do you feel?"

"Great! Really, Edward, you'd be surprised. I think I could have a million babies. There was nothing to it."

"It didn't hurt?"

"Oh, a little. . . . Not much."

"When did it happen?"

"Just last night. . . . I woke up and suddenly, there I was!"

"How did you get to the hospital?"

"I found a cab."

"Well." There was a moment's silence. Rachel sat back, smiling, contented as a cat with a bowl of cream. "What do they look like?" Edward said.

She smiled even more. "Oh, I don't know. You know, all babies look alike to me. Sort of wrinkly."

"Do they look like anyone special?"

She pretended to consider. "Oh, I guess like me a little. . . . They have black hair."

"Oh, they have hair already?"

"Yes, a bit. . . . Not too much."

There was a very long pause. Finally Edward brought himself to say, "What color are they?"

Rachel paused. Power, power! Oh, this was delicious! Let me die now and I will die happy. "Gee, Edward," she said. "I'd send you a swatch, but they're a little young for skin grafting."

As always, he let her joke pass by. "When are your visiting hours?"

"Three to six."

"I'll see you then," he said and hung up.

After lunch the babies were brought in again briefly and then wheeled away. Rachel went down the hall to take a shower. She found her progress curiously slow, because of the pain from the episiotomy stitches. Like an old lady, she eased herself along, occasionally holding onto the wall for support. But after the hot shower—she washed her hair too—she felt wonderful. She changed into the closest thing she had to a sexy nightgown, splashed herself with perfume, and even did a perfunctory job of making herself up, powdering her nose and putting on lipstick. Then she lay back in bed and waited.

Three o'clock came, then three thirty, finally four. Outside, she could hear the bustle of visitors, people talking, walking up and down. Her room was as silent as a tomb. She felt immensely sleepy and immensely sad. If Edward didn't show up soon, she could tell she was in for rather a large case of postpartum depression. Finally, at four thirty, she got out of bed. She wanted to go peek at the babies herself.

The glass wall in front of the baby room was as crowded with onlookers as the monkey house at the zoo on a sunny day. To one side Edward was standing, his hands behind his back, his face close to the glass. Slowly, very slowly and quietly she sidled up beside him.

"How do you like them?" she said.

He started, not having heard her approach. He smiled. "They're wonderful," he said fervently. "They're beautiful."

Rachel peeked through at them. "Do you think they are? I don't know what's wrong with me, I just can't think newborn babies are nice-looking. I mean, as babies go, they're pretty good. . . ." But he was staring transfixed as one of the two stretched and waved a small fist.

"Look at that," he said. "She's going to be a fighter."

"Like her mother?" Rachel suggested, but he wouldn't reply.

"What are you going to name them?" he wanted to know.

"I thought Angela and Kathleen . . . Angela for Angela Davis and Kathleen for Kathleen Cleaver."

Edward allowed himself a broad smile, but his voice when he

spoke was fond, not caustic. "I should have guessed." He looked thoughtful. "Well, Angie and Kathy . . . that sounds nice."

"I thought Kate, not Kathy," Rachel corrected him. "Like in *The Taming of the Shrew*."

"Well, you have all your heroines there, don't you?" he said dryly.

"Guess so." They stood smiling at each other.

Edward lowered his voice. "I don't know if they allow this here, but I thought we might have something to drink." He indicated a paper shopping bag he had set down on the floor. "Something to celebrate, you know? A little champagne?" His eyes were twinkling.

"That sounds like rather a good idea," Rachel said. "I don't see how it could hurt."

He let his eyes rove over her body. "You look different somehow. . . . You're really burgeoning, Mom."

Rachel looked down at her breasts, which were still abnormally full as they had been during pregnancy. "I guess I couldn't very well be virgining, could I?"

"Guess not." He put his hand on her shoulder. "So what do you say?"

"So I say, let's do it . . . whatever it is." She walked slowly after him back to the room, taking a sidelong glance at the champagne bottle. If she knew Edward, it would be the best champagne.

He stayed throughout the visiting hours and, when he came the next day, got to meet Rugoff, Beatrice, and Ibert, who all managed to put in an appearance. Rugoff was touching. He came bounding into the room with an immense bouquet of yellow roses, took one look at Edward, who was sitting calmly reading the *Wall Street Journal*, went out to look at the babies, came back, took another look at Edward, and said to Rachel in a soft voice, "They're very pretty babies . . . Rach."

"Ya, I kind of like them," Rachel said. She had had her hair done and felt, propped up in bed with all the flowers around her, like a queen holding court.

"Who was that?" Edward wanted to know after he had left. "One of your beaus?"

"Ya, how'd you like him?"

He would not rise to the bait. "He seemed like a very nice fellow."

Beatrice, of course, scarcely looked at the babies. At first she even looked at Edward with some hostility, as though a dog with rabies had been set loose in the room. But then, surprisingly, she and Edward got into a long conversation about stocks —who would have suspected that Beatrice had stocks or, having them, knew the first thing about it!—and soon they were chatting away while Rachel, leaning back, dozed on her pillow to the tune of a Mozart quintet on her transistor radio.

Ibert was very dapper, brought a box of the most beautiful chocolates Rachel had ever seen. "Why are you tempting me?" she asked him. "These are fantastic."

"Well, I've always wanted to go into that store," he said breezily. "This gave me an excuse."

Whether he assumed Edward was the father of the babies or just a new lover, it was hard to say. But he chatted urbanely, and they went out to inspect the babies together to make sure they had undergone no radical change in the last three hours. "Motherhood becomes you, my dear," he said, kissing her hand gallantly before he left.

Edward raised one eyebrow. "He's not another—"

Rachel shook her head. "Just a friend. . . . You met him at our wedding, in fact."

"I did?"

"Yup . . . I guess you've forgotten that memorable occasion."

"I have certain vague memories."

"How did you like Beatrice?"

"She seemed a little . . . strident at first," he said evasively, "but I'm sure underneath—"

"Underneath she's strident, too," Rachel said.

Alone that evening, after the babies had been brought in and then taken away, she allowed herself the luxury of tears. She was glad she was having trouble sleeping because of the stitches; it gave her something to worry about.

Chapter Eight

EDWARD's mother was delighted to see Rachel again, so she said frequently in the next few months. She took the tack that Rachel's absence had been like a stay in a T.B. sanatorium or a mental hospital, the kind of thing you didn't refer to directly, but would hint at from time to time. "Oh, that was when you . . ." (eyes averted) or "I guess you weren't here when. . . ." But it was Edward's father who was really delighted, not so much at the reappearance of Rachel as at the appearance of the babies. He carried their photos everywhere, did all but waylay strangers on the street with stories of their remarkable progress.

"I wouldn't have suspected it of him," Rachel said. They were in bed, and she was lying staring at the ceiling. The slow healing of the stitches made intercourse still a little painful, but she almost relished this. It was like magically becoming a virgin again, the illusion she could be created anew.

"Oh, sure," Edward said, stroking her. "Well, men are more sentimental than women basically."

"They are?" He always said things so categorically you couldn't disagree.

"In terms of true sentiment, yes."

Edward's father had a friend, Henry Wadsworth Gilian, who had been best man at his wedding and who had married the very same year but had no children and hence no grandchildren. "I was showing him these photos," Mr. Wittiker said to Rachel of the latest baby snapshots taken on their third month birthday, "and it was sad, in a way, I felt a little guilty. You should have seen the expression on his face! You could just see, he felt . . . he would never have anything like this . . . I shouldn't do it," he admonished himself, putting the photos back.

In fact, that particular photo showed the two girls with all six or seven chins in full display and Rachel scarcely imagined that Henry had been subject to quite the pangs of loss and regret which Edward's father delighted in attributing to him, but it seemed a harmless vice.

Rita was stiff, but then, as Edward pointed out, Ali's coming marriage had thrown her into an angry, repressed rage, not unlike a middle-aged woman with menopause. What angered her especially, so she claimed, was the fact that Rachel, now that the babies were on a regular schedule, was back at school, doing coursework for a doctorate in zoology. Rachel herself could not but agree that, as usual, her motives were somewhat suspect. No doubt were they living in Berkeley where such a move toward intellectual attainment would have been greeted with kudos by her parents, she would have lounged around the house, eating peanut brittle and reading dime store novels. But here, where the only fitting careers for women were considered things like airline hostesses, models, or interior decorators, she had to rock the boat by donning her blue stockings after a considerable hiatus. A freckle-faced Finnish girl took care of the babies in her absence, getting along with them famously, but Rita still made dark hints of neglect and lack of the proper motherly concern.

"She's only thirty-six," Rachel said. "Let her lead her own life!"

"She feels like fifty-six," Edward said. "No, I understand. I feel sorry for her."

It was nearly Christmas now, and Ali's wedding was to be on Christmas Eve. Rachel was standing in the bedroom, fastening a pin on her red velvet dress. Edward was putting on his socks. The babies were sitting in their infant seats, each clutching a rattle. Agnes, the maid, had got them all dolled up in matching pink outfits, although Rachel had told her she hated pink and hated things to match. They sat, egregiously overfed, looking pleased with themselves and the world. Rachel looked up, the seas of middle-class respectability closing over her head like waves over a drowning man.

"I always meant to ask you why you and Magda split," she said. For six months she had found herself literally unable to acknowledge Magda's existence, or speak her name, although she knew she had moved to some distant city after the marriage with Edward had not materialized.

Edward pulled on his second sock. "We didn't see eye to eye on certain matters," he said.

Rachel looked at him, but his eyes had that vague, blank look they got when he removed his glasses. "Wasn't white enough, huh?" she couldn't resist adding. "Edward, if you ever really leave me, you know who it's going to be for—an albino."

Edward said, "Let me make one point, my dear."

"Do, by all means."

"You claim I'm antiblack."

"I said—"

"Or anyhow, not pro, which in your book amounts to the same thing. . . . Now I don't call you anti-Semitic, do I? But have you ever considered all the pro-Arab remarks you make if anyone brings up the Israelis? Or the slighting references to Sol Spiegelman as a 'greasy Jew'—"

"But he is a—"

"And so forth and so on. . . . Just drawing an analogy," he said.

Rachel grimaced. "A case of the pot calling the kettle anti-Semitic, eh?" she said. "Well, maybe. . . . I thought you were going to say I wasn't a real revolutionary, so why keep going on about it?"

Edward straightened his tie. "Oh, that too," he said.

Later, as they went down the steps to the car, she said lightly, hand on his arm, "So do I love you because of the way you are or in *spite* of the way you are?"

"I don't know, baby."

"Well, do you think you love *me* because of the way I am or in spite of the way I am?"

Edward chuckled. "You're always after answers, aren't you?"

Rachel sighed. "Am I? I don't seem to come up with a hell of a lot of them."

The reception at Edward's parents was large—nearly a hundred people, the usual discreet mingling of black and white. Edward's mother in a green silk dress held court quietly in one corner. Ali, in a jazzy white pants suit, was dancing with Ronald, Edward's cousin who had almost been disowned by the family for wanting to be a jazz musician but who had saved the day by becoming, instead, a photographer for *Life*. Edward's father sat, a grandbaby on each knee, smiling broadly and benignly at all who passed by. Rachel tapped Edward's shoulder. "I'll be back in a second," she said.

Her bag was in the corner of the bathroom where she'd deposited it on their arrival. Its size was explained as necessary for "baby supplies." Now, having locked the door, she whisked out the pot of black greasepaint and quickly smeared it over her face. Her lips she painted in an exaggerated pale pink. The Afro wig was scuffed by now, but her hair tucked under it neatly enough. Then off with her dress which she stuffed in the bag and on with the old baggy clown costume which had served her in such good stead in the past. A pair of floppy shoes and a banjo completed the outfit.

As Rachel entered the room, singing softly, no one noticed at first. People were nibbling, sipping, circulating from room to room.

"Swanee, Swanee, how I love ya, how I love ya, my dear old Swanee!"

People began looking up. Rachel continued her slow saunter around the room. She had left her old identity behind and felt no trace of self-consciousness or awkwardness. In the corner she saw Edward pouring someone a drink.

"I'd give the world to be! Back home again in D.I.X.I. Even know my Mammy's . . ."

Several faces were smiling; others looked puzzled. Slowly various members of Edward's family were turning in her direction, their positions rigid like children caught in a game of statues. Edward looked up from his drink pouring. He knew. He closed his eyes.

But Rachel was passing on to the next room, the strumming louder, her voice rising. It seemed to her that she had never been nor would ever be this happy again.

". . . waiting for me, praying for me, down by the Swanee . . ."

Magic

"LOOK at this: 'Marilyn Monroe Dead,'" Hermione said to her son Grant's fiancée, holding up the New York *Times*. "Can you imagine?" She was standing near the window in a purple Oriental dressing gown, and her face, as Melissa walked in, was half lit up from the sunlight. Her wild, unruly cascade of gray hair made her look like a benign, if eccentric, lioness.

"How terrible!" Melissa said, frowning and glancing down at the paper.

Hermione gave a brief, mirthless laugh. "Well, she had enough in her short life, didn't she? Four husbands. . . ."

"Three," Melissa said steadily, looking right at her.

"Was it three? These women—they're like children, blundering from one man to another. They never learn, it seems." She smiled at Melissa. "Well, it's funny, but in this photo she looks quite a lot like you, my dear. It's amazing."

Melissa looked at the photo of a smiling blond girl in a tight print blouse. She laughed nervously, trying to balance irony and politeness in her voice. "Why, how can you say that, Hermione?" she said tensely. "It doesn't look like me at all."

But Hermione just patted her arm and smiled slyly. "Oh, it does, it does. Her smile, her hair—"

"Well, we're both blondes, if that's what you mean," Melissa said, still frowning, somewhat hurt. She felt an obscure insult to herself in this. It seemed to her another of Hermione's ways—not always so subtle—of voicing her disapproval of her son's engagement, a disapproval not so much of Melissa herself as of the idea that one of her sons should be leaving her. "Look, Mother's just like that," Grant had said after a similar incident a few days earlier. "You've got to understand. All her life she's been the only woman in the family—a husband, two sons, even teaching all these years at an all boys' school. She's used to being the center of attention herself. She doesn't like sharing it. . . . God, I hate to imagine the treatment she'd give a fiancée of Paul's! This is mild in comparison."

Melissa was glad that her upbringing had trained her so well in the art of concealment. She was able to meet all of Hermione's remarks with seeming detachment. Anyway, the ordeal was only for ten days, six of which were already over. It was to be, as Grant had put it, an unofficial vacation, an introduction of Melissa to the small Pennsylvania town in which he had been brought up, until Andover and then Harvard had made him almost a stranger to it. When they returned to New York in mid-August, Grant would start work at the law firm he had entered and Melissa would return to her secretarial job at a publishing house for art books. The marriage was planned for Thanksgiving, when Grant's father, who was in Europe for an academic convention, would return home.

Grant wanted Melissa to quit her job after their marriage. "So it's two hundred and ten dollars a week," he said when he heard. "It's insane! Your father's got money; I've got some. What's the point in it?" Melissa had tried to explain that although she knew her father could well afford it, she hated the idea of taking money from him. She had resisted asking him to pay for her two night courses in Chinese—she was working toward an MA in Oriental civilization at NYU—because she had known he would protest and feel the money better spent on a mink coat. As for being psychoanalyzed, he would never have given a penny toward that if the psychoanalyst father of one of Melissa's friends had not called up and yelled at him over the phone for half an hour. But on that point Grant agreed with him. "What the hell do you need to be analyzed for?" he had said when he heard. "Of all people!"

Melissa knew Grant was right about the job. It was dull, tiring; she came home each day worn-out and simply fell asleep on her studio-couch bed, without taking off her clothes. But somehow, it was still better than having endless days stretching before her in which to sit around and be depressed. "Why be depressed?" Grant had said in bewilderment when she had tried to explain how she felt. "I don't know. I just would be," was all that Melissa could reply.

As for Dr. Kaufman, Melissa's analyst, he didn't like the idea of Grant any more than Grant liked the idea of him. "This man knows nothing about you," the doctor had said. "You've said this yourself. He's made a snap judgment based on a few superficial things. To him you're just a conventional, poised, attractive young lady, evidently just what he wants in a wife. But you know yourself that's only a deception. That's not the real you. The real you spends half the day depressed, indecisive, drifting along through life without knowing where you're going, feeling a failure for some reason we still don't know. I'm not saying he'll fall out of love with you. I'm saying you don't know yourself well enough at this point to know *who* you could love. There's a side of yourself you're not taking into consideration at all."

But I *hate* that side of me, Melissa thought to herself. Her hope was that by marrying Grant she would in time become like his image of her. She felt certain he truly was all the things people commonly assumed to be true of her—conventional, poised, attractive. Together they would lead a life like a couple out of a *New Yorker* ad, comfortably well-off, relaxed, secure, playing chess in the evening—she in her hostess gown before the fireplace, sipping cream sherry and he sipping scotch. What a tempting image! Rather than stay and defend these ideas to Dr. Kaufman, however, she abandoned the analysis.

"You've made a good decision," Grant had said when he heard. "You won't regret it for a minute." Whether he was referring to her stopping the analysis or to her deciding to marry him, Melissa was not absolutely certain. But even if she felt she could not share his firm sense of conviction, she nonetheless wanted to convince Grant's mother, Hermione, and his older brother, Paul, that she would make Grant a good wife. If she had deceived Grant (though perhaps deception was too strong a word) why not them?

There was a sound of typing from out on the porch, and through the window, Melissa could see Paul, his back bent, his face scowling.

"Paul and I were going over his dissertation last night," Hermione said. "It has some interesting ideas, but they need to be worked on. And did he tell you about the controversy he's gotten into with that lady don at Oxford? Oh, I wish he'd withdraw the whole thing. He'll just get into trouble."

"No," Melissa said. "Grant mentioned it, though." She turned and sat down at the breakfast table.

"It would be good if Grant would talk to him about this controversy thing," Hermione said, idly stirring a cup of coffee. "Paul respects his opinions so much. It's as though Grant were the older." She smiled at Melissa encouragingly. "Or you could say something to him yourself, dear. It's your field, isn't it?"

Melissa looked embarrassed. "Well, not my field, really," she said. "I mean, I'm just taking these two courses."

"Still," Hermione persisted. "You're working toward a degree, aren't you? An MA? And it *is* odd, isn't it, an odd coincidence, both you and Paul being in such an unusual field. There can't be that many people in it. . . . What made you pick that particular field?"

"Well, I don't know," Melissa said, picking her words carefully. "I've always liked Chinese poetry, and I'd like to go to China one day, to visit or study or. . . ." She stopped, remembering that when she married, these hopes were hardly likely to be fulfilled.

But Hermione was too distracted to listen. Looking out at Paul again, she said, "I think now that Paul's passed his orals, he's gotten over the big hurdle, you know? I think that was the great divide, in a way. . . . It's just that I wish he would see *people* more, take out a girl now and then."

"At our engagement party he brought this one girl," Melissa said, glad to convey one bit of good news. "She seemed very nice. She's the secretary in his department at Columbia. . . . But then suddenly he stopped seeing her. I guess it never amounted to anything."

"No, his relations with girls never do. I think he scares them off, somehow. And yet he's quite shy, really." Hermione's face, usually so determinedly cheerful and bright, clouded over slightly. "He'll never marry," she said. "I don't even expect that anymore. I just thought perhaps. . . ."

But she left her thought unfinished. Grant must be such a relief to her, Melissa reflected, being a success in everything, carrying everything off so easily, a well-paying job, his cheerful, open disposition, so much like Hermione's own, his fiancée—yes, even she, Melissa, was part of his success, taken not so much as a person, but as a thing composed of a double strand of cultured pearls, a pair of black alligator heels, a pretty hairdo, and a faint smell of Chanel No. 5. Paul stood outside this. Even though he had partly recovered now, the nervous breakdown he had had eight years earlier, when he was twenty-four, had left its mark on him. "You should have seen him before," Grant said. "He was always full of the devil, playing tricks, kidding around. I was so proud of him. He was my idol practically."

It was hard for Melissa to relate this image of the fun-loving, good-natured Paul to the person he was now. At this point he led a solitary life, rarely even went to plays or movies, studied all day by himself, ate heartily, and only showed his eccentricities in his mannerisms and in the occasional off-color jokes that he would tell and then burst into loud, nervous laughter. Melissa could not feel at ease with him. It was awkward trying to think of congenial things to say, yet underneath, a secret, silent, but barely acknowledged current of sympathy extended from him to her. He was like her, she thought; they were a pair, separated by some fine but clear-cut line from Grant and Hermione, who also, in her mind, stood grouped together, like characters about to begin a dance.

". . . be coming to the magic show tonight?" Melissa, breaking out of her reverie, heard Hermione say.

She looked up and found Hermione's bright, curious eyes resting upon her hands. Without realizing it, she had been shredding the napkin into little pieces. She laughed, embarrassed, and scooped them all together. "I didn't know there was one," she said.

"Yes, it's an annual thing with the summer school, giving a show at the end of the term. Paul's going to help out by donating his services for a magic show. He's very good, you know. He always liked to give home magic shows when he was little. Grant used to help him. Where *is* Grant, anyway? That boy! Isn't he up yet?"

"I imagine not," Melissa said. "He would have come down."

"Well, yes, he needs the rest. He's so pale and run-down," Hermione said. "He worked so hard on his bar exams." She reached over and patted Melissa's hand. "And you, too," she said. "I want the two of you to have a nice rest and do just whatever you please."

Grant lay in bed, half-asleep, wondering if he should get up. Groping for his watch on the bed table, he saw it was past eleven. He had a vague feeling he had dreamed something, and he couldn't remember what it was. Well, the hell with it. Melissa was always telling him that if he wrote down his dreams and then wrote down whatever came into his head about each thing in the dream, he would see something important about himself. Sometimes, for fun or to make up to her for teasing her about her analyst, he'd do it. He even kept a little pad near his bed for that purpose; but nine times out of ten, in the rush to get to work on time and to walk Melissa's poodle (since the engagement they had been living together and he had acquired that chore), he forgot, and by the time he thought of it again, the dream had vanished. Well, this was vacation. Down with dreams. He stretched and lay back again.

The door opened. It was Melissa, who quickly closed the door behind her. She was in her blue robe, her light hair falling loose and slightly messed up on her shoulders, giving her a sexy, languid look that he liked.

"Sloth," she said, smiling. "It's eleven."

"I know."

She came over and stood by the bed. Reaching up, he pulled her down next to him and smiled. She frowned, nervously sweeping back her hair. "What if your mother. . . ."

"Oh, Mother, schmother! Let her worry about it. Anyway, it'll give her a vicarious thrill if she does come in. She and Dad have slept in separate bedrooms for so long. . . ."

Melissa laughed. "Have they really? How funny!"

His face kept the same amused, half-teasing expression. "You know. She likes to sleep with the windows open, he likes them closed, things like that."

But Melissa's face looked worried again. "What about Paul?"

"Oh, he'll be working all morning."

"He could stop early."

"It's possible."

Melissa crossed the room and lay down on the other bed. Paul's. Grant watched her. Part of his impulse had died away from her lack of response. But even this did not take away from his good humor and sense of well-being. There would be other times. "Sleep well?" he asked.

"Umm-hmm. . . . You?"

"I *always* sleep well," he said, smiling.

"That's right. I forget."

They lay there in silence. Through the half-drawn venetian blinds a stream of sunlight fell on the wooden floor.

"Marilyn Monroe died," Melissa said.

"Did she?"

"Yes, it was in the paper. She took an overdose of sleeping pills."

"Hmm."

"I felt sad about it, somehow . . . I don't know why."

"It *is* a sad thing. She was fairly young, wasn't she?"

"Thirty-eight or something. I don't know. I can't explain it, but I felt badly."

Grant looked at her sorrowful face. He had only seen Marilyn Monroe once in a movie and hadn't been struck by her, but it was typical of Melissa to react to something like that. She never read the newspapers thoroughly, yet always found some obscure notice about an animal that was becoming extinct or a play that had been forced to close which would make her brood all day.

"It's funny sleeping alone," said Grant, to change the subject.

Melissa reached over and pressed his hand. "For me, too. But it's only four days more."

"No, I know. I can wait."

If only Melissa had something to do, Grant thought. That was the trouble with this visit, something he hadn't foreseen. He had a whole stack of briefs to study. He could relax part of the day —swimming, playing tennis—but the rest of the time he had to work in the library. That left Melissa with no other company than Paul, who was certainly not much fun, and Hermione, who, Grant well knew, was inclined to be chattery and nerve-racking, even in her desire to be nice.

"Why don't you try some sketching today?" Grant suggested. "You said you'd like to."

"Well, I'll see."

Grant swung his legs out of bed and gave her a perfunctory kiss. "That's the spirit," he said.

"Don't let me disturb you," Hermione said, tiptoeing through the porch. "I brought you that article, though, in case you want to look at it."

"Oh, thanks, Mother," Paul said. He had sensed rather than seen her hovering around in the kitchen, ostensibly making preparations for lunch, but actually watching him; he could tell. It had made him so uncomfortable that he wasn't concentrating. He had just gone over her corrections on the outline for his dissertation, rereading her remarks, but unable to look at them objectively. He hated it when she felt it necessary to help him as though he were still a schoolboy and hated himself for accepting the help. And somehow the whole morning had drifted by. Incredible!

"You just go right on working," Hermione said. "You can see it later."

"No, I'm about ready to quit now," Paul said abruptly. He tilted his chair back, balancing on two legs, something he knew made Hermione nervous.

"Did you work at all on that point we were discussing last night?" Hermione asked, peering over his shoulder.

Deliberately he shuffled the papers together and turned them facedown. "No, I did something else."

Paul could see the conflict in Hermione's face about whether or not she should pursue it. After a moment she said, "Well, maybe just for now it would be best if you stuck to the outline, don't you think? I mean, so you can get it down on time for Professor Herman?"

He looked outside, as though he hadn't heard her. "Melissa and Grant up?" he asked.

"Melissa was just here a moment ago. I don't know about Grant."

"We were going to play some tennis today."

"You and Grant? How nice!"

He fiddled with the scissors. "Of course, I'm not a 'champion' like Grant, but I thought it might be good to get some exercise."

"Yes, I heartily agree with that," Hermione said. "It'll be good for both of you." She turned to go inside. "That film star Marilyn Monroe died, you know. Melissa was very upset about it."

The sky had clouded over. Melissa went inside to get a sweater, then came out again. Grant had gone over to the library, saying he'd be back at one. Hermione was preparing her class for the following day. Melissa had promised to gather some raspberries in back of the house, and she began slowly, bending down so all she saw were the dusty bushes in front of her.

"You won't find too many," Paul said.

Melissa stood up, her face flushed from stooping over. "I didn't hear you come up," she said.

"Cat's feet," he said, pointing to his sneakers. "Grant at the library?"

"He has some briefs to go over," Melissa said, trying to sound noncommittal.

"Yes, he always does, doesn't he? Well, it's just as well. There's not much else to do in this town."

Melissa tried to smile. "Yes, you must have had a dull summer."

"It isn't the Riviera. . . . Oh, well, there are such startling compensations as tea with Miss Landy and picking raspberries. I say you won't find many because I went over them just last Wednesday."

"Your mother mentioned something about a controversy you're in," Melissa said lightly, trying to win him over.

He smiled sardonically. "Yes, of all things, a lady don, Millicent Tushingham, has taken it upon herself to disagree with a defense I wrote of one of her articles. She's been writing some rather amazing letters to me."

"I'd like to see them."

"Would you?" He looked at her suspiciously. "You haven't read the article so you wouldn't understand it," he said.

"I know the gist of it."

Convinced, he brought a whole sheaf of papers out on the lawn. "I want to read you the whole thing," he said.

Melissa propped herself against a tree to listen to him. At first, she tried to follow the essence of his dispute with the lady don. But it was an intricate, scholarly point, involving the meaning of two words from a Lady Murasaki story, and she soon gave up. Why did he get involved in these entanglements? To put such energy and interest in it! If it had been a more wide-ranging creative essay, it would have been one thing. Yet she sensed somehow that the narrowness of the topic was deliberate on his part, as though he only wanted to look straight ahead at a single point, like a horse with blinders on. He has nothing else in his life, she argued to herself. What else can he do?

If only he had someone, some girlfriend. But who would accept him with his strange mannerisms and peculiarities, his sarcasm, his abrupt sense of humor? Paul's eyes were lowered to read, and taking advantage of this, Melissa looked at him closely, studying him, as though to find the clue to his character. He was a large, muscularly built man with an unusual, powerful face, quite unlike the typical, bespectacled image of the scholar she had expected. Yes, he would be attractive to women, she thought, but whom? Perhaps some nurse, some strong, capable woman who would be a source of security for him as Grant was for her. The strong with the weak: that was the only way things could work out.

". . . do you think?" he was saying.

Melissa came back to reality with a jump. Daydreaming again —the second time that morning. She realized she hadn't heard a thing he had said for the last ten minutes.

"Woolgathering?" he said. "I admit it isn't the most fascinating of topics."

She blushed, embarrassed. "No, it was terribly interesting, really. . . . I know that story, actually. I once did a paper on it. . . . Yes, I think you're right. You should stick to what you've said."

"Mother doesn't. She thinks it can only lead to trouble."

"Well, that's silly, you've a right to your opinions."

"Mother says you feel badly about the death of Marilyn Monroe," he said, pronouncing the name in an odd way, as though he had never heard it before.

"Yes, I do," Melissa said, thinking: Why does she have to tell everything?

"Suicide is a sin," he said flatly, still staring at her in his rude, abrupt way.

"I feel differently about it," Melissa said very quietly.

"Do you?" He smiled in a strange way. "Is that Grant's opinion or yours?"

Her face reddened. "It's mine. Why should I take up his opinions?"

"I thought you were one in everything."

"You know that's not true. Why do you say it?" Despite herself, she had done precisely what she had intended not to do: She had lost her temper with him. She looked down and was silent. Damn him.

"Perhaps you ought to go back to your raspberries," he said.

"I will," Melissa said. "That's a good idea."

And she did. But he was right; there were hardly any, just a handful or two, and those already brown from the heat.

"What's the score?" Paul said. He was standing at the net, having just bent down to retrieve the ball while Grant strolled back to the base line. "Your ad, isn't it?"

"I thought it was deuce," Grant said, squinting into the sun. "I might be wrong, though."

He was wrong; he knew it himself, and most likely these small devices on his part to give Paul a point now and then did more harm than good. But there was no way out of it. If he played his best, it would be slaughter. And right now, as it happened, he was in good form, whereas Paul's game had deteriorated since the last time they'd played, probably from lack of practice. Now Paul either threw games away, in anger at himself, or deliberately played his worst so as to negate any advantages Grant tried to give him. The best way was to forget about it and play normally, with good steady strokes, no curves or short shots.

"I'm pretty sure it was your ad," Paul said, still standing there. "Don't you remember? I hit that return of yours out before."

"Did you?" Grant said. "Yes, that's right. I forgot. Okay. My ad, then." He smiled. "It's getting pretty hot, don't you think? Maybe we should quit after this game—or soon, anyway."

"Whatever you want."

"Well, I mean, I can go on, if *you* want to. I just thought. . . ."

"Look, if you want to play, I'm perfectly willing. It's up to you."

"I am a little beat." Grant grinned again, but Paul's straight stare with his usual hint of sarcasm took whatever good humor there might have been out of his remark. Caught lying again. Well, the hell with it.

Paul's next serve came just over the net, veering slightly to one side. Grant rushed in and hit a long, smooth shot into the backcourt. He moved back to get in position for the return, but Paul, rushing forward too quickly, tripped on the white tape. He fell forward, his racket flying out of his hand.

"Hey, are you okay?" Grant jumped over the net. Paul was examining his knee. The skin had been broken, and there was some blood; but it was not a severe cut.

"It's nothing much," Paul said.

"Well, still, we'd better wash it off."

"Maybe we should finish the point."

"Oh, it's not worth it," Grant said.

This remark hung in the air between them for several moments before Paul said in a low voice, "That's right. It was your game, anyway, wasn't it, with that last point."

"You can't count the last point," Grant said heartily.

They gathered up the scattered balls and walked across the court toward the car. Grant felt in a good mood. Grinning, he put his arm loosely over his brother's shoulder. "Your serve is a lot better," he said. "You know that? If you could just get it in more consistently, your game would improve a hundred percent. . . . If you'd let me, we could come out and practice. I'll show you a few things. I think it would make a big difference."

But Paul said nothing, and they drove home in silence.

*   *   *

"Isn't Melissa's hair nice?" Hermione said as they all got into the car to drive down to the lake. "How do you get it so high up? It's just like a little hat on top of your head."

"I just put it up," Melissa said, getting into the back seat next to Grant. Paul was driving, and Hermione sat beside him.

"You don't do that thing—what is it called—teasing? That's very bad for your hair, evidently. There was an article on it somewhere."

"No, I don't tease it," Melissa said.

"Melissa hates to be teased," said Paul. He drove down the driveway and turned left. "Miss Landy, who as you know was kind enough to invite me to tea several times this summer, told me that a woman in town got a beehive hairdo and a bee got into it and stung her. She went into the beauty parlor all dripping with blood, and the next day she died."

For a moment no one said anything. Then Hermione said, "Well, really, that's ridiculous. I've never *heard* anything so foolish."

"It's the gospel truth, as Miss Landy herself will tell you," Paul said.

Hermione made a disgusted face. "Oh, you just like to carry on," she said huffily.

"He's just pulling your leg, Mother," Grant said, putting his arm around Melissa.

"I suppose he is," Hermione said.

"Just pulling one of your beautiful gams, Mother," Paul said. "Watch out one doesn't get longer than the other." And tilting back his head, he began singing a song that went "Those beautiful gams, oh, my, what beautiful gams, as white as lambs, oh, where, oh, where did you get those beautiful gams?"

"What song is that?" Melissa said.

"That is a song of my own creation," Paul said. "Do you like it, Melissa?"

"It has a nice tune," Melissa said softly.

"Mother, did you say Williams Hall for you?" Paul asked, slowing up.

"Right here is all right," Hermione said. "Well, I'll tell you, why don't you drop Grant and Melissa off now, as long as we're so near the dock, and then you drive me around, if that's all right."

As Grant and Melissa walked hand in hand down to the lake, Hermione turned to look at them once more. "I wonder if that's Melissa's only suit," she said, frowning. "I don't mind myself. I'm sure it's very comfortable. One must get so much more sun that way. But I just thought if some of the neighbors were down there. . . . Well, of course, it is a pretty little suit, though, isn't it? And you can't tell Melissa what to do. If I live to be a hundred, I'll never understand what goes on in that little head of hers—I mean, not that I expect or even want to live to be a hundred," she added.

Paul drove up in front of the big red-brick building. "The expression is usually used figuratively, I believe, " he said.

Floating out on the lake, Paul closed his eyes and gave himself up to the enjoyment of the sun. It was nice to be this far out where the yells of the kids jumping off the dock could hardly be heard, where the sounds of cars passing on the road nearby were almost inaudible. The water right on top was warm. It was only when he dangled his feet farther down, treading water and breathing through his nose, that he touched the cold bottom.

A plane was passing overhead. Odd, the sense of dread he still felt at the sound of planes. The mental hospital had been near an airport, and his earliest memories of the place were of planes flying over. At the time, he had got them confused with planes in war movies he had seen, and their droning, as he had lain on his back in the dark for an endless stretch of time, had awakened in him a feeling of terror that even now had not entirely vanished.

Lifting his head slightly, he could see the red spot of color that was Melissa's bikini and the blue that was Grant. Lying in the sun, talking. Grant holding forth on one of his theories. Wasn't she bored? Or did she want that? Maybe she did. Boredom equals security. Even Melissa was willing to accept boredom in preference to fear.

He had read her diary once, gone into her room, or rather his father's room, which she now occupied, and found the diary facedown in the drawer. Scattered phrases, drawings. "I have nothing to talk about with Hermione. . . . Up at eight, went in to see Grant. Can't get through to him. We talk about trifles. Why do I feel so detached with him? It doesn't do any good to condemn oneself for it, yet I can't help feeling guilty about it. . . . Wish I knew how to drive so I could go off by myself during the day. . . ." Nothing about him, though! His vanity had been offended. Not even a slighting or nasty word: Paul is being difficult again. If only Paul would leave us alone. Nothing. And yet when she looked at him this morning in the raspberry patch, wasn't there some feeling there? Or was he just foisting his own longings onto her?

Slowly with firm, sure strokes, Paul began swimming back to shore. As he climbed onto the sand, he heard Grant saying to Melissa, "I just hate guys like that."

"Like what?" Paul asked, reaching for a towel.

"Oh, I was just telling Melissa about these lawyers at the firm —you know, the kind that will only take on a 'perfect' case, nothing involving any element of risk. Christ, it makes you think the whole profession is just a bunch of pompous bastards."

"But *you're* not a pompous bastard," Paul said. A second later he added in a low voice, "At least I don't *think* you are."

Melissa broke up at this. She began laughing so hard tears streamed down her face. Grant looked at her, puzzled, but Paul, catching her infectious laughter, began to laugh himself. For nearly five minutes the two of them sat there, gasping, clutching their sides, until Melissa managed to compose herself. "I'm sorry," she said to Grant. "It just struck me as so funny."

Grant eyed her suspiciously. "I didn't even hear what the joke was," he said. And getting up, he folded the three wet towels neatly into the straw basket.

*　　*　　*

"You said nothing about a magic show, Mother." Grant looked annoyed. "Why didn't you say so before?"

"Didn't I? I thought I did. Perhaps it was to Melissa." Hermione looked flustered. "It's nothing so much, really. The faculty of the summer school always puts on these skits every year, and I thought, why not have Paul do a little something? It was just an idea, but I mentioned it to him a few weeks ago, and he was glad. You know, he always liked doing tricks. Why, he even went to a magicians' convention in Rochester to get some pointers."

Grant gave a snort of laughter. "Are there magicians' conventions? How crazy! What do they do, go around pulling rabbits out of each other's hats?" He drummed impatiently with his fingers on the desk. "No, the point is, I wish you'd let us know earlier. We have plans for the evening."

"Well, dear. . . ." Hermione looked at him helplessly. "He'd be so pleased if you'd come."

"Yes, I'm sure, but that's not the point. . . ."

"Melissa can forgo a little evening's entertainment," Hermione said. "You've been out almost every night."

"Well, aside from that not being true, it's not Melissa, it's me, too. . . . Look, we'll see what we can do. That's the most I can say."

There was a NO TRESPASSING sign in front of the fence. "That doesn't matter," Grant said. "It's just old land. No one'll see us."

"Are you sure?" Melissa stood uncertainly and did not move. It was just barely dark out, that instant of twilight before darkness falls.

"I'll help you over the fence," Grant said. "Give me your hand. You won't fall."

Clutching him, Melissa jumped and fell, not hurting herself, in a pile of leaves.

They wandered through the forest. It was cooler than it had been walking along the road, since here the sun had been shut out all day. Grant walked ahead of Melissa, holding back the branches so she could proceed. He, too, was silent now. When they had set out, it had been on his mind that he wanted to make love to her. All day he had been distracted by the thought: when she had lain beside him on the beach, when she had come into the bedroom in the morning. The tentative abstinence he had planned for these weeks—sublimate everything into sports!—had suddenly seemed impossible. He felt that he could literally not survive this stay, which was awkward enough anyway, without making love to her.

When the road was no longer visible, he stopped, pulled her down beside him on the ground, and began kissing her. He had intended to be gentle, to soothe her into the proper mood with tender endearments, but as the kisses lasted longer, all that blanked out of his mind. He drew her dress over her head.

"It's so hot," she said, drawing away from him.

Grant smiled at her. "Why don't we, Lissy? It's so lovely here."

"There are too many mosquitoes," Melissa said, laughing nervously. "We're too near the road."

"We can go farther in."

He walked ahead again, and she followed, nude except for her sandals, her dress draped over her arm. Within a few minutes they were deep into the forest. Once again they lay down. Grant spread out his shorts and shirt for Melissa to lie down on.

Above her, Melissa watched the trees that arched together, blocking out the sky. Up until this moment she had felt she wanted him also. But now, suddenly, a feeling of loneliness assaulted her. She thought: This is how he thinks of me—a sexy blonde, to sleep with in the woods. What does he care what I feel? And yet even this mood passed, as quickly and mysteriously as it had come. He made love to her slowly and half without her will; a feeling of passion overcame her; she forgot everything else.

Afterward she dozed off and had a dream: She was lying next to Paul, and he was kissing her; but these kisses were extraordinarily sweet, sweeter than any real kisses. He was leaning over her and saying, "You pretended not to be interested in me, but I could tell you were." Then, suddenly, the dream changed. He had cancer and would die in two years, and if she loved him, she would catch the cancer and die also. And with that, the sweetness of the dream vanished, for she knew she loved him and would die.

"Honey," Grant said. "Are you sleeping? Do you want to go?" He bent over her and grazed his lips against her neck.

Melissa awoke and looked up, startled to see Grant. His touch on her, his kiss, seemed crude and flat compared to the kisses in the dream.

"That was nice, wasn't it?" Grant said.

"Umm," Melissa said, afraid he would realize what she was feeling.

"We always wanted to do it out-of-doors, remember?" he said. "I'm glad we did. . . . It's strange, but nice—to escape like this. . . ."

"Go back to a primitive state," Melissa said, trying to joke.

"There's something beautiful in just being here, in nature," Grant said.

Melissa smiled.

"It *is* a beautiful forest," she agreed, turning her head. "But these damn mosquitoes—there are never mosquitoes in D. H. Lawrence."

Grant laughed. "You'll never be a romantic," he said.

"Are you?" The dream still possessed her, and she could not help looking at him as though he were a stranger.

"Maybe more of one," he said, grinning. "I don't know."

It was hard to sleep. Downstairs, the faucet in the kitchen was dripping, and she found herself lying awake to listen to it. *Ping* . . . *ping*. . . . Where was it she had read of someone dying who had heard the sounds: *pitti pitti*. Someone was dying—who was it? Marilyn Monroe. Why had that been haunting her all day? A silly blonde, a movie star. Someone trapped by a false image of herself, which she could not escape. And yet it was her fault!

She preserved the image willfully! Her fault! She killed herself because of it! No, that was no good. She'd never get to sleep that way. Melissa sat up, hugging her arms around her legs. Well, it was silly to get all upset. She would not be a suicide, certainly—there was something too melodramatic about it.

She got out of bed and quietly tiptoed downstairs. There was no carpet on the stairs, and the wood felt cold and slippery under her feet. Hugging her bathrobe around her, she walked into the kitchen. Everything was still, and the furniture sat silently, like props on a deserted stage. What was that! A tapping on the window startled her, and whirling around, Melissa saw Paul outside on the lawn, leaning toward the window, his face near the glass. She opened the window and found herself face to face with him. He had left on the makeup from the magic show. His skin was unnaturally pale, and a dark mustache had been corked on his upper lip. He was wearing a cape tied around his neck.

"How did it go?" Melissa said, feeling guilty about their not having shown up.

"Didn't you hear?" he said mockingly.

"What? We just got back a little while ago." She looked at him gravely. "Wasn't it held?"

"No, it was held." He put out his hand to her. "Why don't you come outside?" he said. "It is beautiful out."

Melissa hesitated only a moment. "Okay."

When she came outside, he was standing on the back lawn, looking up at the stars. "There's another one," he said.

"What?" Melissa looked with him. The sky was black with a haze of stars, so many that they made the sky oddly radiant. Standing there in the darkness beside him, she felt peaceful for the first time all day.

"Shooting stars. Look, there's another." He grabbed her arm and pointed.

"Where? I don't see." Melissa looked back and forth. The sudden, abrupt touch of his hand on her arm stirred her profoundly.

"It's over." His voice became flat and uninterested again. He turned to her. "There're a lot of them this time of the year. I've counted fifty in one night."

"So many," Melissa said softly.

They were silent a moment.

"You didn't see Mother when you got back?" Paul said.

Melissa shook her head. "I think she was asleep."

"That's right. She would have been." He put his hands together lightly, as though he were praying. "Well, you missed something," he said in his former ironic voice.

"Did the tricks go over well?" Melissa asked.

"Oh, the tricks were fine." He smiled and, reaching into his pocket, pulled out a red silk scarf which he draped over his hand and whipped back a moment later to reveal a bunch of flowers. Melissa smiled.

"But at the end," he said, "there was something in the nature of a fiasco, you might say." He paused, but Melissa said nothing. "I was going to do a prophetic trick," he continued, "you know, the old one of picking someone in the audience and getting him to help you guess certain things. So I took out this crystal ball I use and said, 'You may not see anything so unusual about this. You may think all magicians have crystal balls.'" He looked at her, waiting for a reaction. "You don't think that's funny? Well, senses of humor differ. Anyhow, it broke up the show. They roared. It was just one of those things that you couldn't stop once it got started. I just stood there, tried to start over. They wouldn't let me. They whistled, screamed. Finally I walked off the stage and went home which, so I hear, upset everyone because they were waiting for the rest of the act." He dug his heel into the ground and moved it back and forth. "I thought I'd given them enough entertainment for one night," he said. "Don't you agree?"

The pain in his voice was just barely concealed by the irony. Melissa stared at him, deeply touched. For that one instant he seemed incredibly close to her, someone she could love in a way she had never loved Grant or anyone before.

"What do you think, Melissa?" he said, using her name for the first time and giving the word undue emphasis. "Do you think people always make mistakes like that, always spoil what they want once it's within their reach?"

"I don't know," Melissa said uneasily. The change in his voice frightened her.

"Do you *want* Grant?" he said, continuing in the same way. "Is that your goal in life? Well, it's an interesting goal, a worthy one. . . . It's a mistake, though, to leave your diary around. One might assume from a perusal of it that your feelings weren't so simple, and that would be a mistake, wouldn't it?" He reached out to touch her, his hand on her shoulder, near her neck. Melissa, looking at him for an instant, saw a flicker of fear cross his eyes, and it was this, as much as the touch of his hand, that made her pull back.

"I don't know," she said in a whisper, almost pleading. She began backing away toward the house.

"What do you think?" Paul cried after her. "Tell me, Melissa, tell me what you think? Am I a failure? Tell me!" His voice, trembling, followed her as she fumbled with the door.

"Yes," she flung at him, her voice rising. She turned a second to see him standing there on the lawn with the dark cape hanging lopsided off one shoulder. "Yes! You are!" Melissa whispered.

Going into the house, she nearly bumped into Hermione.

"Oh, dear, I just happened to be passing your room," Hermione said, "and I saw the door open and your bed empty, I wondered. . . . A pity you couldn't make it to the magic show tonight." She stood near Melissa, her face large and pale in the darkness.

"Yes, yes, it was," Melissa said, hearing nothing, dazed.

"Paul did so well," she said, "so well till the very end—and then it was just this little thing that upset it all. He's so hypersensitive, you know. Just a little joke. But where did you and Grant go? I thought—"

"Please, I'm terribly tired," Melissa said, trying to brush past her, her whole body trembling uncontrollably.

"Always sneaking off—you two—like lovebirds." Her voice suddenly turned reproachful. "But, you know, it's just as well you weren't there in a way. It would just have made him feel worse, knowing you saw everything."

"Please, stop it, stop it!" Melissa heard her own voice burst out in a terrible scream. For a moment she was not even aware of who had screamed, but wondered who was making so much noise so late at night.

"My God, Mother, what's going on?" Grant appeared in the doorway, dressed in his pajama bottoms. He went over to Melissa and took her in his arms. "Darling, what's wrong? What happened?"

Melissa tried to speak and couldn't; the tears poured out of her.

"What—have you and Paul been pestering her again? Christ, I'm sick of the two of you! I bring her home and all week it's this same business—innuendos, gossip, everyone picking away at everyone. Look, this girl is going to be my wife!"

"No one's denying that," Paul said dryly. He had come in so quietly no one heard him. "The case is conceded."

"Oh, hell! Why don't you cut out all that stuff? 'The case is conceded,'" Grant mimicked. "Can't you say something straight out? All this damn Chinese courtesy!"

Paul raised his eyebrows and bowed slightly. "Honorable sir," he said, drawling his *r*'s in an Oriental way.

"It's not that," Melissa said. "It's not that."

"Well, what is it, then?" Grant said angrily. "What's all the commotion about?"

"I was just showing Melissa a few of the magic tricks I did in the show," Paul said, exquisitely polite. "And one of them scared her. She isn't *used* to magic tricks."

Grant looked suspicious. "Were you?" he said belligerently. "What tricks?"

Paul smiled, sleepily. "Oh, nothing unusual, really, making things appear and disappear, a few transformation tricks, the old routine."

"You remember? You and Paul used to do them together once," Hermione said, looking anxiously from one to the other. "That summer you both put on that act, remember? You cut Mademoiselle Bijou, the French teacher, in half."

Grant relaxed. "Yes, I *do* remember," he said. "Whatever happened to her?"

"She got false teeth and married a dentist from Duluth," Paul said. "They have eight children."

"Eight! Good God!" Grant said. He shook his head. By now he was almost in a good humor.

"Yes, and she's a weak woman," Hermione said, grasping at this straw. "I said to your father more than once, 'Mademoiselle Bijou is a weak woman.' She had liver trouble; she had diabetes. Why, do you know that that last semester she was so tired she had to teach sitting down! She came to me especially one afternoon. 'Mrs. Fordyce, I have to teach sitting down. I just don't have the energy to stand.' That's what she said. And yet she had all those children!"

"Maybe she had *them* sitting down," Paul said.

Grant laughed, and even Melissa smiled.

Later Grant came into Melissa's room to put her to bed. She was tired and drained of feeling, almost light-headed. Grant sat on the edge of the bed, holding her hand. The lights were off, and the house still again.

"Listen, if Paul acted funny tonight," Grant said, "you've got to understand. He still isn't really all. . . ."

"No, I understand," Melissa said quickly.

"It's too bad Dad isn't here," Grant said. "Things always get out of hand when he's away. He's terrific. You'll love him. He has a great sense of humor. And he plays a damn good game of tennis for a man his age. He keeps himself in shape. . . . You'll see at our wedding."

"Yes, I'm looking forward to meeting him," Melissa said formally, knowing now for the first time that there would be no wedding.

He kissed her lightly before he left. "I'm glad we didn't go to the magic show, actually." He smiled intimately at her.

She smiled too and lay there, the smile remaining on her face almost by inertia. Listening, she heard his footsteps retreating down the hall into his room. Several moments later Hermione passed by and closed her door with a sharp click. And last of all came Paul, his step slow and light, as light, it seemed to Melissa, as the gesture he had made when he had flipped back the red silk scarf, revealing the three perfect rosebuds underneath.

A Sense of Ritual

ON the way up from New York it was stuffy in the car. The windows had to be shut because of the cats, and outside it was ninety-three degrees of an August afternoon.

"As soon as we get on the highway," Sam said from the driver's seat, "there'll be more air."

"Couldn't we open it just a crack?" pleaded Maggie, who was in the back seat wearing shorts and a sleeveless blouse, a scarf over her head to protect the elaborate hairdo she had had done that morning at a downtown beauty parlor. She was afraid Sam and Liz would think it decadent and silly of her to have had her hair done, even if it was for her own wedding, which was to be the following day. Because of this, Maggie had made Dave promise not to tell them. "After all, it *is* an occasion," she had said to him to justify it. "It's only once."

But the fact was that it was precisely because it was "an occasion" that Maggie was worried about her own wedding. For years—she was now all of twenty-three—she had gone around telling everyone, her friends, her parents, that she despised convention, thought things such as weddings, graduations, and birthdays, all those ceremonial marking points, were a lot of hooey. The prospect of getting married herself made her feel as though she were giving in to all the voices of convention and respectability against which she had clamored for so long. I am betraying my ideals, thought Maggie, though what these ideals were was somewhat foggy even in her own mind.

The drive up, once they were on the road, did not seem long.

Although it was Friday, it was no special holiday weekend, and they had started early enough to avoid most of the traffic. Liz entertained them all with a comic description of her and Sam's wedding, describing how the minister, whom she knew very well, had kissed her before Sam had a chance.

"Later I told him about it," Liz said, smiling, "and he turned beet red and said, 'Ah, Lizzie, it was a moment of truth.'" She looked at them. "I wish so much you could have had Scottie, too," she said. "You would have liked him."

"Well, ours is okay," Maggie said without much enthusiasm.

In fact, they had had trouble getting a minister. City Hall and a justice of the peace had seemed too cut and dried, and yet an elaborate ceremony made them both uneasy. It was Dave who had had the idea of going back to his old college campus where he knew the chaplain and having him perform the rites.

They had gone to see him one Saturday morning just as he was leaving his chaplain's office to go get a white shirt for a wedding. He was an outgoing, hearty man with a crew cut, dressed in a tight navy blue shirt, khaki pants and sneakers, who, once he had bought the shirt at the Co-op, had sat them down on the lawn and questioned them about their religious beliefs. It turned out he felt he could not marry them, not because Maggie was Jewish and Dave Protestant but because neither of them believed in God. "I mean, if one of you had *some* belief," he said, looking at them hopefully, but neither of them could lie about it, Dave because of his conscience and Maggie because, having come from a family of agnostics, she couldn't quite believe he was serious.

The lawn had been deserted as they sat there except for tables and big, soft chairs which were being carried out for storage over the summer, and the chaplain's voice had seemed very loud in the enclosed Gothic courtyard. "You're reading Dostoevsky," he said to Maggie, who at the time had a worn paperback copy of *The Brothers Karamazov* in her hand. "What do you think Dostoevsky thinks about salvation?"

Maggie, caught between indignation and shyness, could say

nothing, and Dave had to answer for her. When they left him, he shook both their hands with a strong, muscular handshake and said he was sorry about Dave's dwindling religious interests and that the young people of today were losing a sense of moral responsibility.

Afterward on their way back to the house where Liz and Sam were waiting, trudging up the hill past modern, white Colonial houses, Maggie blew up.

"What does he think you are?" she said. "I certainly wouldn't be marrying you if you were as religious as all that."

Dave shook his head and smiled. "Yes, but you've got to realize that when I was in college it was different. I admit, I played a sort of ambiguous role even then, but I was head of the magazine sponsored by the Christian Association—things like that—so in the eyes of people like him, I stood for—well, I don't know. . . . Anyway, he feels he has to bring me back into the fold."

But this did not calm Maggie down. "Do you know what he said?" she announced to Liz and Sam when they were back at the house and stretched out on the lawn again in bathing suits. "He said, 'You've got to learn to play volleyball with God.' Can you imagine?"

Sam laughed. "You mean, you've got to be careful not to kick him in the shins," he said.

"Just about," said Maggie.

"Sweetie, you're distorting what he said," Dave said patiently. "He said there were some ministers today who tried to get young people interested in religion by using catchphrases like that. He didn't use the phrase himself."

"Oh, he did use it, Davie, he did!" Maggie protested, though, in truth, she couldn't remember exactly what the chaplain *had* said. She only remembered the feelings he had aroused in her, and she was glad when, even if it was because she was exaggerating, Sam and Liz took her side and laughed at him, too.

But even though the chaplain would not perform the ceremony himself, he recommended someone else, a Unitarian whom they had driven out to see the following day. The Unitarian met them in a very modern church with a modern office. There were wall-to-wall bookshelves and in the corner a black leather couch and reclining chair. "I saw it in Bonnier's for five hundred dollars," Maggie said later. "I think he does a little therapy on the side," Dave said. He had them sit down in chairs facing his large desk and handed them little slips of paper, fastened by paper clips on which were typed the different services from which they could choose. There was a "Traditional Service" in which a couple whose names, Michael and Miranda, were scrawled in pencil, agreed to cherish, to have and to hold, where the name of God was invoked to look over this couple and preserve their happiness; there was a "Semi-traditional" in which another couple, this time Mary and Richard, agreed to do similar things but in which the name of God was mentioned less often, and there was a third in which Rita and Alex agreed to do various vaguely humanistic things in which the name of God was not mentioned at all.

"I guess the modern is best," Maggie said dubiously.

"But with the traditional vows," said Dave. "They're nice, the 'Do you, so and so, take this woman. . . .'"

"Very good. Modern service with the traditional vows," the reverend said. "Fine."

As they walked out into the sunlight, Dave said, "Don't you get a picture of those anonymous couples from their names—Michael and Miranda, very stiff and proper—"

"I know, and Rita and Alex sort of wild and bohemian. You have the feeling Rita wore hoop earrings and a handwoven skirt and Alex collected folk songs and studied music at Oberlin."

"They really should have a Super-traditional with Ezekiel and Rachel, him with a beard, her with her hair parted in the middle."

"Do you like him?" Liz had asked anxiously when they returned from this second safari.

"Well, he's a *nebbish*, but that's good, I think," Maggie said.

"Good?"

"Well, you notice him less. He'll just be there like an ornament. He won't distract. . . . And he didn't ask about what religion we were or if we were religious or anything."

"That's good. . . . I guess Unitarians just don't care that much."

All this, the visits to the two ministers, had taken place three weeks earlier, and at the time Maggie had been relieved to have the whole thing settled. But now, sitting in the car, listening to Liz, with the wedding scheduled for tomorrow, she began brooding silently over the Unitarian and wondering if he had been a good idea. Seeing her worried face, Liz, too, fell silent and turned around front again. But a moment later a mischievous smile appeared on Maggie's face. "The nice thing," she said, "is that I don't have to promise to obey."

Liz laughed. "I didn't either. Scottie knew it would be silly for me to make a promise like that, so he just left it out."

Sam shook his head. "These women," he said. "It's terrible."

It was time to exit; he turned off the road.

"You must sign here," said the large, officious-looking woman in the Marriage License Bureau. "No, not in ball-point," she said, pushing Maggie's hand away. "In ink. Ball-point doesn't last."

"Your name is so funny," Maggie said as they walked out and down to the elevator, "and it's hard to pronounce."

"What's so hard about it?" said Dave. "Thattcher."

"It's spelled in a funny way with the two *t*'s. People always get it wrong. . . . I like my name. It's easier. . . . It's too bad your name doesn't go with mine in some way . . . Maggie Montgomery."

"Oh, God!"

"Don't you like it? . . . Or something like that. Maggie Kaufman Thattcher doesn't sound like anything. . . . Anyway, why should I have to give up my name? Really, it's not fair."

"You can keep it—in the middle."

"Yes, but Mrs. Thattcher makes me think of your mother. She's Mrs. Thattcher—not me."

"What are you then?"

"I don't know." A moment later. "Do you see what I mean, though?"

"I see you're tired."

Maggie sighed. "I am actually. I'm bestially tired. Aren't you? You said you were in the car."

"No, actually right now I feel rather good, getting away from those damn cats."

"That's good," said Maggie glumly.

Dave smiled. "Good spirits and health seem to be a ball we pass between us. There's never enough for both."

"Do you think it's psychological?" Maggie said in a worried voice. "On my part, I mean? Because of the wedding?"

"Could be."

"What do you think, though? Is it?"

"Probably partly."

"That's terrible, then."

"No, it's not. The main thing is not to worry."

"Is it?"

"Yes."

"I guess you're right." A moment later she said, "The thing is, though—" but just then the elevator came, and they got in in silence and rode down.

When they got out, Dave said, "The thing is—what?"

"I forget what I was going to say. . . . Oh, yes, the thing is, I mean, you don't feel like we're backing down by doing it, do you?"

Dave took her by the arm. "Of course not. First of all, we love each other. And that's what marriage is for."

"Do you think so? Seriously?"

"I do think so," Dave said earnestly, looking straight at her. "That's the secret of its popularity."

"Maybe you're right," Maggie said, but she did not sound totally convinced.

"There are times, you know, when you just have a drink because it's that time of day," Maggie said, coming into the kitchen," but other times you really feel like you need one." She slipped off her shoes. "I feel like I need one right now."

The drinks had already been made. Liz was sipping hers, and Dave and Sam had gone outdoors with theirs to start the fire for dinner. It had become a ritual in the few times they had come up to the house for Dave and Sam to go outside at dinnertime to start making the fire or at least Sam would make it and Dave would stand near by, talking to him and offering a helping hand when it was necessary. Maggie and Liz would stay in the kitchen and sip strong, cold gin and tonics, get slightly high, prepare the salad, and exchange intimate confidences about their pasts. This ritual was especially dear to Maggie who felt that to Liz, as though to some older cousin or sister she had never had, it was possible for her to say all sorts of things, even things she would not have told Dave, and this was a comfort to her. She took a long swallow of the drink and said, "Jesus, what did he put in here?"

"Well, we had to finish off the gin," Liz said.

"It just may finish me off."

Maggie began helping Liz by washing off the lettuce leaves. She washed one leaf and took a sip of the drink, washed another and took another sip, and gradually she began feeling very good. "You know, it's odd," she said. "I've known Dave longer than you've known Sam. I figured it out. We met two and a half years ago when I was in my junior year at college and you met two months later."

Liz smiled. "It *is* odd." She stood a moment watching Maggie. "How come you didn't get married sooner?" she said.

Maggie flushed. "Oh, gosh, a million things. Dave wanted to get his PhD finished so he could support me. And then neither of us wanted to rush into marriage—"

"Why was that?" Liz said.

"Oh, I don't know." Maggie felt pinned down under Liz's sharp questioning. "We wanted to know how we felt about each other first. We just couldn't face the whole bit of engagement rings and showers and electric coffeepots. That's why we're only having you two at the wedding and the Witkins."

"You're lucky your parents understand about it," Liz said. "Most parents would be mad as hatters."

"Oh, yes, well, my parents are very liberal," Maggie said. "They always understand."

They finished the salad and, having nothing to do until dinner was ready, sat down at the kitchen table.

"Still, I thought of our sleeping in separate beds tonight," Maggie said, "just so there could be one night of abstinence."

Liz smiled. "It's funny, I thought of that with us too. Only I thought one month."

Maggie laughed. "So one month, one night, what's the difference? It's the principle that counts."

"True."

"Anyway, it was easier for you," Maggie said defensively. "You weren't living together whereas we have been for the last six months."

"No, I had an apartment," Liz conceded. "Sam used to come up to see me."

"So that makes a difference," Maggie said.

"Oh, look, I didn't mean—"

"No, I know, I was just—"

But before she could finish the sentence, Sam came rushing in with the hamburgers on an aluminum pan. "Look out," he said. "This is hot. Stand back!"

Getting undressed in the room upstairs, Maggie let her clothes drop to the floor. She was too tired to pick them up. Standing before the mirror of Liz's mother's dressing table, she pulled the bobby pins out of her hair. On the table was a framed picture of Liz and Sam on their wedding day, Liz in a suit, squinting into the sun, a cigarette in her hand and a half-smile on her face, Sam in a plaid vest, holding a champagne glass and looking pleased. For a long time Maggie stared at the photo, her bra hanging from her hand. Then she went over and got into bed, fastening around her head the black Flents sleep mask she wore to keep herself from being awakened by light in the morning. A few minutes later Dave came upstairs and began getting undressed.

"It's hot up here," he said.

"It's bestial," Maggie said, peeking out at him from a crack in her Flents.

He clicked off the light, got into bed beside her, his arms around her neck. They lay like this without saying anything. Finally Maggie said, "I'm as horny as a great horned owl."

"So let's make love."

"We could, I guess. . . . But maybe we should wait."

"That's true."

"The only thing is, if we were going to wait, we should have done it for longer, like for a month. We should have planned it."

"But we didn't think of it."

"That's true. . . . Liz said she and Sam didn't for a month before."

Dave laughed. "And we've got to do exactly what Liz and Sam do, of course."

"No, seriously, we should, sweetheart," Maggie said in a half-joking voice.

"Well, I'm glad you girls have cleared up all these essential points."

"Don't you and Sam ever talk about things like that?"

"Not exactly."

"It's odd."

"Well, I don't know how odd it is."

There was a few minutes' pause before Maggie said, "We *should* have waited a month, Davie. We *should* have."

"Why?"

"To give it a sense of ritual."

"Oh, well, you can't have everything."

"That's true," Maggie said in a worried voice, but a moment later she laughed. "We would have gotten hideously horny if we had," she said.

"Sure."

"And you were finishing your dissertation, so it would have been bad to suddenly change things. It might have had a bad effect."

"Of course it would have."

On the way to going to sleep, Maggie had vague sleepy thoughts about getting married. She wondered if it would make any difference. She didn't see how it could. What was there left? It wasn't just a matter of sex—that was the least of it—it wasn't just that they had already slept together; it was living together in general. Didn't she already do things like make beds and prepare Viennese chicken the way he liked it and subscribe to the *New Republic* and bring his bag of dirty socks and shirts to the laundry on the corner and arrange dinner parties for their friends and see that there was enough toothpaste left and send away for theater tickets, and didn't he already put up shelves in the kitchen and read her master's essay and give suggestions and bring her English muffins with Golden Blossom honey and a pot of hot tea when she had cramps from her period and was in bed, rereading Jane Austen, and teach her tricks about her serve in tennis and help her choose dining-room chairs at International Home Furnishings and walk the dog at seven in the morning before he left for work and at eleven at night when she had already taken a hot bath and was in pajamas? What was there left? Still, there had to be some change. Somehow there would be.

"Well, we'll see," Maggie said, without knowing she had spoken aloud.

"See what?" said Dave vaguely. He was nearly asleep.

"Just things in general," Maggie said softly.

She hated it when he fell asleep before she did. There was nothing worse than lying there listening to someone else already asleep and not being able to sleep oneself.

*　　*　　*

Maggie followed Liz down into the cellar. It was dark and cool there and seemed quieter than any other part of the house. Upstairs, the afternoon sun made the air stifling. Side by side in a corner of the cellar stood a double bed and a single one. "Maybe we'll sleep here tonight," Maggie said.

"You can," Liz said.

The two girls sprawled out on the two beds. Liz, who was tired from all the preparations for the wedding, closed her eyes for a few minutes while Maggie looked around the room. In the corner opposite were old boxes and piles of books. The light came from a light bulb near the ceiling that you had to pull a string to turn on. Maggie touched the string, and it swung back and forth gently.

"Did you use to store things down here?" Maggie said. She herself was always storing things and had at home countless old papers and diaries and Christmas cards from years back. She had offered to let Dave read all her diaries from the age of thirteen to nineteen (she had stopped keeping them after that), but he had only got through three volumes and then petered out. It had hurt Maggie's feelings at the time, but she had consoled herself with the thought that he never finished books either; he'd even stopped right in the middle of *Anna Karenina*.

"Oh, sometimes," Liz said. "Old drawings and things. Mother would always root them out, though. She's the kind of person who will let things sit for years but then suddenly gets this demon in her and cleans everything out, throws out everything, old diaries, papers. Dad's practically killed her sometimes for it. . . . But you know what she once found down here? There were these two old vases, brass ones, that no one cared about— they'd just been thrown down here—so one day she took them up and began cleaning one of them and you know what she found in it? A star sapphire!"

"What did she do with it?" Maggie asked.

"Oh, had it made into something, I guess. But the crazy thing is she just put the other one away and then about five years later she was cleaning that and she found another sapphire. I mean, that's her for you. She wasn't even curious enough to look in the other one."

"How odd," Maggie said, but vaguely; her thoughts were elsewhere. She leaned back in the bed. "I like it here," she said. "It's cool."

"We should go up," Liz said.

"I know."

"So," Liz said. "You're on the verge—"

"Of what?" Maggie said quickly. "I'm sure marriage won't change anything for us."

Liz smiled. She swept her long hair back so it was spread out on the pillow. "Oh, it does, somehow," she said. "There is some difference."

"Is there?" Maggie frowned. She was willing to take Liz's word for it, almost.

"Well," Liz said. "Marriage is a strange thing."

"As Henry James would say," Maggie said, teasing her.

Liz smiled too, an enigmatic smile. "Not quite," she said.

But Maggie persisted, not wanting to be serious. "Or at least it would take him two hundred pages to say it."

"Maybe."

Maggie would have asked Liz what she meant by saying marriage would make a difference, but she didn't because she felt she wanted to find out herself. Besides, the difference would not be the same for everyone. She jumped up. "Come on," she said. "Let's go out on the lawn and you can spray me."

Two minutes later they were outside, and Sam, who had just come back with Dave from ordering the flowers, was directing the hose at Maggie, who whirled around and around, laughing and crying, "Oh, Sam, don't! Not so high! You'll get my hair wet!"

At four o'clock in the afternoon Maggie went upstairs to get dressed. It was hot there; it seemed at least ten degrees hotter than the rest of the house. The Witkins, Ronald and Judy, had just arrived. Dave's brother, Henry, had been there for over an hour. Silently and swiftly Maggie dressed, struggling with her girdle, which clung to her moist skin and would not go on. The bra she put on backward so she could see the fastening and then turned it around to the front, stuffing her breasts into it. Dave had said it was the kind of bra that made you look like the cover of a historical novel. She went into the bathroom to put on her makeup. There was a knock at the door; it was Dave.

Maggie kissed him, and they held the kiss nearly a minute. When they came out of it, they smiled at each other.

"Would you stick this in?" Maggie said, handing him a hair clip which was to hold down the veil.

He fastened it, saying, "That's not all I'd like to stick in."

"Oh, sweetie," Maggie said with mock disapproval, but actually she was pleased.

He watched her fixing her hair.

"Dave?" Maggie said, frowning.

"What?"

"Do you think that if I'm happy, it means something bad is bound to happen?"

"Of course not. Why should it?" He sat on the edge of the tub.

She tried to explain. "Just as penance or something. You know what I mean."

"No, I don't."

"You think if you're happy, it's perfectly all right and nothing to worry about?"

"Sure."

"Anyway, bad things are bound to happen anyway," Maggie continued with her argument that was mainly with herself. "So why not be happy as you can. Don't you think that's true?"

He stood up and kissed her neck. "I think you're a darling. That's what I think."

"Do you really?"

"Yes, I do."

"Do I look all right?"

"Terrific."

"Davie"—she was done now—"I'm bestially scared, aren't you?"

"Don't be silly," he said, and taking her hand, he took her downstairs, where everyone was waiting.

When Maggie came down, Liz had just emerged from the study where she had changed into her dress. Self-consciously Maggie adjusted her veil. She had to keep holding it under her chin to make it stay and this felt uncomfortable. Sam came over to her.

"Hey, very nice," he said.

Everyone smiled at Maggie, and she tried to look absorbed, as though she were wondering if she had forgotten anything. She was disappointed more people didn't say: you look beautiful, the way people did in books to brides, and it worried her: Did she look all right?

"Your strap is showing," Liz said, coming over and pulling up the strap of Maggie's slip, which had fallen down.

"I know," Maggie said mournfully. "It won't stay up."

Out on the lawn they gathered together for a picture. The sun was shining, and it was hard to look into it. First Sam took a picture; then he joined the others, and Dave took a picture with him in it, and then they all got in the car. Liz sat next to Maggie. With a paper clip she fastened her strap. "I feel as nervous as though I were getting married all over again," she said.

Sam made Dave sit in the front seat.

"It's true, we should be separated a certain time at least," Maggie said, "for a sense of ritual."

"That's right," Sam said. "I thoroughly approve. No intercourse for at least ten minutes before the ceremony."

Maggie and Dave looked at each other and laughed.

"Look at each other while I'm reading," the minister said beforehand. Maggie looked once at Dave in the middle of the ceremony. The tips of his hands, touching hers, were icy cold as she knew they got when he was very nervous, as they had been when they heard Richter play the Beethoven Ninth Piano Sonata at Carnegie and as they had been when he was about to take his orals. His face was unusually pale, and when it came his turn to speak, his voice quavered with emotion. The fact of this—Dave being nervous!—practically made Maggie pass out right there and then. She looked away and did not glance at him again until the ceremony was over. When she started reciting her own vows, the solemnity of everything, the quietness in the chapel, the fact that Liz and Sam and Henry and Ronald and Judy Witkin were all there, watching both of them with serious, intent faces—thank God they had not had more people!—so overwhelmed her with shyness that she could barely speak above a whisper. She tried to focus on the minister's hands, on the ring on his right hand which looked like some sort of ring from a family crest. In it was a pale-blue stone with a figure of an animal—was it a bear?—carved on it, and it seemed to Maggie that even this bear had a solemn, determined expression. When it came time for the exchange of rings, Dave tried to push the ring on Maggie's finger, but it got stuck—from the heat her fingers had got swollen—and she had to put her hand on his and help him. They glanced at each other for an instant and smiled. And then it was over—finally!—and they kissed, a relieved, passionate kiss, somewhat moist since both their faces were drenched with perspiration.

They went out from the cool, dark chapel to the lawn outside. The relief from having the ceremony over made Maggie giddy. She began laughing, drinking champagne and feeling good again. She looked forward to being kissed by everyone. The minister, who became quite outgoing after two glasses of champagne, nipped her directly on the lips, but Sam just darted forward and in an instant pulled back again so she hardly knew if he'd kissed her at all.

"Ooh, talk about unconscious guilt feelings," Ronald Witkin said, and Sam turned bright red.

Maggie felt it was a nice thing to be married. First, you could flirt with other men as much as you wanted and not have to worry about what they thought of you and if they wanted to ask you out. It seemed to her as she stood there on the lawn, sipping what was left of her champagne and laughing at everyone's jokes that she liked all the men there, even the minister who had seemed so stern and official during the ceremony.

Afterward, back at the house, Maggie went upstairs, feeling bubbly, gay and happy from the champagne. Everyone was changing out of their formal wedding clothes into shorts and skirts because it was so hot.

Maggie reached into her suitcase and took out her bikini. She had never worn it before. Two weeks ago, passing a store along Fifth Avenue, she had seen it and, on an impulse, gone in and tried it on, along with a lot of other sensible, dark-colored lastex models. She had sneaked with it into the dressing room and in it —it was shocking pink and orange—had stood and regarded her own image and thought: Every woman has a secret desire for a bikini. If I don't get one now, at twenty-three, when I weigh a hundred and five, I may end up getting one when I'm fifty-five and weigh a hundred and forty-five. So, guiltily replacing the others on the rack, she had paid her fourteen dollars and ninety-five cents and taken it home. Before Dave got back from work in the evening, she had tried it on once more, trying to stand up straight, suck in her belly, put her shoulders back and her behind in. She had even shaved on either side of the suit's skimpy bottom (why was it in *Vogue* and *Harper's Bazaar* the models in bikinis never had pubic hair? Or hair under the arms even?). When Dave had come home, she had modeled it for him, and he said it was very nice but suggested that for the trip to his hometown to visit his parents which they were then planning, she wear her old, falling-apart green one. And so she had never worn the bikini. But now, elated with champagne and general excitement, she slipped the bikini on and skipped down the steps to help Liz with dinner, smiling happily to herself.

Dave looked at her disapprovingly as she came down the stairs.

"What happened to your dress?" he said.

"It felt hot," said Maggie.

She helped Liz in the kitchen, crushing garlic for the steak and preparing lumps of cheese to put on crackers for hors d'oeuvres. Outside, through the window, she could see the Witkins, Dave and Henry out on the lawn. Sam was bent over the barbecue tending the fire.

For dinner they used paper plates. There were tremendous chunks of steak for everyone, more than anyone could eat, ears and ears of roasted corn, red wine, and strong garlic bread. Sam had a lot of wine and began telling jokes he had heard in the Army. He talked in a loud voice, and Liz seemed embarrassed, though Maggie and Dave laughed. The candles dripped wax on the table, and Maggie dipped her finger into it while it was hot and began molding a small wax animal. For dessert there was watermelon and coffee, and Sam offered them cigars. Maggie took one and puffed on it all through dessert until once Sam called out, "Hey, you've got a big ash there, bridie. Better shake it off." Everyone laughed, and Maggie turned red. She went inside to help Liz with the dishes.

Suddenly she felt drunk and hot and ashamed she had worn her bikini. She even wished she and Dave had done the conventional thing and gone off after the wedding on a proper honeymoon. What would have been so wrong with that? Dave was sitting in the armchair out on the porch, talking to the Witkins. Silently Maggie went over and sat down next to him, her head leaning against his shoulder.

Later Maggie and Dave went down to the cellar, which Maggie had chosen as their sleeping place. The beds were made. Liz had gone down while Maggie was dressing and made them. Maggie found on the pillow of the double bed a small yellow flower which Liz had placed there. It was cool in the cellar and dank. No light came in except from a side window which looked out on the street. They took off their clothes and made love. Afterward they had to turn on the light to find the pajamas. Maggie had brought her pink drip-dry pajamas; she had no lacy trousseau of elegant nightgowns. She put on just the tops but decided it was too hot and that it would be more comfortable not to wear anything. They lay down together in the double bed, but neither of them could sleep.

"I feel drunk," Maggie said. "I had too much champagne. I shouldn't have worn my bikini."

"I told you not to," Dave said, but not in an unkindly way.

"I know," Maggie admitted. "I should have listened to you." She touched his shoulder. "Do you know where my Flents are?" she said.

"I'm not sure," said Dave. "You must have left them somewhere."

"I think I left them upstairs in the bathroom. . . . Should I go get them?"

"Sure. . . . Why don't you?"

Maggie felt her way cautiously out of bed and up the stairs of the cellar. On the way past the door she sniffed. There was a funny smell from the cat's box. The downstairs part of the house was totally silent. Light coming in from the windows cast strange shapes, and Maggie felt scared. She went upstairs and found her Flents in the bathroom near the sink. There she also saw cosmetics which she had left out from just before the wedding. Carefully, she went downstairs again and on her way down was startled by the image of herself in the hall mirror as she descended. She saw a nude figure, hair loose and wild-looking, carrying the Flents. Her face looked frightened. The floor of the cellar was cool underfoot as she padded over to the bed. With the Flents secured, they tried to sleep again, but it was hot and humid, despite being in the cellar.

"I think I'll move to the other bed," Dave said.

"Are you sure that will be all right?" Maggie said.

She was sorry he was going to the other bed because the idea of sleeping in the double bed was nice, but she was glad because now she had more room. Alone in the big bed she stretched out and kicked off the covers. Without knowing when, she fell asleep.

"Halloo! Halloo!"

Maggie, from the depths of sleep, heard a far-off calling. The sound grew louder, then faded, and was replaced by a rattling sound. Half-awake now, she realized someone was trying to shake open the back door. She got sleepily out of bed, put on her pajamas, and went upstairs. There, leaning against the screen door, was Henry.

"I locked myself out," he said mournfully. "I went for a walk, and I forgot about the door."

Maggie let him in.

"You don't suppose there's any chance of breakfast, do you?" he said. "I just thought—"

"Everyone seems to be sleeping," Maggie said. She squinted at the light. "What time is it, anyhow?"

"Nine thirty."

She stifled a yawn. "If you wait awhile," she said, "maybe—"

"Oh, no, I better get going," Henry said. "It's a pretty long drive I have ahead of me. . . . My bags are all ready." He went into the study to get his bags while Maggie followed him, too sleepy to say anything.

When he left, they shook hands, and smiled. "Thank you for the presents," she said. "Have a nice trip."

She stood outside the door, watching him disappear around the house to his car. It was a clear perfect morning. You could tell that once again it would be hot, but now the sun, filtering through the trees and onto the grass, looked fresh and warm. Maggie felt the cool wetness of the grass under her feet. Scattered on the lawn were various things left out over the night: Liz's copy of *The Iliad*, some cornstalks tucked under the grill, Dave's blue sweater, someone's sunglasses (hers?). One of the cats, who must have got out when she opened the door, romped over the yard and disappeared into the ivy. Picking up the sunglasses, she went back inside and down into the cellar.

Dave was lying asleep on the single bed, one arm thrown over his eyes. She wanted to get into bed beside him but was afraid she might wake him. But then she thought she would anyway. That was the change, then, that being married, she could do all the things out of love which before she had done out of rebelliousness. In that love was her sense of ritual. There was no more need for bikinis at her wedding dinner, but of course she could not have known that a day ago. Quietly, carefully, Maggie got into bed beside Dave, pulling the sheet up over her; her last thought before falling asleep was of Liz's mother who had found a star sapphire in a brass vase and then, years later, without even looking, found another one.

The Boy
in the Green Hat

"THE strangest thing happened in the park today," his wife said.

Lange, standing in the entrance hall, had thought she was about to take his coat and hang it up, but she just stood staring at him with her large, lustrous eyes which, with their milky gray color, had a peculiar, almost manic intensity. He went to hang it up himself. He had had a difficult day at work, but even if he had not, he was always taken aback, unpleasantly, by his wife's habit of bursting out with her "events of the day" before he had had a chance to relax, make himself a drink, and ease out of the strain of his own worries. Of course, he reminded himself, hunting for a sturdy, wooden hanger—he was always telling her to throw out these twisted metal ones—she was alone all day or most of the day with only the maid and their five-year-old son, Avram, to talk to. This explained why her need to communicate to him was so much greater than his need to communicate to her. He found a hanger, draped the coat over it, and started into the kitchen.

"What was it that happened?" he said.

"This boy," she said, "this boy in a green hat."

"What boy?" He opened the refrigerator door and withdrew the Rose's Lime Juice with which he intended to make himself a gimlet. It would have been nice, too, he could not help thinking, if she had thought of preparing his drink for him, having it ready when he came home.

"There was this boy," she said. She stood near the refrigerator, watching him, her arms crossed tensely over her breasts. "He kept following Avie and me."

"Following you?" Lange, selecting a large glass, measured out a precise amount of vodka. He always kept the vodka chilling so that no ice cubes would be necessary.

"Yes," she said, her voice breathless, shrill, insistent. "He followed us."

"From where to where?"

"Well, first in the playground. He kept circling around Avie—"

"Talking to him?"

"No."

"Then what?" The drink prepared, Lange walked out, after her, into the living room. He sat down on the large scarlet couch and arranged himself comfortably. It was an enormous room, almost circular, with a terrace running half the length of the apartment. Lange's advertising company allowed him to deduct the rent from his income tax. From the couch, without even stepping onto the terrace, a wide expanse of New York was visible. Now, at dusk, with the lights on in the living room and the faint, glimmering lights of the city outside, he took the first sips of his drink which was perfectly cold, the way he liked it. He turned to his wife more genially, crossed his legs and said, with almost guilty attentiveness, "How old was this boy?"

"I'd say he was nine or ten," she said. She remained standing, as though hovering over him, like a bird about to take flight.

He motioned to the couch beside him, but she shook her head, evidently too absorbed in her story to sit. "Well, there's nothing so unusual about a boy of nine or ten being in the playground," he said.

"Yes, but he followed us," she said. "Later we went down to One Hundredth Street. I told you—I was going to meet Janie McGregor there. And I was sitting talking to her and looked up —there he was again."

"Maybe his mother just happened to go down there, too."

"But he had no mother," she said.

"Really?" Lange sipped his drink reflectively, trying to listen and to piece it all together. "Still, he could have been playing by himself at that age."

"Maybe. But why would he follow us?" Her eyes, fixed on him, were demanding, impatient.

"I don't *know* why," said Lange, impatient himself. "Need there have been a reason? Anyway, if he wasn't harming you, why does it matter?"

"But he might have! He might have!" Her voice became so agonized that he set down his drink. "He was staring so."

Lange stood up and put his arm around her. He felt that her whole body was trembling uncontrollably; she was terrified. "Have a sip of my drink," he said quietly.

She took the drink and mechanically, as though it were medicine, swallowed what remained in the glass.

"You're tired," he said, half-suggesting this possibility as a partial explanation; she was three months pregnant, and although it scarcely showed, he felt it might have told already on her nerves.

"No," she said stubbornly. "No, it isn't that."

She was always cleverer than he expected, seeing through these attempted excuses on his part; he felt defeated. The pleasantness of the half hour in which he was to have had his drink, a half hour he had looked forward to almost throughout the day, was marred. He thought of making himself another drink, then decided against it. A few minutes later the maid announced that dinner was ready.

After dinner he went into his son's room to say good-night to him. Katherine was in the kitchen, discussing something with the maid. His son's room was almost as large as their own master bedroom. Gaily colored paintings hung on the wall. In the corner was his bed, painted bright red and decorated by hand with Amish designs.

"So how's the boy?" he said, coming to sit beside him.

"Okay," Avie said cheerfully.

He was always surprised at his son's good nature, his outgoingness. Perhaps he expected that somehow the boy was doomed to become some combination of himself and his mother, whereas, on the contrary, he seemed far better adjusted than either of them, at ease with strangers, rarely intimidated.

"I hear you went to the park today," he said. "Wasn't it cold?"

"Noo," the boy replied, considering. "It rained later," he said after a minute.

"Who'd you play with?" Lange asked. "Was Billy there?"

"Ya, we played a little."

"What'd you play?"

"Oh, different things."

"Were there a lot of kids there?"

"Sure." Avie lay back, looking at his father with large, dark eyes.

Lange felt confused by the directness of this glance. He hesitated, then said very quickly, as though it were of no importance, "Was there some boy in a green hat?"

"What boy?" Avie said.

"Was anyone—trying to bother you? You know—"

"Nobody had a green hat," he said.

"You just played with Billy?"

"Ya."

Lange sat there, abstracted, not speaking. He stared at the wall where a tapestry of a shocking pink bull hung slightly off center. Its eye, a vivid purple shade, seemed unusually bright and angry, even though the dark room muted the color.

"Aren't you going to tell me a story?" Avie said.

Lange started. Then he said, stroking his son's pajama-clad foot, "I really can't tonight, Ave. I've got to do a lot of things. Tomorrow—tomorrow I'll tell you one—twice as long if you like."

"Okay." The boy accepted this readily and burrowed down under his covers as he always did before going to sleep. Lange tucked him in, kissed him lightly on the cheek, and left the room.

Standing in the hall outside the boy's room, Lange frowned. A dead end. What would Avie know or remember anyway? There were so many children—he didn't keep track of all of them. Oh, let it go, he thought, impatient with himself. But he couldn't, not so easily. He felt he had to know if there had been a boy in a green hat.

Katherine was standing in the living room, looking out over the terrace. He approached and said in a quiet voice, "You feel better now?"

For a minute she didn't reply. Her body, next to his, seemed very still and languid, almost limp. "Yes, I feel fine," she said in a vague voice.

"You can get to bed early," he suggested. "Read in bed."

"Yes." Again her voice had that dreamy, not quite paying attention quality.

"I might go into my study," Lange said. "I have some papers to go over. I'll be in later. Should I carry the TV into the bedroom?"

To this also she agreed. He left her in the bedroom, getting undressed to take her nightly bath.

He did go to his study, but only for a few minutes. If he could have worked, he would have—he had not been lying about having things to do—but he was restless and distracted and merely sat at his desk, drumming on the broad teak surface with his fingers. Then he had an idea. Leaving the room quietly, he took his coat from the hall closet, and, equally quietly, closed the door behind him. There was a chance Katherine would miss him, but it was unlikely. If he hurried, he would be up before she had finished her bath. He knew that often she liked to soak there for at least half an hour. He could, he thought, waiting for the elevator, have used the study phone, but there was the chance she might lift it up to make a call herself, and although the study was soundproofed with a double layer of Portuguese cork, he would not have felt completely safe.

Outside it was gray and rainy, unusually cold for April. He hurried across the street, ducking his head to shield himself from the rain. Most of the stores along the block were still open, the delicatessen, the beauty parlor which was reputedly a hangout for all the call girls of the neighborhood; he had always looked with suspicion and curiosity at its glossy exterior of spun-glass wigs and artificial nails. He went into the drugstore. The middle-aged Jew behind the counter smiled at him genially. Usually he would have stopped to exchange a word. Now he just smiled, trying not to seem curt, and ducked into the phone booth at the back of the store.

It was a small booth with no stool. For a moment Lange stood there, staring at the advertisement glued to the inside of the booth. "Have you made your ten calls?" it read. "Groceries? Invitations? Business Matters?" Under which category, he wondered, did his present call belong? He withdrew from his pocket the slip of paper on which he had written the number, inserted two nickels, and dialed. He was in luck; Janie answered.

"Hello, Janie? Sol Lange."

"Sol! Hi! How *are* you?"

"Fine, very well." He hesitated.

"Bill isn't here," she said quickly. "He's at a meeting. Did you want to leave a message for him?"

Lange cleared his throat. "No, actually, I wanted to ask you, Janie. There's a favor I wanted to ask—well, not a favor, I just wanted to find out— You were in the park with Katherine today, weren't you?"

"Yes, yes, I was," she said, sounding mildly surprised.

"How did she seem to you? I mean, did she seem—nervous or upset in any way?"

"Upset?" She paused just a second, then said, "Maybe a little keyed up. Nothing much."

"Did she by any chance mention anything to you about a boy in a green hat?"

"No-o, not that I remember."

"I see." He was silent a moment, staring out the booth at a customer who was coming in to get a newspaper. "Well, could you tell me this, then? Did you yourself happen to notice a boy in a green hat—you know, just playing in the park anywhere."

"A boy in a green hat," she said, obviously trying to remember.

"Think a minute. There's no hurry."

There was silence at both ends of the line for several moments. Then Janie said, "Yes, yes, I did, come to think of it."

Lange swallowed hard; his heart was beating quickly. "You did?" he said, trying to keep the eagerness from his voice.

"Yes, I remember now."

"How old would you say he was?"

"Oh, maybe seven."

Seven, nine; that was close enough. A tremendous relief settled over him. He said, "Thanks so much, Janie. . . . Listen, just one more thing, though—how long after Katherine arrived did this boy appear? Do you happen to recall that?"

"Oh, he was there before she came," Janie said right away without any hesitation.

"Before she came?"

"Yes, he was there all afternoon."

"You're *sure* of that?"

"Yes, positive. Well, I know his mother, Mrs. Model—I was even talking with her earlier in the afternoon."

"He has a mother?" Lange said, dismayed.

Janie laughed. "Well, of course he has a mother! Sol, don't be silly! He has a sister too—they were playing together."

"A sister too." He frowned, despair and unquiet seizing him again. "Then it may not be the same boy," he said, troubled.

"What boy? What do you mean?" she said. "What is all this about?"

Lange hesitated. In general he did not discuss his wife with anyone, but now he was compelled, not so much by closeness to Janie McGregor as from a desire to talk to someone about it, to hear what she might have to say, to create order out of this chaos. "It's—" he began slowly. "Well, you remember when Katherine went into the hospital the last time?"

"Bellevue?"

"No, the time after that when she was just in Mount Sinai for a few months. Right after Avie was born."

"Yes, I remember."

"Well then, the thing that started it off, or seemed to, was her imagining that certain people were following her—sometimes real people, people we knew, but sometimes just imaginary people. But she would describe them in great detail—what they wore, what they looked like. Maybe she was describing people she had really seen on the street, maybe taking bits of this person and that and combining them. Anyway, she would become obsessed with these people, what they were doing, what they wanted of her—"

"Paranoia," Janie said quickly, proud, Lange thought, to be able, so quickly, to put a label on it; this annoyed him.

"In a sense," he said impatiently. "There's more to it than that."

"Of course."

Again her tone irritated him; he wondered if this whole thing wasn't a mistake. She was obviously delighted to be hearing all of this, to be treated as confidante—she had always resented his abruptness with her, he knew. But he felt compelled to go on, having gone this far. "Well, at that time, when she was released, the doctor said this was one thing I ought to be watchful for—this tendency to imagine people, that it might be the beginning of something."

"I see," Janie said. She added, "Katherine is always so observant of people, anyway."

What did that have to do with it! Oh, he regretted this! What folly to talk to this woman! "Anyway, that's all," he said quickly, wanting to get off the phone. "So I just wanted to check with you about this boy."

"Yes, yes, well, I'm glad you did, Sol." Even her use of his first name bothered him as some attempt at an unwarranted intimacy. "And listen, if anything should happen, I'll let you know."

"I doubt that it will," he said, trying to be genial and at the same time trying to discourage her from getting further involved. "Thank you, anyway."

Going upstairs, he felt angry with himself. What had been the purpose of that? What had it accomplished? Was there any point, really, in playing private detective, tracking down all these minor clues which, nine times out of ten, might mean nothing?

The long, carpeted corridor of the floor on which he lived was silent. There had always seemed to Lange something faintly ominous about that long corridor. It was so totally impersonal, each door marked only by a number or possibly a mat placed outside. It was as though the coldness and uniformity must conceal in each case, as in his own, some peculiarities going on within, fights, tensions of one kind or another. Perhaps such people, he thought, musing on this, perhaps people who had something to hide selected these buildings unconsciously, wanting to conceal themselves in their bland uniformity like animals hiding under a rock.

He turned to his study, moving quietly through the darkened apartment. He decided to stay there just a little while, long enough so that he could then enter the bedroom and feel calm and collected. He took up the papers he had been trying to study before he had gone down and was just beginning to get absorbed in them when the door opened. "Janie McGregor called," Katherine said, standing in the study door.

Lange started; he had imagined, hoped, she might be asleep. But she stood at the door, alert as a sentry, her body outlined in the transparent nightgown, her hair bound up sleek and tight in a turban.

"Janie McGregor?" he said, uneasy. "What did she want?"

"She was just calling to invite us over for dinner in two weeks." She paused, still not moving an inch from the doorway. "She said she had just spoken to you."

He was silent one second, then said, "Yes, I called her. Well, I wanted to speak to Bill, but he wasn't in."

"I came in here after she called, but you weren't here." She gazed at him with an intense, inexorable glance. "Why did you call from downstairs?"

"I was down—to get an evening paper," Lange said quickly, remembering in a flash that he had forgotten to get the paper. "And I thought I'd just call from there."

"She said you called about me."

Damn the woman! Damn her to eternal hell! And damn himself for his idiot foolishness in trusting her to keep her mouth shut for one second. He sat at his desk, fury making him clench his fists, at the same time knowing he was trapped now.

She stepped farther into the room, closer to the desk. "Didn't you believe me?" she said. "About the boy? Didn't you believe me?"

He frowned painfully. "I wasn't—sure." He paused. "I *wanted* to believe you," he said, staring at her intently and inwardly willing her to believe him.

She smiled at him strangely, her face in the tight turban Oriental, mysterious, the eyes seeming elongated like the eyes of an Arab woman. "You never have faith in me," she said. "Never."

"I do have faith in you," Lange said. He stood up and went over to comfort her. He felt that his touch, more than what he could say in words, would calm her.

But she drew back as soon as he had laid his hand on her arm. "You never do," she said. "You never have. Right from the first time. You always think of me as someone crazy, not to be trusted. I always sense it."

"It's not true," he said. "You simply think that."

"No." She shook her head. "I can tell. I always sense that in you. You act as though I were some wild animal that could never be trained."

"But I want you to get well," he said, trying to make his voice quiet and patient. "Surely you can't doubt that. . . . And not just for your sake," he felt compelled to add. "For mine. For our children."

"But I never will," she said in a desperate voice, "because you'll never trust me. And one can't get well without trust."

He said nothing, touched by some truth in this. "I have trust," he said, reaching out for her again.

"You pretend to have trust," she said. "It isn't the same thing."

Lange was silent, tired, finally, of denials, disguises. "Perhaps you're right," he said. "I only pretend to. That's so." He stood, exhausted, staring at her.

He had expected that this confession would arouse her still further, but suddenly, as though the words were a needle which he had sunk into her arm, bringing sudden peace, she became quiet. She let him approach her, and as they went inside, her whole body went completely limp and unresisting while he, in a kind of stilled fury, tried to vent on her body the anger he felt, not so much at himself or even at her, but at her illness which, like a knife, lay between them, making trust and belief impossible.

The next Saturday he took Avie to the park alone; Katherine was at home preparing for a dinner party they were to give that evening. The weather had suddenly cleared, turned mild, although it was still hazy and not quite spring. He walked alone, feeling in a good mood, relaxed, having slept well, his nerves at rest. The playground was crowded with pretty young mothers, chatting beside carriages and, perhaps because of the spring weather, they looked to him unusually fresh and attractive in their brightly colored coats and scarves. He stood to one side of the playground while Avie went off on his tricycle, pedaling furiously. Lange stared around, bemused, at the children playing, digging in the large sandbox with their shovels. Then suddenly his eyes stopped roaming and stared. Right near the sandbox, standing to one side, leaning against a tree, was a boy in a green wool hat. He might have been playing and stopped or was just about to play, but now he stood with a peculiar, dreamy expression, watching the other children. Lange's throat felt dry. He stood motionless, staring at the boy. At that moment Avie came peddling over. "Let's go back," Lange said hastily. "It's time for lunch."

"But we just came," the boy wailed. "We just got here."

"We have to go back. Your mother's expecting us," Lange said and hurried his son out of the playground and up the hill to their house.

At home Katherine was in the kitchen, standing at the counter, slicing tomatoes. Lange came into the kitchen, his coat still on.

"Was it nice out?" she asked.

"Yes, quite nice," Lange said. He paused a moment. "But, Kath, you were right. I saw that boy. The one you mentioned. . . . The boy in the green hat," he added as she continued to look at him with a blank, uncomprehending expression.

But when she spoke her voice was bland and unrevealing; she continued to slice the tomatoes. "What boy do you mean?" she said.

An American Marriage

B EFORE calling it quits definitely, Carol and Mike Bonner agreed to both try being analyzed.

Carol's analyst was a tall, thin Viennese man who looked like an Austrian version of T. S. Eliot. He was famous as a theoretician; since Carol's parents were paying, she could afford someone well known. His office was dark and messy with books and papers stacked all over the place and a green velvet couch in one corner. It looked like the pictures of Freud's office that Carol had seen in photographs. There was even a cocker spaniel who came to the door when she entered, though he did not, like Freud's spaniel, remain in the office during the session.

Carol could not help feeling the bridge in age, experience, and background between herself and this man. She would not have wanted a woman, God forbid, but sometimes she wondered: Wouldn't an American have been better? Of course, her parents had wanted her to have the best, just as when she was growing up, they had wanted her to have the best education, the best clothes, the best summer vacations. The best, in this case, meant a man old enough to have studied with Freud; from his person wisdom would trickle down, as it had from the disciples. But Dr. Furstenberg terrified her with his German accent and his dry, ironic laugh. He was as remote from any influence of feminine charm as a man could be, and Carol, who was not averse to using such influence when it might be helpful, disliked him for it. The old prig!

She felt terribly small and petty as she sank, mink-clad, sunglasses pushed visorlike against her streaked blond hair, into the green wool basket chair and told all about herself. She could not help feeling that he despised her, though he would not admit it, for the disorder of her life. But of course, he was too wonderfully discreet to say anything of the kind. She hated the doorman, too, and the way, recognizing her, he smiled obsequiously each time she entered the building. She hated the little, crouched waiting room with its copies of *Medical Newsletter* and *M.D.* which were never up to date. Especially she hated the other patients who all looked so god-awful: the fat lady in suede boots, the gawky lawyer who asked her for a date, the little girl (or midget) dressed always in plaid who carried a bright-red patent leather purse. She even resented the money, though she knew her father, an ear, nose, and throat man with a lavish office on Park Avenue, could easily afford it. Usually Carol would have derived some pleasure out of knowing she was spending his money. It made her feel loved and wanted to run up huge bills at Bergdorf's and overtip cabdrivers and waiters. But now, seeing some Pucci lounging pajamas on sale for two hundred dollars, she would think: For four lousy hours, I could get a whole outfit! Why, if you took all those hours and added them up, she'd be the best-dressed manic-depressive in New York! For revenge—though at whom the revenge was aimed was a mystery—she tried cutting sessions or arriving late, but of course, the next time she had to talk about "why she had felt the urge to 'act out.'" You just couldn't win with these characters; they had all the answers.

It was worst during the time when Ben, her first husband, came to New York for a month, and she began seeing him again and sleeping with him. She knew it was bad, bad for herself—she had been down this one-way road to nowhere too many times—and bad for the kids who could not help getting mixed up with Ben leaving at ten Saturday morning and Mike arriving half an hour later to pick them up for their weekly "day with father" outing. But hell, why must she account for everything she did? She was an adult, wasn't she? For what that was worth.

Mike was going to an American analyst who, though he belonged to the New York Psychoanalytic Institute, had an office in the Village. It was a trek for Mike who worked as an editor for a magazine in midtown Manhattan. But he had no choice. He was going to the Treatment Center in order to pay less; he was still supporting Carol and the girls.

His analyst was the swinging type, a short, stout man with longish black hair and a wrinkled, but friendly basset-hound face. He wore dark sports shirts and flowing navy blue ties with giant red polka dots. His waiting room had a dozen doors, each leading off to some unknown, mysterious realm. One door was painted bright orange, another a scarcely less subdued shade of violet. The plastic coffee table was littered with copies of *Ramparts* and *Mad* comics and large white bowls of leafy plants were suspended from the ceiling by chains. Over the couch an Andy Warhol cluster of vibrant flowers made a blotch of color against the white wall.

As analyst Dr. Nachmanson was scarcely the conventional type either. Mike had expected a silent presence, stern, patriarchal, sparing in remarks of any kind, but Nachmanson reacted to everything. Guffaws, chuckles, snorts, hoots—all these sounds came trumpeting forth with unrepressed vigor from behind Mike's head, interspersed with terse, but vivid comments: "She really bitched you up that time, huh?" or "Let *them* eat shit for a change, Bonner. How about that?"

In general, Mike found he had a harder time with his analysis than he had expected. He had, of course, read a lot of Freud, and consequently it had seemed to him that his case would be a pushover. Certainly there were no suggestions about his character that he would have any qualms about entertaining, nothing that would take him aback. He had wanted to sleep with his mother? Sure, why not? He'd go along with that (though the memory of her squeezing into her size eighteen girdle was hardly calculated to evoke the most erotic memories). "Just tell me," he said at one of the first sessions, "tell me honestly what you think is my problem and I'll go home and think about it. I

won't say I'll change right away, but I'll take it into consideration."

But Nachmanson didn't see it that way. "You have enough
ideas rattling around in your head," he said, puffing on his cigar
(he always smoked Schimmel Pennicks during the hour, giving
the air in the room a strangely acrid smell). "That's one of your
hang-ups, pal . . . Did you ever stop and think how many times
you say, 'On the one hand . . . on the other hand'?"

Though taken aback by this, Mike could acknowledge it to be
valid. But in his work it was precisely this quality for which he
was valued, his tendency to look at things calmly, from all angles, not to fly off the handle. Did he really want to change all
that?

One Friday evening in December Mike came over to Carol's
apartment to spend a half hour with the girls. He was leaving
that night for a weekend in Boston to give a lecture and visit
some friends, the Langens. Hence he would be unable to make
his usual Saturday morning visit. On the way in, following
Carol, he glanced at himself in the hall mirror. Tall, heavyset,
beginning to be gray, he still had a deceptively boyish, genial
appearance, as though he had been cast for the wrong part in a
play. Under his arm he had his leather briefcase, an old battered
one, dating from graduate school days. It contained, along with
the notes for his lecture, a pair of wrinkled blue pajamas. He
thought of how the fact that he never had his pajamas ironed
used to drive Carol crazy. But they got wrinkled in bed anyway,
didn't they?

He had just had a crummy session with his analyst. He always
hated going late in the day. By six o'clock he was pretty exhausted, and the long drive downtown, plus the search for a
parking space, was a final irritant. This session he began quite
unexpectedly to talk about Carol and the affairs she had had,
both when they were together and now that they were apart.
Some had been with people he knew. Others he had only
suspected or heard about. It seemed to him he had resolved all

this; he could talk about it with detachment. He could see it her way. She had a right to have affairs, in a certain sense. Maybe he had been too uncommunicative, too. . . . "Is that what you really think about it?" Nachmanson said. He kept battering Mike with questions, one after the other, until finally, at the end of the hour, Mike yelled, "Okay, I hate her for it! I hate her! I hate *them!* Does that satisfy you?" Naturally Nachmanson said nothing to indicate either satisfaction or dissatisfaction. The smiling Freudian bastard! What did it matter to him if she'd gone down for the whole Bulgarian merchant marine corps! Mike hurried out, only nodding to him briefly. When he got out in the cold December evening, wrapping his maroon scarf around his neck, he felt more than a little shaken at this burst of dark feeling that seemed to have come from nowhere and momentarily overwhelmed him.

Carol was going out on a date with a girlfriend, the wife of the professor of Slavic languages at whose house she and Mike had met eight years earlier. The professor had a gourmet society meeting—he was taking lessons in Chinese cooking—and the two girls (they called each other girls, though Carol was thirty-three and the professor's wife forty-one) were going to see a double feature at Loew's: a sexy Swedish picture and a Japanese horror movie that someone had said had remarkably good photography. Carol always went to the movies when she was depressed: good movies, bad movies, any movies. She sat benumbed, munching Snicker bars, as entranced as a ten-year-old at Radio City. Mike had never liked movies—but then he was never depressed; he always sublimated. But for his sake, although she told herself the time for these childish games was past, she would have liked it to be a man with whom she was spending the evening. Two women of a certain age, husbandless: the classic farce. Maybe, if we're lucky, we'll be picked up by two fairies in the lounge and get a free caffè espresso at the Coffee Mill afterward—great! She had arranged to meet Virginia at the theater.

She, too, had just come out of an analytic session. Hers was at five thirty, leaving her just time to bolt home and give the girls their usual Friday night supper: chicken chow mein, matzos, raspberry ripple ice cream. She was fuming when she came out. It was the first time she had said nothing, not one solitary word the whole hour. Oh, she had been silent before, deliberately or not, for five minutes, ten, but never once had she thought a whole hour would go by without a single exchange, even of hostilities. But once it had started, the silence, as though by inertia, had gone on and on until finally she felt that even if she had wanted to, she could not have broken it. Sitting there in the chair, Carol had glanced up once and seen Dr. Furstenberg's intent, colorless eyes fixed on her, just the trace, she thought, of a smile on his lipless lips. Oh, how she hated him! He reminded her, sitting there, of her father, who would always come home after work and plotz into a chair in front of the seven o'clock news, not wanting or caring to talk to her or her sister, even if something special had happened at school. He reminded her of Mike, who, at dinner, would listen to her when she was telling about the Women Strike for Peace group, outwardly sympathetic, inwardly detached, eyes glazed ("Can you repeat what I just said?" "Yes, I can. You just said . . ." Even there he never missed a trick!). A kind of rage, a cold fury built up in her until she felt she wanted to get up and smash every damn Chinese vase in the office (Dr. Furstenberg collected Chinese vases set into small lighted alcoves, like prayer stands. Ought one to put pennies there? God, make me a more interesting neurotic). At the end of the hour he got up, smiled, openly this time, and said, "So . . . we'll continue next time." Continue *what?* It was like Alice and having more tea when you hadn't had any to begin with.

For the first half hour Mike played with the girls. Carol stayed in the bathroom, ostensibly getting ready for her big night on the town, in fact sitting morosely on the toilet seat reading the second half of the New York *Times*. When it was time for the girls to go to bed, Carol emerged, perfumed, gleaming, in a new striped dress. Mike looked at her with that blank

I-refuse-to-comment expression she had seen on his face when he was lusting after some forbidden creature at a party. This gave her a small token of satisfaction.

They returned to the living room and sat warily facing each other.

"How're tricks?" she said.

"Okay." He still had that expression: I will say nothing that can be used against me. Did he think the place was bugged?

"You're going to—"

"Boston." He watched her cross her legs and begin unclipping her watchband, a habit she had when she was ill at ease. Why the perfume? She never wore it. He didn't like perfume. To show— someone does. Please, that's been proved, he felt like saying. Proved, proven.

She sat back and regarded him.

"I hear Ben was in town," he said.

"Oh, who was your source?"

"Muriel said she saw you at the Pinter."

"Yes, it wasn't very good."

"How *is* he?"

"Well enough. . . . His wife may be divorcing him."

"That's a pity."

"Why?"

"Well. . . . A two-time loser."

She sat forward, suddenly hostile. "Is *that* losing? What's winning then?"

"Okay."

She continued examining him. "What's with the tie? Is this your mod phase?"

"Isn't it conservative enough? I thought you liked outlandish things and people."

"You're not the type."

"Maybe I'll *become* the type."

Carol smiled. "We could do this all night, couldn't we?"

"Sure."

"Why don't we not?"

"What, then?"

"Leave, if you like. . . . Don't you have a train to catch?"

"Ultimately."

She poured herself some sherry and sat coiled with the glass in her hand. "So let's screw."

She said it just to test him, for no more or less devious motive.

"No thanks," he said.

"No time between trains?"

"There's time."

"Just not interested?"

In fact, he had had this fantasy a hundred times—coming back, screwing her, and leaving—and if it could have been just like that, as coldly and nastily satisfying as it was in his fantasy, he wouldn't have hesitated one second. Just do it and leave her to howl and scream and pull whatever tantrums she had up her sleeve at the moment, leave her to complain about too many orgasms or not enough—whatever! But it wouldn't work that way, and he didn't feel like chancing anything else.

"Not interested," he said.

She said nothing. So he was going to Boston. She knew whom he'd stay with too—the Langens, probably that bastard Hank Langen, who, while she had been married to Mike, always used to take her aside, hold her hand, tell her how much he commiserated with her and now, under the influence of his wife, that prissy slob, had dropped her completely, wouldn't even say hello when they met once in F. A. O. Schwarz's in front of the teddy bears. Murder, she thought. One day I will commit murder. Not suicide: That would make Mike too happy. She said, "I took Janie around to Dalton today."

"Oh?" Mike lit a cigarette and didn't look at her. Having rebuffed her sexually, he felt, at the same time, an enormous sense of pride and an equally great sense of uneasiness. He would not be allowed to escape free for that. Probably as a gesture it had been gratuitous.

"They have this special program for two-and-a-half-year-olds. I want to get her in it if I can."

"I thought there were all these local nursery schools," Mike said. "I thought you were going to try one of those."

"You don't *do* that," Carol said sharply.

"Why not?"

"Because they're lousy, that's why."

"I thought Margie Klinger said——"

"Who cares what Margie Klinger said? . . . Look at her kid! She's a fat Mongoloid."

"But Dalton is pretty expensive, isn't it?" He tried to sit back and regard her calmly. He shouldn't have come, should have just skipped a week and come next Saturday.

"Sixteen hundred," Carol said flatly, looking up at him deliberately, challenge in her eyes.

Mike tried to smile. "For nursery school? That's crazy!"

She stiffened. "In what *sense* is it crazy?"

"No, I take it back, not crazy—it's just, well, it's a hell of a lot of money, isn't it? I mean——"

"As a matter of fact, it isn't. No! Not at all. Nursery school is the most important experience a child can have. . . . Are you going to ship them off to some pound, some——"

"Anyway, two and a half!" He crushed the cigarette out, not having taken two puffs. Wasn't he giving up smoking? "Can't she wait a year? That seems so young."

"No, she cannot wait a year." She sat on the edge of the couch, legs crossed, looking tense and ready to leap at his throat.

Mike stood up. "Carol, listen, let's not get embroiled in some unnecessary thing. . . . I'd love to send her. I don't have the money. That's it. That's all there is to it."

"You do have it."

"I don't."

For a moment she wouldn't even answer him. Then she blurted out, "You don't have it for us, but you have it for the things you want, for your damn records, for your causes. You can donate to them, you do plenty, if you want. Don't give me that."

"I don't have the money," Mike said, trying to hold back.

Suddenly Carol leaped up. She rose so quickly that her stocking caught; there was a tearing sound as the run slithered down her leg. "You do have it. Why do you lie?" she cried. Rushing into the bedroom where the girls were asleep, she stood, pointing, shouting, "Here! Tell them you don't have anything! Tell them you won't give us a cent! Here they are—tell them!"

"Damn it, why do you drag them into it?" Mike, furious, grabbed his coat and briefcase and headed for the door. "What kind of hell do you want to make for them?" In a minute, he thought, he would have hit her, something he had never done; he wasn't sure he was sorry to have been spared the satisfaction.

That spring Carol went with her father and stepmother to Miami Beach for a three-week vacation. They thought she was looking run-down and needed a rest. Her father rented a suite in a big luxury hotel overlooking the sea. Every day they all went down to swim. The girls loved it. They discovered a drink called piña colada, half pineapple juice, half coconut milk, which they consumed three or four times a day. The rest of the time they spent on the beach, running into the waves, playing in the sand, collecting seashells. Carol's stepmother was a heavy woman with coarse, dyed red hair and a tendency to overdress. She wore cashmere sweaters with sequins all over them and plastic sandals through which you could see her purple-pink painted toenails. Each afternoon she and Carol went up to the solarium and lay nude in the sun. Like a town through which a flood has passed, leaving its mauled and mutilated victims, the terrace was littered with the bodies of middle-aged women in varying stages of disintegration. Once, between marriages, Carol's stepmother had been a masseuse, going to the homes of rich women and massaging their opulent backs and bellies with firm, unsparing hands. She offered to massage Carol; it would "relax" her, she said. Carol refused and then, one day, accepted. With the sun beating down on all parts of her body, Carol lay on a red-and-

white-striped mat while her stepmother, like a butcher
tenderizing a piece of beef, pounded her all over with quick au-
thoritarian gestures. It was not relaxing, it was a punishment,
and Carol accepted it as such. With each blow Carol's stepmother kept on talking, derided men, accused them of infidelity,
lust, cruelty, stupidity, and incompetence. These remarks, too,
Carol accepted as a punishment, seeing in her stepmother the
woman she would someday become. But she said nothing, simply lay as still as a corpse, her eyes masked with blobs of cotton
soaked in witch hazel, offering her beautiful, tanned face to the
hot rays of the sun. At dinner she flirted with the hotel manager,
a fattish man in a straw hat who would have liked her to do it
more graciously, as long as she was making the effort, and after
that they all went down to watch little dogs racing around and
around on a sandy track. Carol's father won a lot of money.

Mike was invited, in the month of July, to be a judge for a lit-
erary contest on an island off Italy. He was glad to go, not giving beans for the contest, for the sake of the free vacation and
the chance of escape from Carol's lawyers, who were pursuing
him with impossible demands for money. The island was nice; it
was sunny. Mike was given a room in a villa with a British homosexual of fifty, a withered man with a face like a lump of
Roquefort cheese, who, over Italian vermouth in the late afternoon, related long, droning stories about his hopeless love for an
American boy who took his money and blackmailed him among
his friends. Mike felt sorry for the man and was repelled by him.
He was glad when he met a girl, someone connected with the
business end of the contest, who attached herself to him and
with whom he began having an affair. She was an Italian girl,
homely, with a long face and somber, suffering eyes. She knew
English quite well, bit her nails, and always insisted on paying
her own way at cafés and in the theater, calling this
independence. She had read his essays in Italian and admired
them. He liked her because she was quiet and didn't wear a girdle and cooked incredibly good meals for him which they ate in

a courtyard in back of her house. He stayed with her in the evenings, usually leaving the next morning for one of the meetings connected with the contest.

One morning he woke up late—it was after eleven—and decided: the hell with the contest. Filemina, as usual, had rushed out to her job. Alone in the airy, sun-lit apartment, Mike made himself a large pot of coffee. Relishing his leisure, he sipped the coffee slowly, adding an extra pour of milk to mask its bitter taste. The house was near the sea, and through the window came fresh sea breezes and the honk of boats. It reminded him of an apartment on Riverside Drive he and Carol had rented when they were first in New York. One night, out of motives known to no one, a middle-aged housewife in a flowered dust wrapper had leaped from a six-story window to death in the courtyard below. An ambulance had come and taken the body away. Gradually the noises created by the incident—children crying, dogs barking, neighbors shouting—died away. They had gone back to bed and, without a word, made love twice. They had each other: what fear need they have of death and the unknown despair of strangers?

Apocalypse at the Plaza

THIS was the time of year Pomerantz liked best: summer weekends in New York. Sitting in his small, airless, unair-conditioned apartment or idly roaming the deserted streets with the knowledge of being one of the few who could not afford to go away either for the month or, at the very least, for the week-end, who could not manage to sponge off some anonymous friend at Fire Island or Westport—this gave him a special pleas-ure. Now, at home, sinking into the red canvas swing chair which hung precariously from the ceiling, he stared at the collage scotch-taped to the wall.

It was a big one, the biggest he had ever done: ten feet long and six feet high, extending almost the length of the room. His last show had been all collages, but mainly smaller ones, eight inches by twelve. This one, which he had been working on for four months already, was going to be called "Apocalypse." By now the large sheet of paper was about three-quarters filled in with pastings from magazines and newspapers, some in color, some black and white. Two cars with fashion model eyes and obscenely grinning mouths were colliding head on while build-ings toppled into a raging fire. A woman painted entirely in gold (he had gotten that from an article on *Goldfinger* in an old issue of *Life*) clung to a rocket which was soaring into the air. Below, a turbid sea charged, afloat with precarious objects—sewing ma-chines, boxes of shredded wheat, electric toastmasters—rem-nants of the civilization that had just been destroyed. Three

243

begirdled women sank, smiling, into a vat of Progresso marinara sauce.

The phone rang. Pomerantz debated not answering it. Usually for days at a time he left the phone off the hook until the gentle, beeping sound distracted him as he passed and, almost out of mercy, as for a dying animal, he would replace the receiver. Now, slowly, he ambled over to the phone, weeding his way through his art supplies and, without thinking, said, "Yes? Hello?"

"Murray?" It was his ex-wife, her voice sounding more hesitant than usual. "Is that you?"

"None other," Pomerantz said. He sat down on the sink and began, with his free hand, to peel an avocado that was lying there.

"I've been trying to get you for days," she said, "but you're always busy. Do you spend your whole *life* on the phone?"

"Almost," Pomerantz said cheerfully. "I've become adjusted to it. It's like an iron lung. Take it away and I'd cease to breathe. That cord is like an umbilical cord, connecting me to—"

"Are you all right?" she asked. "I mean, you're okay?"

"Sure," he said mildly.

"I thought you might be out of the city for the Fourth. Almost everyone is."

"Why? I can be just as unpatriotic right here at home," Pomerantz said, peeling the last trace of skin from the avocado and biting it, as though it were a peach. "I have the flag lying on the floor. I—"

"I thought Alice Montgomery or someone would have lured you out," she said, emphasizing the word "lured."

"Haven't heard from her in months," he said.

"Haven't you? How odd. She always had such a thing about you."

"So you claimed." Pomerantz stood absently, holding the phone, munching the avocado, which was a good one, and not speaking, almost forgetting what he was doing there.

She, too, was silent for the moment. "Do you have air conditioning *at least?*" she said suddenly.

Without moving, Pomerantz shook his head. Then, realizing she could not interpret this gesture over the phone, said, "No."

"You *don't?* But you were *going* to. You promised me. How can you do any work in this heat?"

"A good question."

"You must be dying." He could almost see her pursed lips and frowning, rosy face. "That's incredible."

Again Pomerantz was silent, wondering why the hell she had called. He had an urge to replace the phone quietly, so quietly she would not hear and would go on talking to herself.

"The reason I called," she said, as always leaping to his mental cues, "is that Harry and I are in town just this fortnight and we'd like to see you."

"You would? Both of you?" He tried to sound ironic, but it fell flat.

"Why don't you come up and meet us? We're at the Plaza. You can meet us for lunch, if you like."

"I've eaten," Pomerantz said. This had a certain technical veracity since he had, in fact, just consumed the avocado. But apart from that he had not eaten since the night before. His usual means of sustenance, when he was working and too lazy to cook, was cold soup, eaten directly out of the can, and Mallomars.

"Meet us for coffee then," she said, not giving up so easily. "Or a drink."

Pomerantz hesitated. "What time are you having lunch?" he asked, still cagey.

"Right now. . . . So—"

"Okay, I'll be right over," Pomerantz said agreeably. "I'll see you then."

He was ready to hang up when she said suddenly, "Murray, you'll be sure—"

"What?" he said, startled.

"Oh, never mind," she said. "Okay, see you."

Was that just another ploy to give her, for whatever reason, the last word? Or did she really have some last-minute message to communicate? God knew. It was no longer his business, anyway, to deal with all those subtleties.

Halfway down the stairs, he suddenly turned, rushed up again, and made a beeline for a magazine at one end of the pile. With great care he cut out a woman's breast, thus partially mutilating a Playmate of the Month and, with equal care, pasted it onto one end of the collage. Bobbing there among the waves, it looked like a rubber beach toy. With a small, secret smile, Pomerantz left the room.

They were sitting at a small table near the back of the room. Pomerantz entered slowly. He liked the Plaza, just as he liked all old buildings. Seeing them being torn down, even reading about this in the paper, gave him a distinct pang, as though he had heard of the death of a friend. Now, sauntering toward the table, he had only a peripheral sense of the restaurant, the other diners, the tables, set with silver and flowers and glasses—these all existed on the outside of his consciousness, like designs on the rim of a plate. What he was most aware of, especially as he came closer, was the color of Virginia's dress. It was yellow, but a bright sun yellow, like a Van Gogh sunflower. It stood out, almost radiated light, so that her face and limbs seemed minor, almost nonexistent appendages to this first, brilliant glow of color. As he was almost at the table, he noticed also, by contrast, Harrison's tie, a paisley pattern of green and purple, rich, deep, baroque colors.

"Murray!" Virginia rose from her seat to kiss him lightly on the cheek. Pomerantz had a feeling of light coming closer, as though the gold of her dress were an actual flame that could burn. "We're so glad you could make it."

"That's an extraordinary tie," he said, ignoring her, looking directly at Harrison. "Fantastic."

Harrison, plump, solid figure, almost blushed. He had that peculiar combination of suavity—the effect of his early success as a businessman, taking over and remodeling a large restaurant chain —and an almost childlike awkwardness. He had always reminded Pomerantz of those precocious little boys at school who were shoved several grades ahead, who delighted the teachers, and yet were always the butt of jokes among their schoolmates, never quite fitting in, despite endless geniality, even obsequiousness. "Do you like it?" he said, fingering the tie nervously. "I hesitated actually, before buying it. I wasn't sure it was my type, to be frank."

"On the contrary," Pomerantz said. "It says something about you. A tie like that isn't just a tie. It makes a statement. That is, it can—and that tie does."

"The thing about ties," said Virginia, who had been eyeing the two of them uneasily throughout this exchange, "is that it's almost the only area where a man can exert any taste in clothes. I mean, most things like suits are so bland—always gray or blue or whatever."

"Precisely," Pomerantz said. "Show me a man's tie and I'll show you the key to his character." He leaned forward confidentially and said in a lower voice, "I've often thought one could make a business out of that—you know, the way some people read character by handwriting or tea leaves. Why not by ties?"

"Why not?" Harrison said genially. He was smoking a cigar and offered one to Pomerantz.

Pomerantz shook his head.

"He doesn't smoke," Virginia said.

Pomerantz stared at her. Now, close up, he realized a strange new fact about her appearance. Her dress, which he had taken for a uniform yellow, was, in fact, cut out at various places to reveal bare flesh. One such place was a circle around her stomach in the middle of which, like a bull's-eye on an archery target, her belly button was revealed. The other was toward the back, curving down dangerously low almost to the point where her spine ended and going up to some thin strip near the neck. Idly, he wondered how such a dress was made. Did you make a regular dress and then, at random, cut a hole wherever it suited you? An interesting concept. Pomerantz imagined a designer, equipped with a large pair of sharp scissors, going down a line of models, clipping away, revealing a breast here, a buttock there.

Evidently disconcerted by his absorbed stare, she laughed and said, "Do you like the dress? I bought it on an impulse."

"You must get an interesting suntan with a dress like that," Pomerantz said seriously.

"Oh, no, well, not necessarily," she said. "I haven't noticed that."

At that point the waiter, who had been hovering discreetly near the table, approached and quietly presented Harrison with a check. He looked at it impassively. "Won't you have something?" he said to Pomerantz. "Some coffee? A little cake?"

"He's like a Jewish mother, always trying to fatten people up," Virginia said, smiling.

"Their pastries are excellent," Harrison said, not at all disconcerted by this analogy.

"No, that's okay," Pomerantz said, "if you're both finished. . . ." He was still fascinated by that hole cut out around her belly button. "You should wear a diamond in your navel," he said as they got up, "like a belly dancer."

"How do they keep those in, though?" she said. "I've always wondered about that."

Upstairs in their suite it was even colder than in the lobby. A large air conditioner, coiled on the windowsill like an animal, was purring in the corner.

"Oh, that reminds me," Harrison said. "Virginia mentioned you don't have an air conditioner. Well, it just happens that the New York office has an extra one—we've been storing it—it used to be used for an extra room there. And I'd be delighted, really, if you'd take it over. We could have it installed for you with no trouble at all."

"I don't like air conditioners," Pomerantz said. "Otherwise, of course—"

Harrison smiled uneasily. "Oh, well, you don't need to have it on all the time."

"I just don't like them," Pomerantz said. "I never have. I hate that *sound* they make."

"Oh, well, that needn't bother you. This one is unusually silent. You can hardly tell it's in the room with you."

"Exactly!" Pomerantz said, leaping up. "That's perfect. You can't tell it's in the room with you. That's just the feeling you have with these things, as though someone were in the room with you, breathing over your shoulder."

Harrison said nothing. He looked at Pomerantz in silence. Finally he said, "I never thought of it quite like that."

"Most people don't," Pomerantz said. "I guess I just have an unusually vivid imagination."

Harrison nodded. "Yes, so Virginia told me. Well, I'm sorry you—"

"Oh, don't be silly, he'll take it," Virginia said, reentering the room. "Don't pay attention to that. That's absurd."

Harrison looked uncomfortable. So he hadn't quite got used to her taking over yet, Pomerantz thought with a small, inward feeling of pleasure. Well, he would. Give him time. "I think if he *genuinely* doesn't," he began, but Virginia interrupted him.

"He's just teasing you. Of course he would like it," she said, just as though Pomerantz were not present or were a child too young to be expected to take part in the conversation. "No one *likes* to suffer."

Harrison cleared his throat. "Well, my dear, of course I'm delighted to have it installed, as I said—" He looked hesitantly from one to the other, and since neither said anything, he stopped. "You two will excuse me for a moment," he said, "won't you? I have to make a call, somewhat private, and I thought I might—" He hurried out of the room, evidently pleased to leave the scene of battle.

"You mustn't tease Harry," Virginia said, pretending to pout. "It's unkind. He can never tell when he's being teased."

"I wasn't teasing him," Pomerantz said flatly. "I was perfectly serious."

"You mean you're *really* able to work in this terrible heat without an air conditioner?" she said, looking at him suspiciously.

"When Ethel will let me," he said.

"Ethel?" She frowned. "Ethel who? What Ethel?"

"Didn't I mention Ethel?" Pomerantz said innocently.

"I don't remember," Virginia said, still concerned. "Did you? I don't think so." She looked at him with large blue eyes. "Where did you meet her?"

Pomerantz cleared his throat. "It's interesting you ask that," he said, "because the way we met is rather unusual, actually. . . . I met her in my analyst's office."

"Oh? She's a patient of his also?"

"No, her son is."

"Her son?"

"Yes, her ten-year-old son."

Virginia considered this. "He's ten? Then she must be—she's older than you?"

"Actually not. She's only twenty-four, but she's from the South. She married young."

She looked at him curiously. "Well, I suppose they do things like that down there. . . . Who was her husband?"

"Oh, some—some political figure."

"*Political?* In what sense?"

Pomerantz said nothing for a moment. "Well, to be frank, I had to promise not to reveal his identity. You see, when they got the divorce, she had to promise—"

"For the sake of his career?" Virginia said quickly.

"Exactly," Pomerantz said.

She sat down on the edge of the bed and crossed her legs. Her skirt in this position reached nearly to mid-thigh. Pomerantz watched her look down, lost in thought, evidently absorbing all this. Finally she looked up and said, "Doesn't your analyst mind?

I mean, does he think it's all right for people to meet in his office that way? I thought they were always—"

"You're right technically," Pomerantz said, "but I think he was glad, considering the circumstances."

"What circumstances?"

"I think," he spoke more slowly, almost bashfully, "he thought it would help take my mind off Juanita."

"Juanita?"

"Didn't I mention? I thought I—"

"Noo," she said, actually reddening. "Well, no wonder you haven't been getting that much work done."

"It has been a problem," Pomerantz admitted, "but you know how these things are."

"Of course," she said, crossing and recrossing her legs. It seemed to Pomerantz that the irritation and jealousy she kept so carefully from her face revealed itself in this quick, annoyed gesture. He stood there, regarding her in the yellow dress, and feeling, for the moment, a pure sense of pleasure. If only life could always be so pleasantly conceived! He opened the terrace door and stepped out. "What floor are you on?" he said.

Virginia arose and followed him, smoothing her dress down around her hips. "I don't know, really. Maybe the twenty something."

Pomerantz stared down at the plaza below, fascinated by the patterns, the shapes of color which seemed to move in and out like an abstract painting come to life. He stood on a chair to get a better view and then climbed onto the railing and sat there, holding onto the chair arm for support.

"Murray!" Virginia's voice suddenly rose almost hysterically. "What are you doing? Get down! Stop it!"

"Stop what?" Pomerantz said amiably, not taking his eyes from the view below.

"You mustn't," she said. "Things can't be that bad. It isn't worth it."

"Worth what?" Pomerantz said, not turning.

"Murray, please, I beg you." She put her hand out to touch him, but tentatively. "Please come down."

"But it's so beautiful," he said. "Look! Look at it."

What he wanted to communicate to her—the strangest thing of all—was the feeling that he was not looking down, but up, that suddenly he had the sensation, perfectly vivid, although in the back of his mind he knew it was not so, that he was lying in a hammock, gazing up at the sky. The trees below, splotches of uneven green, were the trees supporting him, the gray of the pavement, a sky of muted blue, the horses and carriages—figures from a Chagall painting, floating through the air. Extraordinary!

". . . didn't mean to upset you," she was saying. "If there's anything wrong, you ought to have. . . . Oh, where is Harry? Why doesn't he come back?"

"Fantastic," he murmured, swaying slightly. "Look at it!"

"Darling! Please, I beg you!"

Her voice rose so high and shrill that, for the first time, he turned to look at her in surprise. "What's wrong?" he said. "Aren't you feeling well?"

"I'm fine," she said. "I'm fine, really, but you. Oh, please, come down, Murray. Just as a favor to me. Won't you—"

Obediently, Pomerantz climbed down and wandered back into the suite. Virginia rushed in after him and flung herself down into the nearest chair, her hand over her eyes. "Oh, my God," she said. "My God."

Pomerantz looked at her curiously. "What's the matter?" he said suspiciously. "What are you—pregnant or something?"

She shook her head loosely from side to side like a rag doll. "I thought I'd faint," she said. "Oh, dear, I never—could you get me a glass of water?"

"Sure," Pomerantz said. He filled a glass in the bathroom, regarded his face a moment in the mirror with interest, as though he had never seen it before and came back. She took the glass and drank all the water in one gulp, swallowing heavily, like a horse. "You aren't used to the heat," Pomerantz said gently, touched in spite of himself. "You never liked the heat."

"It's not that," she said. She set down the glass and stared at him with her huge, beautiful eyes. "It's—oh, never mind. Did you really—or were you just joking?" She put out her hand and touched his arm. "You must take care of yourself," she said. "Promise me you will."

"Of course I will," Pomerantz said, standing a foot or so away from the chair, staring at her dreamily, bemused.

"All those women," she said. "It's probably not good for you —all that distraction. You need peace and quiet. . . . Let Harry install the air conditioner, why don't you?"

"If it'll make you happy," Pomerantz said. "*I* don't care."

Staring at her as she sat in the chair, her legs out straight, her shoes off, he was fascinated once again by that hole around her navel. Suddenly, like a former alcoholic seized by an irresistible desire to drink, he wanted, more than anything in the world, to bury his face in her stomach and kiss her navel. The round, succulent pink of the skin was like some ripe peach waiting to be eaten. "Virginia," he said, taking a step closer to her.

She smiled at him. "Poor darling," she said, looking at him both sadly and appealingly. "You poor darling."

This was too much for Pomerantz. With a rush, like a bull suddenly heading for the spot of red before its nose, he rushed at her and buried his face in her stomach, clasping her around the waist. Her skin felt cool, faintly fragrant, with just a trace of sweat. "Oh, dear," she murmured, turning this way and that. "Oh, dear."

It did not occur to Pomerantz until several days later that, if he had wanted, he probably could have made love to her right then and there. But for one second the loneliness and emptiness of his fantasy-ridden days took revenge on him. Desire rushed over his head, knocking him to his feet. He knelt there, his head pressing against her as though into a pillow with a freshly changed pillowcase, immobilized by the intensity of his feeling. "I love you," he said to her navel.

"I—a—it seems," Harrison said. He had evidently entered the room and was standing at the door behind them.

Pomerantz leaped up, struck, above everything, by the ludicrousness of his position, squatting like that on the floor. Virginia stood up from the chair and rearranged her dress. She, too, seemed perfectly calm and collected, as though nothing had happened. "Darling," she said, coming toward Harrison. "You know, I was wondering—couldn't Murray stay here this afternoon if he likes since we'll be going out? He feels a bit tired and I thought if he wanted to just rest and—"

"Sounds fine by me," Harrison said.

"But I don't need to rest," Pomerantz said. "I feel fine."

"You just lie down on the bed here," she said. "Ring up Room Service, if you want anything. Whatever you like." She bent down and kissed him on the cheek. "You'll feel better in a little while," she said.

After they had left, Pomerantz lay there, motionless, staring at the ceiling for a long time. He felt as though he were totally drained of feeling of any kind and could not imagine how he could so have lost his head as to rush at her like that. He didn't even *like* navels, really. What had possessed him? Sitting up, he reached for the phone at the bedside table. "Is this Room Service? This is Room—wait a second—" He got up and looked outside the door. "Room 2317. Could you send up a magnum of champagne, please? Extra dry. . . . Yes, that'll be fine. . . . And also, could you—do you have some fresh bagels and lox? Great. Send those up too. Oh, maybe three or four. And if you possibly have some raw scallions, just plain. Ya, I'll be in here."

Hanging up, Pomerantz began wandering around the room, waiting for the food. He opened both closet doors. Virginia had her usual row of multicolored, expensive dresses. Like flowers they hung there—scarlet, kelly green, purple blue. He had noticed her first at that party because of the colors of her dress—he still remembered it—a bright pink and yellow, like a Matisse odalisque. To one side of the closet lay a sewing basket. It was open and within, lying on top, was a small pair of gold scissors in the shape of a crane. Lifting up the scissors, Pomerantz turned them around in his hand, feeling the smooth, delicate blade.

Then he had an idea. Holding up one dress, hanging it in front of the closet, he cut a round, kidney-shaped hole just over the left breast. He stood back to consider it, made it a little larger and added another somewhere toward the back. Satisfied, he put it back and took out another dress. Perhaps a sleeve on this one? Or maybe a hole just below the navel? He was just onto the fourth dress and really getting into his element when the bell rang.

"Just come right in," Pomerantz called from the closet. "Set it right down." He was really hungry now. Those bagels would go down in a jiffy. The champagne, too. Nice of them to think of it.